the Chaldean Star

A NOVEL BY
Jaroldeen Edwards

Deseret Book Company
Salt Lake City, Utah

No part of this book may be reproduced in any
form or by any means without permission in writing
from the publisher, Deseret Book Company,
P.O. Box 30178, Salt Lake City, Utah 84130.
Deseret Book is a registered trademark of
Deseret Book Company, Inc.

First printing August 1986
Second printing September 1986

Library of Congress Cataloging-in-Publication Data

Edwards, Jaroldeen
    The Chaldean Star.

    I. Title.
PS3555.D935C46   1986   813'.54   86-11501
ISBN 0-87579-040-2

With love to
William F. Edwards
and Catherine Eyring Edwards
for their enduring example

Chapter One

The silver jetliner screamed out of the eastern sky and jolted to a landing on the bleached-white tarmac, which lay shimmering under the desert sun. The brakes shrieked in protest as the plane roared down the bumpy runway until, like a tame and docile beast, it came to a halt on the open asphalt beside the terminal.

Leslie woke up as the plane hit the ground. Her mouth was dry, and her eyes were gritty with weariness. Out of her small window she caught a glimpse of a colorless world flashing by. Beyond the landing field, all she could see was sand, desert, and low rocky hills—no green vegetation. Even the sky seemed bleached of color by the relentless sun.

On top of the hills she saw soldiers in khaki uniforms, as colorless as the hills themselves. Even at this distance she could see distinctly that they were holding their machine guns in readiness position. Beyond the terminal she saw military hangars, camouflaged planes, and a troop of men in battle fatigues marching in drill.

The sight was unnerving, and Leslie shuddered and turned her eyes away from the window. At that moment the doors of the plane were flung open with a clang, and the blast of desert heat was like a sudden blow.

Oh, Susan, Leslie thought in helpless frustration. *This is all your fault!*

As she thought of her absent friend, Leslie pictured Susan as she had last seen her. Susan's pale face, framed by crisp hospital sheets, had been pinched with pain.

"Please, Leslie," Susan had pleaded, clutching Leslie's arm while fighting off the sedative. "Please, please go without me. For your sake—and for mine. Go and find the answers. Please,

Leslie. You know if you don't go now, you never will, and you'll always regret it. Do it for me, Leslie, if not for yourself."

It wasn't fair of Susan to use her accident and my pity to make me agree to this madness, Leslie reflected bitterly. *Now I'm alone on the far side of the world, and I don't even know what I am doing here. I didn't want to take this trip in the first place. It was Susan who wanted to come. And now I'm in Jordan, and she's still in California!*

Leslie glared out the window at the hot, unrelenting desert scene.

"Well, little lady," said a hearty voice. "I see you've decided to wake up at last!"

Leslie clenched her hands in irritation, but said nothing. Hal Johnson, the man assigned to the seat next to her, was everything Leslie abhorred in an American tourist. He wore a flashy diamond ring, a floral shirt, and white shoes. His silver hair looked salon waved, and his hands were manicured.

Although his face was carefully tanned, it was full and flushed, like that of a man who lives too well. Leslie suspected that his body, though trim, was barely kept from the edge of stoutness by exercise and massage. Hal Johnson would have seemed like a caricature of a self-made, small-town business-man except for one puzzling feature, which Leslie had observed quite by chance.

Leslie was an amateur runner as well as a professor of biol-ogy, and she had always been fascinated by the athletes who trained at the university gym where she did her indoor run-ning. As a scientist, it had interested her to see the sophisti-cated and complex way the gymnasts used weights to build enormous strength into their arms without losing flexibility and without creating conspicuous muscle bulk.

Something about Mr. Johnson's arm, as it lay on the arm-rest beside her, reminded Leslie of those gymnasts' muscles. Only a trained eye would have observed it, but as Mr. Johnson did even a very simple task, such as lifting his drink, Leslie was aware of the smooth, hard musculature in his arm. She found herself idly wondering why this real-estate man from North

Shore Chicago would want to spend the hours of complex conditioning required to develop that particular kind of strength.

Vanity, she thought, mentally shrugging off her curiosity. *He probably wanted to improve his golf game.*

Leslie had no desire to ask Mr. Johnson personal questions. Ever since he had boarded the plane at O'Hare Airport, he had bombarded her with conversation even though she had given him no encouragement. She flinched every time he called her "little lady," answering him in monosyllables. Finally, in desperation, she had feigned sleep to stop the barrage of his talking.

Undeterred, Hal Johnson had prowled the plane's aisle during most of the night introducing himself to fellow passengers and striking up conversations.

"Hal Johnson's the name," he would begin in his hearty voice. "Real estate's my business—Chicago, North Shore— maybe you've heard of my company—Golden Shore Realty. Been mighty lucky, I want to tell you. Started the company right after the Big War on nothing but a shoestring. Evanston was just beginning to expand, and before I knew it, all up and down Lake Shore Drive, not just estates, mind you, but regular homes. All the families wanted to move north, and we were there—Golden Shore Realty—the right place at the right time.

"Now don't get me wrong. I know it wasn't luck. Someone up there was helping me all along, and I sort of made myself a promise that when I slowed down a little—I wouldn't say I was retiring, but, you know, taking it a little easier—well, I promised the good Lord that I'd sort of make a visit to his homeland to say a proper thanks. I guess you could call this trip a sort of personal pilgrimage—you know what I mean."

The other passengers responded eagerly to his friendly, jovial manner, but Leslie could not shake her feeling of discomfort toward him. *Have I become so private and introverted that I distrust even simple friendliness?* she wondered, disturbed by her own reactions.

When Leslie brought her thoughts back to the present, she realized that Hal was still talking to her, and she made a conscious effort to listen politely. "Tell you, little lady," Hal boomed, "this plane is full of wonderful people. See those two elderly ladies up near the front? They've been in charge of the Arcadia School cafeteria for twenty years, and the PTA is sending them on this trip as a retirement gift. That old couple back there are celebrating their golden wedding anniversary, and their oldest son and his family are with them. The lady sitting there—with the curly hair and the alligator jewelry case—well, she is coming as a tribute to her dead husband, who asked her to make the trip. That group over there is a whole parcel of history teachers from Utah, Idaho, Washington, and the like. I tell you, little lady, people are just wonderful wherever you go— wonderful!"

Leslie said nothing, but she thought if Hal Johnson called her "little lady" one more time she was going to scream!

The other passengers were moving restlessly in the plane, retrieving bags from above their seats, pulling out purses to glance in mirrors, tidying their hair, and retouching their makeup. Most of the passengers, like Leslie, had fallen asleep toward dawn and had missed the final hours of the flight as the plane crossed the Mediterranean Sea, where it lay brooding in darkness far below the scattered clouds. They had also missed the glory of the early morning sunrise and the sight of the sun climbing slowly to its zenith as their jet swept over the plains of Jordan toward their landing place in Amman, a city older than time, which the Greeks called "Philadelphia."

"Now, little lady, time to begin our adventure." Hal stood up and stretched. "A pretty thing like you shouldn't have to lift a finger. Just show me which one of these overhead bags is yours, and I'll get it down for you."

His condescending tone was too much for Leslie. "I am not your little lady," she snapped in a voice as cold as ice. "And I can get my own bags, thank you."

She had lashed out without thinking, and she immediately regretted her rudeness. She expected to see Hal Johnson recoil, to be hurt or insulted by her retort, but instead, as she looked at him, a strange thing happened. For the briefest of moments, she felt as though she saw a mask slip, and in that second, the genial, florid face of the ingratiating real-estate salesman was replaced by a second face: hard, cruel, intelligent, with eyes of granite. It was only a wisp of an impression, almost like a double exposure. Leslie blinked, and again she was looking at Mr. Johnson's familiar, jovial, uncomplicated smile.

"I understand," Hal said smoothly, and his voice was as patronizing as a pat on the head. "You just sit there and rest. It's been a long, hard trip."

Without comment she turned away from him and with a helpless sigh looked out the window once more at the barren landscape. *I never should have come on this trip*, she thought helplessly. *There are no answers for me here. Routine, discipline, work, physical exhaustion, those are my only answers. Why on earth did I let Susan persuade me to make this ridiculous journey?*

The passengers were instructed by the head steward to take their carry-on luggage, collect their other bags at the airport, and pass through customs. As soon as the tourists cleared customs, their tour guide, Miss Pomerance, would instruct them concerning boarding their tour buses.

As the tourists deplaned, the sunlight struck their eyes like a rifle shot. They ducked their heads, blinking against the glare and groping in their travel bags for sunglasses. Leslie noted indifferently that her linen slacks were badly wrinkled. She felt hot and grubby. She was also thirsty, but she knew it was going to be difficult to relieve her thirst. The tourists had been told by the tour officials: "Do not drink anything but bottled water and soda. The best way to relieve thirst is with an orange, but be sure it is not peeled when you buy it."

Chaos reigned in the terminal building. Passengers milled in a large, roped-in section, trying to find their suitcases in the general confusion while crowds of people waited in the customs lines. The room was hot and filled with oppressive odors. The noise was deafening, with voices shouting in French, German, English, but the rich, explosive sound of the Arabic tongue dominated. It was spoken in rapid, expressive bursts by dark, handsome men who, as attendants, officials, airport employees, and tour guides, made up the bulk of the crowd.

Leslie was fascinated by the sight of the Arabic men. They talked in groups, their gestures vivid and articulate. Some of them were dressed in Bedouin robes, others were in western clothes, but they all wore the distinctive flowing headdress of Jordan held in place by a black cord around their head. Leslie thought the headdress was enormously masculine and becoming to the handsome men with their black eyes and vital faces. Fascinated as she was by the foreign scene, the sudden intense realization came to her that she was truly in another world—infinitely removed from everything she understood and took for granted. Leslie felt an unexpected shudder; a sense of isolation and apprehension suddenly overwhelmed her. She felt more alone than she ever had in her life.

Across the room, Leslie saw Hal Johnson waiting in the customs line with the curly-headed widow. She decided she would try to avoid him—indeed, avoid all personal involvement with any of her fellow tour passengers. She would simply remain quiet, inconspicuous, and self-contained. For only two weeks she could steel herself and endure the experience. Squaring her shoulders, Leslie picked up her luggage and moved toward Miss Pomerance who was shouting instructions. Miss Pomerance looked harried and hot, and even though her bleached hair was curled and heavily sprayed, Leslie noted a few stray hairs had escaped and were straggling across the woman's damp forehead.

"Ladies and gentlemen, please listen to your instructions!" Miss Pomerance shrilled, waving her arms like a distraught hen trying to gather up her scattered brood. "Everyone in the World Field Tour, please listen!

"As soon as you clear customs, check the letter of the alphabet posted on your suitcase. That letter will tell you which bus you are assigned to ride for the remainder of the tour. Buses are lined up in front of the airport. They have been waiting for nearly an hour. We must board as quickly as possible. We have a long drive to reach Aqaba before dark.

"Oh!" Miss Pomerance's voice broke, and she cleared her throat and started again. "Once you board your bus, you will be under the care of a local tourist company. Your guide and driver will then become your official guides. My staff and I will remain with you, but we will be acting as only liaisons until we reboard the plane in Tel Aviv two weeks from today. Are there any questions?" People shook their heads and continued what they were doing.

Leslie cleared customs and stepped out of the airport where a long row of dusty Mercedes taxis waited. Beyond the taxis, she saw several well-kept Mercedes buses, each with its door open and a man in a white shirt and dark tie standing by the steps with a clipboard in hand. On each bus was a large, lettered placard. She checked the letter on her suitcase and then headed for the bus with the letter C. To her dismay, she saw Hal Johnson and the woman with the alligator case speaking with the man at the door of bus C. She watched as they began to board the bus together.

The whole process of being herded from line to line and being told what to do and how to do it suddenly made Leslie feel rebellious. She remained standing where she was, feeling reluctant to board the bus—tired of sitting, tired of traveling.

"Hurry up, Mrs. Brinton," Miss Pomerance puffed, tapping Leslie lightly on the shoulder as she hurried down the sidewalk. "We must get boarded."

Leslie glared at Miss Pomerance's retreating back, but with a resigned sigh, she hoisted her shoulder bag, picked up her suitcase, and moved into the line beside the bus.

As she waited, she watched the man who was checking off the list of passengers. He was taller than most Arabs she had seen, and though slender, he had broad, muscular shoulders. He almost had an American build, but his face was strikingly foreign. As a matter of fact, Leslie thought he looked dramatically like a Hollywood version of an Arab sheik. His features were strong and bold, and he had a neat black mustache over incredibly white teeth. Leslie had the distinct impression that

the man was fully aware of his good looks and used them deliberately to charm the female passengers.

"That is a very pretty blue dress," he said, flashing a dazzling smile at one of the plump, elderly women who had been
a cafeteria worker. She blushed at his compliment and giggled
like a girl as the young man took her hand and helped her up
the step into the bus. His voice was smooth, with an accent
that was a combination of the Middle East and Oxford English.

Leslie hesitated as she reached the door of the bus. She
dreaded the thought of being cooped up again. What she needed
was a good run to clear her mind and work off her frustration
and fatigue. She promised herself that as soon as she reached
the hotel she would find somewhere to run at least two or three
miles before bedtime. The thought made her feel a little better.

"Leslie Brinton." She gave her name to the man with the
clipboard. His hand was poised above the list of names, but
when she said her name, his head snapped up and he looked at
her with sudden piercing eyes. For the second time that day,
Leslie had the odd experience of feeling she was seeing double.
Here was a man who, one minute ago, had seemed nothing
more than a gigolo intent upon charming lady tourists, and
suddenly she was looking at the face of a hard, intent man.
Again the image was less than a flash. The Arab's rakish smile
returned, and his dark eyes appraised her confidently.

"Brinton?" The voice was smooth. "You would not by any
chance be related to the Senator Brinton who is a member of
the Middle East Peace Commission convening in Jerusalem
next week?"

"No," Leslie replied flatly. It was a question she was frequently asked, but she had no connection to the famous senator except the name. Ignoring the tour guide's outstretched
hand, she sprang up the bus steps unaided.

The bus driver, a small, wiry man with a huge, dark mustache and twinkly eyes, caught her eye conspiratorially as she
boarded, and with an impish grin, he winked at Leslie. For the
first time since she had climbed on the plane in Los Angeles
almost two days earlier, Leslie, without understanding why,

found herself smiling. Maybe it was because of her small act of defiance in not allowing the tour guide to help her up the stairs, or the fact that the bus driver had understood her defiant gesture and had approved, or maybe it was simply because the bus driver had one of the most infectious smiles she had ever seen, but whatever the reason, the man had made Leslie smile, and for no logical reason, she felt better.

Michelle Green, one of the American tour assistants, sat down next to Leslie. "We're finally on our way," she sighed. "It's always a mess getting everybody sorted out."

The bus driver started the motor immediately and smoothly maneuvered his vehicle out of its parking space ahead of all the other buses. Leslie had to smile at his agility. In the rearview mirror, she could see the other buses far behind, jockeying for position.

The man with the clipboard sat down in the seat behind the driver, directly across the aisle from Leslie and Michelle Green. He picked up a microphone and spoke to the passengers. As he spoke, Leslie could see him watching the tourists in the large rearview mirror. He seemed to be looking at their faces, assessing their reactions like an actor, knowing exactly what to say and how to say it to win their affection. Well, she had no intention of allowing him to work his charms on her. She refused to react like all the others on the bus. She might have no choice about being on the tour, but she refused to behave like a mindless sheep.

"My name is Nephti Ben Abhou," the man introduced himself, his voice carrying through the bus on the microphone. "Your driver's name is Syid Hakem Mojud. Since these are not exactly common names, you may call us 'Nick' and 'Sam.' These are more or less American versions of our names." He laughed and showed his white teeth, and the passengers laughed with him.

Leslie inadvertently caught his eye in the rearview mirror, and she turned her head away quickly. She was not amused and thought to herself, *He acts as though he thinks we're too dumb to pronounce his real name, or maybe he thinks we're not good enough to use it.* Nick noted the flash of irritation in her eyes as he watched her in the mirror. She could have sworn he was laughing at her. *How could anyone with a respected name be willing to compromise and call himself Nick like some pet dog, and then laugh about it?* she wondered irritably. She frowned, breaking contact with his eyes in the mirror.

As Leslie looked away from Nick, her eye caught the profile of the young bus driver, Sam. He seemed like a breath of fresh air to her. The impression Sam gave was one of joy and naturalness. He drove the bus with a grin of pure pleasure, and his quick, dark eyes missed nothing as he maneuvered the large vehicle down the winding road, darting in and out between slower cars. Even his appearance made her smile. It seemed as though his large mustache was an attempt to make up for his compact size. The mustache bloomed bold and amusing like a brush across his upper lip. What a contrast he was to the polished handsomeness of Nick. *Nick!* She thought the name contemptuously. *He looks like a gambler, and the name he has chosen surely suits the stereotype.*

As the bus entered the outskirts of Amman, the capital city of Jordan, Leslie realized how lucky she and the other passengers were to have a competent driver like Sam. The traffic in Amman was wild and disordered. Children, women hidden in long, black veils, and unheeding men crossed the roads at random, dodging or walking without concern or awareness of danger. Cars and trucks drove with a madness that suggested their drivers believed they were given magic immunity by the mere process of clinging to their steering wheels.

The streets of the city twisted and turned. They were actually little more than narrow valleys between the sharp hills and inclines upon which Amman was built. No trees or grass borders relieved the omnipresent sandstone, and the houses, made from the same stone, would be camouflaged into invisibility were it not for the sharp shadows created on their walls by the merciless sun. The hills rose sharply, and small, winding paths, like goat trails, led upward, twisting between the rows of homes.

Rarely, a tiny garden, only a few feet square, would stand out like an emerald against the pale, monochromatic hillside.

Sam drove dexterously through the old marketplace of Amman, and Leslie was fascinated to see market stalls, piles of oranges, brightly printed cloths, pistachio nuts, grains, and rice. The market was teeming with people, and she was struck with the remarkable vivacity of the Jordanians. Their faces were mobile and animated, their hands expressive and graceful, and their children were exquisite—really exquisite. Leslie closed her eyes and felt the old pain. It had been a mistake to look at the children. It hurt too much. She glimpsed two little girls walking hand in hand, smiling up at the tourist bus with wonderful, open, heart-shaped faces, and her heart wrenched. *I won't look again*, she thought, *not at the children.*

Nick was continuing his commentary, and she half-listened as he described the history of Jordan. With interest, she glanced at the ancient ruins of Philadelphia. The modern buildings encroached on the remnants of the old coliseum. The ruins seemed forgotten and unappreciated. High on the opposite hill, Nick pointed out the palace of the king of Jordan. It looked like a park surrounded by trees, flowers, and grass—strangely vivid and isolated in the barren city, like an exotic flower blooming in a desert.

"Why is Jordan called the Hashimite Kingdom?" Leslie asked Michelle Green.

"I'm really not supposed to give you any tourist information," Michelle whispered. "It's part of the deal we make. We are able to get tourists into this part of the world only by agreeing to allow the local tour guides to do all the talking."

Leslie was indignant. "You mean we are told only what they want us to hear."

"Sh-h-h," Michelle whispered in a sharp warning. "You have to remember, we're guests in their part of the world."

Leslie lowered her voice. "You could at least tell me why it's called the Hashimite Kingdom. That's something I could look up in a reference book. It isn't a matter of opinion, or privileged information, it's fact."

Michelle looked nervous, but she sighed and leaned over to speak in a quiet voice close to Leslie's ear. "It's because the king's family was the Hashimite tribe. They were a Bedouin family, and when they took over the throne, they remained in power partly because of Bedouin support. They have done wonders for the Bedouin people." Michelle trailed off, obviously uncomfortable talking about the subject.

Nick had put away his microphone and, unobserved by the two women, was listening to their whispered conversation. He turned in his seat and faced Leslie with an appraising expression that made her feel like a little girl caught whispering in school.

"Miss Green is right," he said in his officially charming voice. "The government has done much for the Bedouins. You will see as we drive along the Desert Highway today. Not long ago, the desert tribes lived far from the perimeters of civilization. They avoided cities and public roads. The trackless desert had been their home for centuries, and they understood it as mariners understand the sea. The Bedouins were fierce and free; they were survivors. They lived a harsh, demanding life where every man was a nobleman and each day was a struggle for existence." He paused. "The government has succeeded in bringing modernization to the Bedouins."

Was it Leslie's imagination, or did he treat the word *modernization* as though it had an evil smell?

"The generous government provides milk and bread for the Bedouins so they no longer have to work or keep flocks. They now live near roads where government trucks can bring them weekly supplies. All they need to do is wait, and their needs are provided for. Bedouin sons serve in the army for two years where they learn modern ways and earn a little money, so after three thousand years of living as nomads, they now have the privilege of becoming . . . civilized. Yes, one must admire such a thing." He smiled, a dazzling flash of white teeth punctuating his last comment, but Leslie noticed the smile did not touch his eyes.

He's lying, she decided. *He hates what is happening to the Bedouins. Why? Why does he allow himself to be a spokesman for something he hates?*

She squirmed in her seat. Everything about this day seemed distorted, strange, and out of focus. Something bothered her about Michelle Green, ostensibly the tour guide but afraid to speak. And what about an Arab driving their bus, while another controlled all the information they heard? Hal Johnson, who was he really—a materialistic man bent on a pilgrimage of piety? It didn't ring true, not even the odd, plump lady and her jewelry case seemed real. They all seemed like characters out of a play. Even the teenagers behind her seemed almost too cute, as though they were acting the way they thought teenagers were expected to act. Perhaps the strangeness of this Eastern country, the strain of the past three years, her unreasonable anger and irritation at Susan, and the long plane ride were all causing her to think, feel, and observe people inaccurately, especially after such a long, deliberate withdrawal from personal relationships. Perhaps she simply had forgotten how to handle being part of the world. Perhaps she was the one who was unnatural and false.

Sam drove out of Amman, while Nick explained that they were now heading toward the city of Aqaba on the northern tip of the Red Sea. Since the bus would need to cover most of the length of Jordan before nightfall, there would not be any stopping for sightseeing along the way.

As the passengers settled down for the long drive, Nick explained that there were two roads, both of them centuries old, which ran the length of Jordan. One road was called the King's Highway, and the other was called the Desert Highway. They would drive the Desert Highway today since it was the faster route, but tomorrow they would drive the King's Highway and visit the lost city of Petra. From there, they would cross into Israel at the Allenby Bridge. Tomorrow evening, they would be in Jericho.

Nick began a long discourse on the Old Testament tribes that had inhabited this desert region. He talked of the Midianites,

the Moabites, the Edomites, and the Ishmaelites. As each tribe
was discussed, he traced its origin to ancestors common both
to the Old Testament and the Koran. Almost all the tribes
were linked in some way to Abraham. As Nick's rich voice
peopled the bus with the age-old history of these tribes and
their primeval land, Leslie could almost feel Abraham's spirit
brooding across the unchanging hills and the flat plains.

Her eyes, searching the landscape, saw the dark goat-hair
tents of the Bedouins, isolated and proud, the design identical
to the tents of Abraham. She saw small villages, and in barren
regions, silent shepherds stood motionless on promontories
watching their scattered flocks of sheep and goats foraging on
the sparse land. She saw herds of camel, and when they passed
a military truck with teenaged, fresh-faced soldiers piled in the
back, a jarring note of the present juxtapositioned with the
past assailed her.

As Nick continued to roll the names of the tribes off his
tongue, the words of Abraham's covenant recurred to her,
"Descendents as numerous as the sands of the sea and the stars
of the sky." These were all descendents of Abraham, all of these
tribes of the desert, Arab and Jew alike—all of one blood, one
fabric. She mused on the centuries of enmity between these
peoples. *It is one family*, she thought as she watched the miles
spin by, half drowsing, half listening to the cadence of Nick's
voice as he entertained and informed the busload of tourists.
Somewhere along the way, the monotony of the desert landscape lulled her to sleep.

Much later, the bus lurched, and Leslie suddenly awakened, startled and disoriented, to a darkening world. The bus
was turning sharply on a narrow mountain road. In her abrupt
awakening, she found herself staring in horror through the bus
window, down the steep, unprotected slope of a precipice. From
her window, the road dropped straight down a sheer, rock-
strewn incline that plunged below her side of the bus into darkness. Her heart pounded frantically as her mind triggered a
vivid replay of her old nightmare. She saw, for the hundredth
time, the image of a small sports car rolling, pounding, and

crashing down a mountainside, bursting into flames and plummeting out of sight into the darkness. She was there—watching. She screamed and threw her hands over her eyes, pressing the image away, desperately trying to block the memory out. The bus continued lurching around the steep curve in the mountain road, as though the driver, Sam, was indifferent to the screams of the passengers.

Michelle Green turned to Leslie quickly, solicitously. "It's all right," she murmured, putting her arm around Leslie's trembling shoulders. "We passed an unexpected car coming the other way, and Sam had to swerve pretty close to the edge to miss it. You don't have to worry; he knows this road blindfolded."

Nick had jumped from his seat and was standing in front of Leslie. "Are you all right, Mrs. Brinton?" he asked, bending over so he could see her face in the dusk.

Leslie was still confused, the raw image of the flaming car continued to dance in her head like a cruel phantom. She gulped for air, trying to calm herself. How long had it been since she had dreamed of the accident? Did this mean the nightmares were going to start again? Why had she come to this harsh and cruel place where the past and present seemed to merge into one moment; where the land itself seemed to proclaim the ancient scriptures; where faith and hatred, family and enemy dwelt side by side in separate solitudes?

Tears of frustration and pain started in her eyes, and she shook off Michelle's gentle hand and turned her face from Nick's dark perusal.

"I'm fine," she said. "I'm terribly embarrassed. I wasn't frightened, you know, it's just that I had a bad start when I awakened." She bit her lip and struggled to bring her emotions under control. Nick said nothing, but continued to study her face with unreadable eyes. *Did he think she was a nervous fool,* she wondered, *a timorous young widow? How ridiculous she must seem to the other passengers—afraid of a mountain road.* Her hands trembled uncontrollably, and she clutched them tightly in her lap.

Without a word, Nick placed his strong hand over hers. His touch was as light as a leaf, but she could feel the warmth of his smooth palm. Neither she nor Nick said anything, but they remained joined by his gentle touch as the bus bounced through the gathering night. Slowly her trembling stopped, and Leslie's hands rested as still as sleeping sparrows in her lap.

Nick did not speak, he simply lifted his hand from hers, and with a deep, penetrating search of her face, he returned to his seat beside Sam.

Leslie stared out the window as darkness gathered across the desert hills, and the bus continued through the night to Aqaba. Unbidden, her mind was remembering, spinning back to Monterey, to memories that would not be denied and could not be forgotten.

Chapter Two

"Good-bye, Mommy!" Kerry had been dancing with excitement, tugging at his father's hand, anxious to be on his way. Why did the sight of Kerry's little red sneakers—hopping, skipping, impatient, and light—still stay in her mind? Sometimes when she could not even recall Kerry's little face, could not summon up each sweet line and feature to her remembrance, the prancing sneakers would still be there, vivid and real in her memory, like little red poppies blowing in a field.

Adam had kissed her and kissed her again, the corner of his mouth smiling against her lips, his voice warm and teasing. "Come on, Honey," he had murmured, "you're sure you can't come? Sure?" Another kiss, this time on her ear.

"Absolutely sure . . . " Another kiss, and she had laughed and gently pushed Adam away.

Leslie was a different woman in those days. Her bright blonde hair was curled, her cheeks were rich with color. She had a pleasant fullness to her figure, delicately curved and womanly. She wore frilly dresses, sandals with tiny straps, and sweet perfume. Her blue eyes were gentle and smiling, and her lips were soft, full, and as inviting as a pomegranate. She loved her husband—loved him more than life itself—and she wanted to be beautiful for him.

Adam had literally exploded into her life. She had been a lab assistant during her senior year of college. On her first day at work, Adam, an indifferent chemistry student at best, misread his lab directions. As she patrolled the lab tables, she saw him add hydrazine instead of water to his chloride, and seeing the gas building in the tubes, she yelled, "Everybody down!" and tackled Adam just as the glass burst. A spume of hot liquid and broken glass blew into the air and fell harmlessly on their prone bodies.

It was a few moments after the explosion before she could think clearly enough to realize that she was lying on top of a tanned and handsome young man, who was grinning at her wickedly. "It was worth it," he whispered. From that moment, she was in love with Adam Brinton.

Leslie was a brilliant student. She had finished her master's degree and was working on her doctorate. Although she had been raised by her widowed mother in a strong Mormon home, she found, as she pursued her education, that it became more and more difficult for her to have faith in spiritual and unseen things. As a scientist, she believed only those things that were demonstrable through observation, facts, and experimentation. In her search for scientific truth, she began to question the existence of any other kind of truth.

After her mother's death, she lost all contact with the Church, by choice. She felt it was hypocritical for her to continue to attend church since she had lost her testimony and now felt that the Church and its teachings had no relevance for her. It was not so much that she felt there was no God as that she concluded it was intellectually and scientifically impossible to prove his existence or lack of existence. She moved in a circle of intellectual friends to whom science was a religion, and she found that their company was exciting and the questions they raised about faith, myth, and the opiate of religion were convincing to her.

It wasn't until she met Adam that she realized her life at the university had become as sterile as her test tubes. Adam opened up the closed and tender places of her heart. He discovered the woman inside of the scientist, and she embraced his love with the same single-minded devotion she formerly gave to her studies. Within a few short weeks, they were married. From that moment on, Leslie filled her life with Adam, and he became her reason for being. All the loneliness and emptiness she had known during her quiet upbringing as an only child, all the bereavement she had felt at the death of her father and mother, all the self-denial of years of intense study, were suddenly swept away by this man who laughed at pretensions, who rejoiced in each day, and who loved her with all his heart.

She had lost the God of her childhood, but any sense of loss she once felt was now assuaged because Adam had become her life and her religion, and through him, she learned to drink in every experience. He opened to her every warm, beautiful, and joyful sensation, and his touch awakened in her a feminine glow and loveliness that transformed her.

During the four years of their marriage, nothing had dimmed her glow. It had taken the full three years since his death for her to change herself from a soft, carefree, open woman into the lean, tightly-controlled, colorless woman she had become: a woman who could never be hurt or touched or moved again. Leslie had become this new impenetrable woman because of the only time she had not let Adam's caresses move her. She had laughed at his entreating kisses that one afternoon, loving him, wanting to go in the car with him and Kerry, but because guests were coming for dinner that night, just once, she had resisted his charms, had resisted her need to be with him.

"Oh, Adam," she had laughed. "You know I can't come with you and Kerry today. You go along and get back in plenty of time for dinner. I've got too much to do." *Too much to do.* How those words came back to haunt her. *Too much to do.* So she had not gone in the car and had missed their final togetherness, had missed the journey all three should have taken together. She, left behind because of too much to do, now faced days of empty, looming gaps filled with routine and numbing repetition—anything to keep from thinking.

Adam had given her a last kiss. "We'll be back by four!" he called. He and Kerry ran to the car hand in hand, and Adam opened the door for Kerry, who scrambled in and wriggled like an excited puppy while Adam fastened his seatbelt. Adam went over to the driver's side and threw her one last kiss before climbing into the car. She took off her apron and waved it at them.

"Good-bye, you two handsome men! Hurry home! I'll have fresh apple pie waiting!"

The car door slammed.

Leslie always wondered why her memory of those last moments with Kerry and Adam was fragmented like pieces of a puzzle. She kept storing it away, locking it up in the back corners of her mind, refusing it the light, but it came pressing back. And always the same stray pieces would stand clear: Kerry's red sneakers, Adam's kisses, the sound of the car door as it slammed, and the smell of burning apple pie. But that had come later— much later—after the telephone call.

She had gone back into the house, anxious to get to her work, anticipating an uninterrupted day of cleaning and baking. She remembered feeling a brief twinge of regret that she had not gone with her husband and son. They had so much fun together; the drive was one they took frequently. She could envision them driving out of Monterey along the seventeen-mile drive past Carmel and on down Big Sur. She had made the drive often with Adam, who was a real estate property manager and handled property and vacation houses from Monterey to the southern end of Big Sur. Usually Leslie drove with him when he visited properties down the coast, but she had spent two days with him already that week, and her house was a mess. Besides, Kerry was excited about having his father all to himself for a few hours.

The police told her it had been a tourist driving a big black sedan. The man was unfamiliar with the seacoast road and pulled into one of the scenic turnouts overlooking the Pacific Ocean. The heavy black car hit Adam's little sports car as it came around the curve of the road. The impact had spun Adam's car with such force that it upended against the guardrails, rolled over on top of them, and crashed down the rock face of the cliff, finally bursting into flames as it hit the boulders in the pounding surf far below. It burned fiercely until the waves and its own devouring heat destroyed the flames.

Someone at the observation point had noted the license number of Adam's car, and the police had called her within the hour. She didn't know how long she sat alone in the house. It wasn't until the smell of smoke from the oven prodded her into action that she finally removed the blackened pies. Outside the windows of her home—her home and Kerry's home and Adam's home—which would never be home to her again— she saw the sky had grown dark, and she suddenly realized that for the rest of her life nighttime would be the worst.

Several days after the funeral, Leslie had driven alone along the familiar highway from Monterey to Carmel. As she came up the steep, narrow road and around the curve to the Big Sur observation point, for one brief, horrible moment she was tempted to let go of the wheel, to allow her car to continue straight to where the guardrail was hideously dented, and to plunge through it, out into the inviting blue of the sky and ocean beyond the rim of the cliff. But she had driven carefully and had parked on the gravel turnout.

Standing on the eminence, she looked down the cliff at the indifferent ocean crashing against the rocks, and there, washed by the spray, was the burned skeleton of Adam's car. A woman next to her was saying to her companion, "Look at that car wreck in the surf. Imagine how awful! I wonder if the people in the car were conscious while the car was falling?"

It hit Leslie like a blow, and she wanted to turn and scream at the woman, to beat against her with her fists. *How can you say such a thing? What a ghastly thing to think. Oh, Kerry! My little boy . . . were you frightened? Did it hurt? Did you see the flames? And Adam . . . what were you thinking? Did you reach out for Kerry? Did you think of me, that I had refused to accompany you on the final journey? Were you in pain?* Her mind was gashed by the thought, and she turned and stumbled back to her car.

After that, the nightmares had grown worse. A hundred times she saw the car falling. Sometimes she would see Kerry's or Adam's face in the flames. They were calling to her. Sometimes she was in the car, and she would try to stop its fall, willing it back up the cliff, straining against the noise and fear and the force of gravity. Somehow, if she were good enough and wise enough, she could make it fly backward, back up the road.

She would awaken, groaning with effort and drenched with perspiration.

She lived for weeks and months in a gray twilight of daily inaction and nightly horror. As her mind went around and around, she became aware that the point at which her thinking always stopped was the moment when she imagined the car hitting the beach. At that moment, Kerry and Adam were dead, of that she was sure. But were they dead? That was the question that hung unanswered in her mind. Before her marriage, she had been a trained scientist. She knew all about the life of cells, but something in her cried out to believe there was something more to Adam and Kerry than protein and DNA and electrical impulse. She wanted desperately to believe there was something immortal in them that could live on, that could wait for her until she could rejoin them. She wanted to return to the simple faith of her forgotten childhood. But she could not. Too many years of disbelief intervened.

She talked with several bishops, but her scientific mind could not accept their answers. She finally tucked her desperate hopes away, considering the answers to be unknowable and refusing to comfort herself with an optimistic dream.

It took about a year to seal all her feelings away. She made a decision to live a Spartan existence, a life devoid of feeling. She learned what she could bear to think about and what she could not. So with scientific precision, she plotted a life for herself that was carefully circumscribed and would allow no emotion or further religious inquiry. She returned to the university, completed her graduate work, and applied for a teaching position at a small southern California college. In the university town, she found herself a frugal apartment close to the campus, and with icy determination, she convinced the administration to give her the fullest teaching load possible. Her students found her organized, precise, prepared—and cold. One young man observed that she taught like a machine.

She was courteous but distant with her colleagues, and after several friendly overtures, they left her alone. Since her work was demanding, the days took care of themselves, but the nights were still impossibly long, and her nightmares recurred. In desperation, Leslie started running to exhaust herself physically so she could sleep. At noon, she spent an hour in the university gym working out in the conditioning room. Then in the evening, before returning to her apartment, she ran on the track. It was a quiet time of day with few runners in evidence, and she ran several miles every night before going home. Running was the perfect physical outlet. It required no thought, it was automatic and tiring, and she could do it alone. That is until Susan came and broke through her careful defenses. *Susan!* she thought with exasperation and affection. Every time Leslie remembered that Susan was in California, while *she* was on this strange and miserable odyssey, she felt a surge of irritation. After all, this was meant to be Susan's pilgrimage—not hers.

Chapter Three

Leslie sat in misery, her nerves raw with memories, as the bus entered the sleepy streets of the Jordanian section of the city of Aqaba. The streets and houses were dark and humble. Palm trees lined the road, and the fragrance of exotic blossoms perfumed the night air. The tourists were staying at a new American hotel situated on the shore of the Red Sea. The hotel was built around a courtyard with a swimming pool from which broad steps led to the beach. Beyond the lighted courtyard, Leslie could see the white line of waves breaking on a stretch of dark sand. The coastline curved around the gulf, and she could see across the water to the metropolitan part of the city, which was built on a hill sloping down to the sea. She noted how much brighter it was in that section. On the far hillside, lights blazed, and she thought she could discern tall, modern-looking buildings. *What a land of contrasts*, she thought, *and what irony to travel this far only to spend my first night in a hotel just like the one on the highway next to my own home.*

The guests were informed that dinner would be served to them, as a group, in one hour in the courtyard.

Leslie could hardly stand the confusion by the bus as her fellow passengers scrambled to claim their luggage. Hal Johnson brushed against her, and she turned with a frown. "Sorry," he said, "quite a crush, isn't it, little lady?" She wondered why she was so aggravated by this innocuous man. After all, he only wanted to be liked.

When Leslie finally got to her room, she leaned against the door with a sigh of relief. It felt wonderful to be away from people, and she wanted to clutch her privacy to her, to find a way to wrap it around herself like some kind of magic protection. The past forty-eight hours had been exhausting. The unfamiliar setting, the press of people, and the feelings of being closed up and programmed by others had unsettled her carefully cultivated defenses. Her long-suppressed emotions were tearing at her, filling her with anger, impatience, and tension—feelings she thought she had left behind forever.

The thought of facing all those people again at supper was almost beyond Leslie, but she was hungry, and she knew if she did not eat, she would be ill.

Perhaps a shower will help, she thought. She opened her suitcase and took out clean clothes. She would eat a light supper and then, hopefully, go running. The thought of physical activity was reassuring because her emotions were her enemy; they must be subdued. Discipline and control were the only traits she would let herself acknowledge. "Never again," she had vowed. Never again would she let herself love anything that could be lost.

"Oh, Adam," she groaned, putting her hands over her face. For a few moments she was motionless, then she resolutely squared her shoulders and entered the shower stall.

After her shower, she pulled on a blue cotton skirt and a sleeveless white T-shirt. All she had time to do was towel her hair, so she slicked it back with a comb, letting it hang damp and smooth to her shoulders.

At the last moment, as she left the room, she grabbed a small book from her bag. *Maybe if I sit and read no one will try to talk to me,* she thought. Her subterfuge worked, and during the simple meal she sat at the end of one of the long tables reading and eating slowly, and no one interrupted her. She tried to close her ears to the flow of conversation around her, but some of the comments filtered through.

"Can you believe it? The Red Sea!"

"Not really the Red Sea—this is technically the Gulf of Aqaba. The sea begins at the far end of the gulf."

"It is thought by some that this is where Moses parted the waters!" someone exclaimed.

"Apparently the sea is very shallow here."

"I, for one, believe the miracles just as they are recorded in the Old Testament. Wherever the parting took place, it was indeed a miraculous occurrence, not just an aberration," a voice asserted.

"Yes, of course," someone else replied, "certainly. The Jews believed that. The martyr Stephen cited the miracle of the Red Sea at his trial. Even after all those centuries, it was still a significant cornerstone of Jewish faith."

"It is a lovely miracle," a woman's voice declared. "I mean, it was so satisfying when the dreadful pursuers were all drowned." Leslie shuddered. That high, piercing voice could only belong to the woman Hal Johnson had befriended.

She was surprised not to see Hal Johnson at the dinner. He didn't seem like the kind of man who would go to bed early or be content to stay in his room alone. He seemed to crave an audience. *Oh, well,* Leslie thought, *wherever he is, it's none of my business.*

Dinner was over, and the tourists began to filter out of the starlit courtyard and up to their rooms. The waiters cleared the tables, and the breeze from the sea stiffened, but the air remained warm and balmy. Leslie, having slept on the plane and bus, found she was wide awake, and the prospect of lying in bed, facing the memories that had been stirred by the day's events, was oppressive to her.

She continued to read in the dim light cast by a small lamp at the side of the courtyard, but the book was not engaging, and she found herself feeling restless. Finally she placed the book on the table and walked across the courtyard, past the swimming pool, and out onto the dark beach. Although the beach was deserted, she saw the pleasant reminders of a happy day in the sand around her. Several towels had been left, and her foot scuffed against a pair of forgotten sandals. Although there was no artificial light, the moon had risen, and the water reflected its brightness. As her eyes grew more accustomed to the night, she was able to look out across the ocean. Far out in the gulf, she could discern the shapes of heavy oceangoing vessels. *Probably oil tankers,* she thought. Behind her was the modern hotel, and before her was the sea, as ancient as the history of man. Again she experienced an odd sense of dislocation and a disbelief that she was actually in this unexpected place.

The sea lapped gently against the beach, and she slipped off her rope espadrilles to test the temperature of the water with her foot. Finding it cool but mild, she waded in a few steps and stood feeling the pull and tug of the sea against her feet. Suddenly she was assailed by a need for physical motion; it was as pressing and urgent as the pull of the tide. The long hours of cramped travel needed to be purged. Looking to her right, she saw the beach continuing unimpeded as far as she could see, curving toward the more brightly lighted portion of the city. Here the beach was dark and bordered by palms and oleander bushes, but the moonlight was bright enough to let her run. On impulse, she darted out of the water and began sprinting along the beach, staying close to the waves where the sand was hard and smooth.

The running felt wonderful. She could feel her slender, powerful legs pumping comfortably; her breathing grew deep and measured. She shook her head in the freshening breeze and felt her hair, dry now, lift like a cloud. For the first time in days she felt free and light. She would run until she felt exhausted, maybe even run to the bright lights further down the shore; they couldn't be more than five or six miles away. So absorbed was she in the physical release of running that it was some minutes before Leslie's mind became alert to the sounds that were following her. As she had run past a dark patch of foliage at the edge of the hotel's property, her subconscious mind had registered two dark figures standing in the shadows in earnest conversation, but the thought had not penetrated. Shortly afterward her silent, bare footsteps were followed by the heavy, slapping footsteps of a large man running swiftly. The man's steps were quiet, but not silent, and he was running with such speed and power that the sound of his breathing was heavy in the night air. Gradually Leslie's mind absorbed the sounds, and she began to concentrate on them. After a few moments of listening, there was no question in her mind that someone was running after her—chasing her! Someone who was heavier than she and running much harder and faster. She could hear the sounds of pursuit growing closer and closer, and she wanted to scream. Panic made her react like a forest animal, and instead of uttering a sound, she drew on her enormous reserves and began running as swiftly as a deer.

Her pursuer remained quiet, but she could hear the cadence of his running feet increase in speed also, and the sound of his powerful breathing came closer. By now she was running head-long, not feeling the bruise of shells and driftwood on her bare feet, uncaring where she was going, and only fleeing in desperate fear down the long, dark corridor of the beach toward the lighted shore in the distance.

"Mrs. Brinton!" a man's voice gasped behind her. The shock of hearing her name caused her to miss a step, and her foot hit a rock in the darkness. She began to fall just as the man's body flung out of the night, and he grasped her at the waist. She and the man fell to the sand in a heavy tangle, both of them breathing hoarsely, gasping for air. Leslie began to beat at the man with her tired fists, but he grabbed her hands and began to shake her.

"Mrs. Brinton! Stop it—stop it! What do you think you're doing?" She was still so frightened that she continued to thresh against him, not listening, until he slapped her smartly on the cheek. The pain cleared her mind, and she looked up into the face of Nick, barely discernible in the wash of the moonlight.

"What do you think you are doing? Do you think you are in Santa Monica?" His voice was fierce with rage, and something else. Perhaps it was concern, although Leslie couldn't imagine that. What was he talking about? What had she done?

"I don't know what you mean," she gasped, still trying to catch her breath. "I always run . . . every night. I don't see how that's any concern of yours."

"You fool!" he said furiously. "You innocent, protected fool! Don't you have any idea what the world is like? Look!" He yanked her roughly to her feet and pointed ahead to a clump of oleander bushes that grew almost to the water's edge.

In front of the bushes, she saw the dark silhouettes of uniformed men with machine guns. Two of the men were walking toward them. She could not see their faces, but she could see the guns they carried trained on her and Nick. Looking up the beach to her right, she saw other sentries standing in the shadows of the palm trees.

He continued to whisper fiercely in her ear. "This marks the beginning of no-man's-land," he said, pointing to the oleanders. "Aqaba is a divided city. If you had listened on the bus, you would have known that. Do you understand? There is no interchange between the two sections. If you had run another ten feet, you would have been shot!"

Leslie's knees suddenly became weak, and if Nick had not been holding her arm with angry strength, she would have collapsed. The sentry called out to them in a harsh staccato voice, and Nick answered, trying to sound as casual as possible. She could not understand a word of the exchange, but she knew she was being described by Nick as a stupid American tourist. Nick was probably saying, "What are we to do with these innocents? It is like watching children when one is a tour guide for the Americans." The sentry listened to Nick's explanation and was silent for a moment. She felt the tension in Nick's hand as they waited unmoving, and she realized they were still in danger. Then Nick said something more, and his voice sounded disdainful. In a quick movement, he picked her up and turned around and began to carry her back toward the hotel beach.

Whatever he had said must have been extremely amusing to the sentry, who gave a harsh bark of laughter and turned away from them. Nick called back a brief acknowledgment of thanks over his shoulder and continued to stride, carrying her back to the lighted hotel.

"You can put me down," she said coldly, but he continued to walk with her, his face set and angry. "I said, you can put me down!" she repeated.

Unceremoniously, he dumped her on the sand. "You idiot," he said, his voice shaking. "Don't you realize you could have been killed?"

"What would that matter to you anyway?" she asked angrily. "It's just one less gullible tourist for your trap—or is it that you would worry about the publicity for your precious guide service? You don't need to worry, I'm sure you have connections and could get the whole thing hushed up."

He took a deep breath as though striving for control, and she had the strange feeling he was restraining himself from hitting her.

It occurred to her that here, in the dark, when she could not see his face clearly, Nick sounded and acted like a different man: direct, powerful, and real. Was this the same Nick who stroked his mustache and eyed the girls, showing his white teeth with self-conscious handsomeness? The same man who gave impeccable tourist speeches with practiced ease? No, this man on the dark beach was strong and commanding, and even though she was furious at the way he had treated her, she knew she owed him her life.

"I'm sorry I said that," she murmured with halting apology. "What I should say is, thank you for my life." She paused. "What do you mean Aqaba is a divided city?"

"When Palestine was partitioned, the city of Aqaba was partitioned as well. It is half Israeli and half Jordanian." He looked out across the water at the brightly lighted Israeli section, and then he glanced down the dark tunnel of the beach where the sentry soldiers were standing unseen in the night. When he spoke again, she could tell he was not speaking to her, but was speaking to himself.

"We are brothers, living beside one another but separated by our own man-made barriers." There was such a quiet intensity in his voice that she was moved.

She exclaimed impulsively, "That's just what I thought today as you were speaking about the various tribes! They are mostly descendents of Abraham in one way or another—all his seed." She looked out across the water to the night sky filled with its billion stars. "Numerous as the sand and the stars," she mused.

"Ah," he said, "I see you know your Old Testament. Did you study it to prepare for your visit to our land?"

She felt herself blush in the dark. "No," she answered, and because of the strange intimacy of the night, she admitted something she had told no one except Susan. "I studied the Bible because I was searching for an answer to the most important question in my life."

"I see," he said quietly. "Then we both have looked to Abraham for answers. I wonder how he feels as he sees his children hating one another."

He had touched her exposed nerve. "You seem very sure that Abraham still exists somewhere, and that he is capable of knowing and caring about such things. That's a rather bold assumption since he has been dead for centuries." Suddenly she resented Nick's bland assumption of a life after death, and she wanted to jar his smugness. "But then, you Muslims do have a primitive belief in heaven, don't you?"

She felt him stiffen at her barbed tone. He turned abruptly to face her, and she could see the moon shining in his dark eyes. What she could not see, however, was the way she herself looked: her face lighted in the reflection from the sea, her skin as pale as the moon itself, her hair a glorious halo around her, and her sweet face filled with naked pain. Her fine-honed athlete's body was dwarfed in the strength and magnetism of his dark shadow. For a moment he stared at her, and then he took a long breath. With effort he smiled, his white teeth gleaming in the darkness, and his face assuming its former suave professional expression. She thought his Arabic accent grew more pronounced as he became, once again, the accommodating tour guide.

"Yes, Mrs. Brinton," Nick said, his voice formal. "I am very happy you have not been hurt. Perhaps next time you wish to go running you will first consult with me. Now, if you will permit me, I will escort you back to your room."

Why had he changed back so suddenly? It was as though the intense, compassionate man who had rescued her had never existed, or had been an illusion she had created out of her own ridiculous imagination. With self-disgust and impatience, she shook off his hand.

"No, thank you, Nick," she said brusquely, deliberately adding his Americanized name, pronouncing it crisply. "I can find my room by myself." She turned on her heel and left him.

It wasn't until hours later, as Leslie lay awake in bed, that she began to wonder why Nick was on the beach in the first place. Where had he been when he saw her running and sprinted after her? Her mind briefly flashed the impression of two men talking in the dark trees behind the hotel—one of them with white hair—but the memory was vague and she fell into a deep and exhausted slumber, still mulling the elusive question in her mind.

Chapter Four

It seemed to Leslie that her travel alarm rang as soon as she fell asleep. She listlessly got out of bed, but then dressed hurriedly, remembering the instructions of the day before. The tour group had been told they must board the bus by eight o'clock in the morning because there was a long day's drive planned with two important stops: one at Petra, the city of rose-colored stone, and one at Mount Pisgah, where Moses had first seen the Promised Land. Leslie did not want to be made conspicuous by keeping the group waiting, so she packed and was ready to go in short order. Michelle Green, the American tour guide, had informed her that at Petra they would probably be riding horses into the ruins, and women were encouraged to wear slacks. With that in mind, Leslie dressed in jeans, a loose cotton shirt and canvas shoes.

The day was already hot, even though it was early morning, and Leslie gathered up the heavy fall of her hair and pulled it into a ponytail with a rubber band. It felt cooler to have the hair off her neck. She snatched her suitcase and her shoulder bag and hurried down to the lobby. There were already several people milling around ahead of her, visiting with one another and waiting for instructions. Sam and Nick were nowhere to be seen, and the bus was still parked where it had been left the night before. Leslie glanced at her watch. It was seven-thirty. She decided to grab some breakfast before leaving.

In the dining room, a buffet table was set with orange juice, milk, coffee, sweet rolls, hash browns, and scrambled eggs. Leslie again thought of the incongruity of this American hotel in the ancient kingdom of Jordan. She ate quickly. A few other passengers came in, nodded to her, and hurriedly ate their own breakfasts. When they reentered the lobby, Michelle Green was fluttering around encouraging everyone to hurry out and board the bus. Leslie could see the bus in front of the hotel doors, Sam was sitting behind the wheel, and two young men were helping load the suitcases into the gaping luggage compartments under the bus. Nick was standing by the open door, clipboard in hand, greeting the passengers as they boarded.

It was a replay of the day before, and Leslie, looking at Nick as he smiled rakishly at the women and held their hands as they stepped onto the bus, could not see any remnant of her companion of the evening before. If anything, Nick's debonair act was thicker this morning than it had been yesterday—and judging from their laughter, the tourists loved it. *He really knows how to get those women to eat right out of his hands,* Leslie thought angrily. *Well, it won't work on me. What a two-bit Don Juan.* She thought about the Nick of last night, and for a moment she had an uncomfortable feeling that he had known, after all, how to work on her too. His honesty and sympathy probably had been another act, an alternate way to handle a maverick tourist. The thought made her harden her resolve not to be involved in any way, and she approached the bus grimly determined to avoid any interchange with Nick.

One of the young men took her bag, and she hurried to the door of the bus. Nick reached out his hand with a mischievous half-grin and a knowing twinkle in his eye. She looked at the outstretched hand coldly and took the high step without his assistance. "Good morning, Mrs. Brinton," his voice said softly, so meticulously courteous that it was like a secret challenge. "I trust you slept well?"

She could think of no answer that would not encourage him, so she said nothing at all. Sam, sitting in the driver's seat, noticed the exchange, and he gave her his saucy grin from beneath his large mustache. Again she found herself smiling and feeling better. Something about the impudent young driver appealed to her. He seemed to be above the petty frustrations and concerns of the rest of the world, as though he lived in an aura of unfailing good cheer.

Determined not to be thrown into Nick's company, Leslie decided she would not sit near the front of the bus, so she chose a seat in the back on the right hand side. As she was busily settling her shoulder bag, she became aware of someone standing in the aisle watching her. "Well, little lady. How did you enjoy your first night in the Near East?" Hal Johnson's voice boomed at her.

She looked up at the florid, silver-haired man. He was not wearing a flowered shirt this morning, but was wearing a modish version of a safari shirt with many well-tailored pockets and buttoned tabs on the shoulders. It was made from a light, buff-colored cotton, and Leslie almost smiled at what she was sure was Mr. Johnson's version of Hemingway, or the great white hunter.

"I thought I was still in California," she said with quiet irony.

He looked at her blankly for a moment, and then gave a forced laugh. "Oh—you mean the Holiday Inn . . . on the Gulf of Aqaba . . . yes, that's a good one." He smiled again and did not move away. There was obviously something more he was planning to say to her, and he felt uncomfortable about saying it. "Er, er, I believe this is Mrs. Platt's seat. I think the plan was that everyone would keep the same seats as they had yesterday. You know, it avoids confusion and it keeps families together . . . that sort of thing."

Leslie blushed. It hadn't occurred to her that if she changed her seat, everyone on the bus would have to find a new seat. "Oh!" she exclaimed in some confusion. "I'm sorry. I simply didn't think."

"No harm done," Hal Johnson answered heartily. "Here, let me carry your bag to your seat."

"No!" Leslie said sharply. Without meaning to, she had rebuffed Hal Johnson a second time. It was just because she felt self-conscious and irritated with herself. She knew she should have accepted his offer graciously. What was happening to her? In her desire to escape notice, she was actually gaining attention, and not very favorable attention at that.

"I'm sorry, Mr. Johnson," she murmured apologetically. "I can manage by myself. It was nice of you to offer." She slid past him as he stood unmoving in the aisle, and again she noticed how little the habitual smile he wore touched his agate eyes—or was it again that she herself was so strange she made people uncomfortable? She didn't know, and she refused to examine her thoughts any further.

Hurriedly she resumed her seat at the front of the bus beside Michelle Green, and moments later, Nick swung up into his seat. As he turned to look over his shoulder to check the passengers, his eye caught hers, and for a long moment, they simply looked at one another. She was the first to look away, but out of the corner of her eye she thought she saw him smile to himself. Oh, *the vanity of that man,* she thought furiously. *He is so sure he has made another conquest with those white teeth and that devilish grin. Well, he has another think coming!*

The bus began its journey toward Petra. The day before they had traveled the Desert Highway, which cut through the interior of Jordan on the high, flat, desert plains. Today they traveled on the other highway, which ran north and south through Jordan. This road was called the King's Highway and was an ancient route close to the western border of Jordan. It had been a caravan route for centuries, and for all of those centuries, it had been plagued by bandits who hid in the surrounding rock cliffs and barren mountains and preyed on the laden travelers in the valley below.

As the bus drove through the desert heat, Leslie found herself captivated by the prehistoric land. It seemed untouched by the passage of time, as though it had remained in exactly the same state it had been in when the hand of the Creator shaped it, barren and eternally old, upon the face of the earth. At one point, the bus stopped so the passengers could watch a herd of camels, their ungainly young calves struggling on spindly, knock-kneed legs to keep up with the ferocious gait of the leaders as they loped across a stretch of desert. Frequently, the tourists saw Bedouin tents made of black or mottled goat hair. The tents were placed far from the road, but close enough that the occupants could, from the distance, observe the passing vehicles. Leslie remembered that the thing that had brought the Bedouins from the deep desert oases and hidden valleys was the government trucks that brought food, milk, and supplies. She thought it sad that these people were caught midway between two worlds, living on the edge of their ancient desert, yet not quite ready to touch the modern world. On the barren and merciless stretches beside the highways of their country, they had created their own no-man's-land.

Nick turned on the microphone and began speaking to the passengers. "In about an hour, we will reach the city of Petra. Petra is a Greek word meaning stone or rock, and the city lives up to its name. It is a city carved out of living stone. At one time, there may have been as many as fifty thousand inhabitants in the city. There are high-rise apartments, as you will see, with homes chiseled into the sheer rock wall of the cliffs and stairs carved on the face of the cliffs so that the dwellers could climb up to their rooms.

"The city was the habitation of the Nabatean tribe. Originally they were nothing more than desert pirates who discovered the hidden rock canyon of Petra; it can only be reached through a narrow earthquake fault in the mountains. This fault was hidden for centuries, and no one could find where the fierce tribe lived. They swooped out upon unsuspecting caravans, then seemed to disappear into the air . . . or into the rock." Nick chuckled at his play on words, and the passengers all joined in.

"Anyway, eventually, the Nabateans, who were very bright, figured out that it would be smarter to spare the lives of the caravan traders and exact a ransom from them than to kill them. It was an offer the caravans could not refuse." Again Nick laughed, and the passengers responded to his humor. *He's even memorized the timing,* Leslie thought, *like some two-bit comedian.*

She was not amused by Nick's attempts at canned wit, but she was interested in the story of Petra, and she listened attentively as Nick continued.

"The Nabateans gave the caravans a choice—your money or your life. The smart ones chose to give the money. Eventually the Nabateans even made their extortion seem quite respectable; they called it protection money—or tax. In the center of Petra, they carved an enormous building into the largest cliff. It was the treasury, and in it they stored the bags of gold and the wealth of generations of plunder. Eventually they became the bankers of known civilization. I told you they were smart. They financed governments, wars, business, and trade. They continued to live in their impregnable city, protected from the world by hundreds of miles of desert and the massive mountain range in whose very heart they were living.

"About the beginning of the first century B.C., the Romans decided to conquer the Nabateans and set about laying siege to Petra. Of course this wasn't hard to do, since the city has only one outlet, and that is through the narrow gorge I told you about that is an old earthquake fault in the midst of the red-rock cliffs. However, the difficulty was that the siege was not a hardship, since the Nabateans were well-provisioned and ready to hold out forever. No one had ever conquered them, you see."

Nick squinted his eyes and looked out the windshield at the massive cliffs they were driving toward. For a moment, Leslie observed that his face lost its gloss of animated charm, and in its place she saw an expression of sorrow and yearning. Almost in a whisper he repeated, "Unconquered . . . " Then he seemed to shake himself, and his smooth, entertaining voice continued, "until, that is, the Roman commander observed a very simple thing. There was no source of water in Petra. All the water was brought in through stone pipes from the river outside. They smashed the stone pipes and waited. Petra was conquered without so much as a battle.

"For a long time, the Romans profitted from the rich trading center that had been established in the city, but the Nabateans lured the caravans away, directing them to Syria. When the caravans stopped coming, Petra died as a city.

"There is one last chapter," Nick added. "The city was forgotten through the centuries and soon what little was known about it was thought to be legend. No one knew where it was until 1812, when it was rediscovered by an adventurous English woman. Because the city is carved into cliffs, some of which rise as high as two hundred feet, and because of the arid climate of Jordan, the city was in a perfect state of preservation. It can still only be reached by riding through the gorge that breaks through the rock."

Leslie found herself eagerly looking forward to seeing the city. Everything Nick had said made her feel that this was a place of incredible uniqueness, and in spite of herself, she felt her spirits lifting to the challenge of a new experience.

The bus stopped at a small way station, and Michelle Green stood up to explain the procedure to the tour group. "Nick is out negotiating for our horses," Michelle said. "If you wish, you may walk into the city by foot, but the path is very rocky, and it is about two miles of walking in the heat. Besides, you will find yourself competing with the horses for space on the trail. Those of you who feel you absolutely cannot ride horseback, however, may walk.

"The horses are handled by their owners, who are Arabian runners. You get on the horse and all you have to do is sit. The Arab who owns your horse will run along beside you holding the horse's bit and guiding the horse. When you arrive in the center court of the city of Petra, you will dismount and pay the runner two dollars—no more, no matter what the man does or says.

"If you are ready, we will go now." Michelle led the way out of the bus, and the tourists hesitantly walked over to a noisy, colorful scene. On a rock field dozens of Arab men, dressed in desert robes and flowing white kaffiyehs bound with woven bands to their heads, milled about with their horses. Each man held the reins of a spirited, lean horse. Each horse had a brilliant saddle, farthingales with silken tassles, and bits and bridles that dangled colorful ornamentation. The horses were high-spirited and small, pure Arabians with flaring nostrils and huge fierce eyes. The Arab men revelled in the fire of their animals, and they shouted and cursed one another and their proud beasts.

More than one tourist blanched at the thought of mounting one of these spirited horses. Even Leslie felt a moment of trepidation, not so much because of the mounts, but because the fierceness and intensity of the Arab men startled her. They were as proud and fiery as their stallions, and she shrank from the thought of putting herself into the hands of men of such strange and menacing cast. Nonetheless, with a semblance of order, Nick and Michelle were getting the tour mounted. Leslie watched in fascination as the Arabs grasped the reins of the horses near their jawline, and with a shouted command, horses and owner trotted off toward the rocky trail that led down the hillside into the deep valley below and toward the rosy-red cliffs looming across the narrow valley.

"Your turn." Nick's voice, close to her ear, made her start. She had been absorbed in the noise and color of the scene and had not seen him approach. He took her elbow and led her toward a white stallion. The horse was slightly taller than the other horses, more muscular and high-spirited. As she walked toward the animal, he tossed his long, magnificent mane and stared at her with a haughty, baleful eye. The horse's owner, a dark-complexioned man as lean and hard as the rocks surrounding Petra, met her gaze boldly. Unlike the other runners who had been all smiles and extravagant gestures, this man gave her no ingratiating smile and made no attempt at verbal communication. He was as proud as his Arabian stallion. With practiced ease, he and Nick helped her mount. Her light, trained body sat easily in the high-pommelled Eastern saddle. As the runner grasped the bit and turned the prancing horse toward the trail, Sam, the bus driver, strolled toward them. He called a greeting to the runner in Arabic. The runner answered, and for the first time, turned and smiled at Sam. With a grin, Sam looked at Nick and then up at Leslie.

"Are you sure you're up to this?" Sam asked, indicating the trail with a nod of his head.

Leslie, holding the reins and feeling the skittish horse with her knees, grinned back. "I figure it's got to be safe. You can't afford to lose any tourists now, can you?" She barely had time to finish the sentence. The horse, trained in its duty, would not be held still any longer. With a shout, the runner leaped into the air and began racing along the trail. The stallion began a murderous canter along the rocky path, his head flinging and his powerful sculpted hooves striking fire from the stones.

Because of the brief conversation with Sam, Leslie had become separated from the group. She could see the others ahead of her on the trail, but she had the uncomfortable feeling of being alone on the back of the powerful white Arabian steed at the mercy of the dark, fierce man who was leading her. She looked surreptitiously at her guide; his face was streaked with sweat, and his skin was like fine, dark leather. His white kaffiyeh billowed around his face as he ran, yet he seemed, like the horse, unwearied by exertion. He was breathing deeply and easily, and he and the horse ran with a perfect synchronization, as though they were one being. Every once in a while she would notice her runner looking at her out of the side of his eyes. He seemed to be measuring her, testing her. His intensity and silence made her uncomfortable.

They descended into the valley, and across a small streambed, Leslie could see the dark opening of the gorge, which led through the cliffs. On either side of the opening, the cliffs rose for over one hundred feet. As Leslie looked into the narrow defile, it looked shadowed and empty. The rest of the tour group were, by now, far ahead. Just as her Arab runner prepared to lead her and her horse into the narrow break between the cliffs, Leslie heard a bloodcurdling cry. Echoing out of the cliffs, trebled in volume by the resonance of the stone walls, came whoops, screams, and wild, high-pitched yells accompanied by the pounding feet of galloping horses and the clang and jingle of bridles and stirrups. Leslie gasped in startled horror, and the runner yanked the horse's bit to stop him and pushed the stallion close to the side of the cliff. From the mouth of the earthquake fault poured out a scene from Lawrence of

Arabia. The Arabic runners, after depositing their tourists, had mounted their steeds themselves, and with wild exuberance, they were showing the pale, pampered foreigners what it was like to be men of the desert—fierce and fearless. They rode out of the defile at charging speed, their horses white eyed and fleet, their robes flying in the wind, and their faces intent on dreams of the past. This magnificent cavalry swept past Leslie, and she felt her steed tramble beneath her in a restless desire to join the pell-mell charge.

It only lasted a moment, and as the Arabs swept onward, across the stream and back up the valley to their way station, they left in their wake only the echoes of their clamor and the gradually settling red dust that their horses' hooves had roused from the stones.

Alone, Leslie and her guide entered the dark and twisting passageway leading to the ancient ruins of Petra. As they trotted through the silence, Leslie felt the magic of the high stone walls, where sunlight barely penetrated. She could see high above her the water conduits, carved into the cliffs, which had served the city and had been its lifeline and ultimately its death. She began to see rooms and apartments, carved like square caves into the rock walls. Windows and doorways cut into the face of the cliffs indicated living quarters, and she could see the narrow stone stairs that led to the higher rooms. *I wonder where the children played*, she thought. *They must have given families with children the lower apartments.*

The gorge had been formed by a prehistoric earthquake, and it twisted and jagged like a giant tear in the middle of the rock cliffs. Often they would turn so abruptly that Leslie would not be able to see more than a few yards in front of her or behind her, and then they would make another sharp turn and the path would suddenly become narrower or broader. Still the runner and the horse kept up their merciless pace, and Leslie began to feel oppressed in the darkness of the pass, with the odd, echoing silence and the barrenness of the red cliff walls. Just then, they turned another sharp corner and Leslie looked down the trail and gasped. A few yards in front of her the gorge widened. She was still in the dark shadows of the cliff walls, but through the width of the opening in front of her, she saw brilliant sunlight streaming like a white-hot spotlight. Centered perfectly in the frame of the opening between the cliff walls and on the face of a cliff across the sunlit square before them was a building carved in rose-colored stone with magnificent Roman columns reaching toward the sky, topped with brilliantly carved adornments that simulated a roof. Above this magnificent facade were carved elaborate window lintels with Roman statuary and columnar decoration. The room thus framed in the cliff wall was a gaping darkness of such immensity that Leslie could scarcely believe her eyes. "The treasury," she whispered to herself.

In a minute she was led into the sunlit square, and enthralled with the immensity of Petra, she paid the runner her two dollars, noting the disdain in his Arabic eyes as he accepted it. Without a word the man sprang into his saddle and shouted to his horse. In a whirl of dust, they were gone. Leslie could not see her group anywhere, so she decided to wander through the city on her own, feeling sure she would run across them before too long.

There were several other groups of tourists in Petra that morning, and as the sun climbed overhead and the heat of the day beat down upon the rocks, Leslie climbed from one apartment to another. Some of the steps were worn and treacherous, but it was fascinating to see how elaborate some of the homes had been, with many rooms carved into the recesses of the cliffs. The rock rooms were pleasantly cool. Leslie was interested to note the blackened ceilings in some of the interior rooms where the smoke from cooking fires, as well as fires for warmth and light, had left an indelible reminder of the people who had lived there.

Some of the rooms had high skylights carved into the roofs or windows fashioned to look out from a narrow face of rock. There were several of the larger living quarters open for the tourists, but after a while Leslie grew impatient with the standard ruins. Her eye was caught by the extent of the city. Most of the places that the tourists visited were centered around the spacious square within full view of the gargantuan treasury building. But Leslie noted with interest passageways that twisted through the cliffs away from the square, leading to many other cliffs, and as far as the eye could see, those cliffs were dotted with doors, windows, and openings. The city was remarkable in size, and Leslie idly wondered if anyone had really explored its vast outer reaches or had any idea what was contained in those hundreds of vacant rock rooms, tucked and hidden through the warrens of rocks, cliffs, and pathways.

On impulse, she left the group to which she had loosely attached herself and turned to climb a winding path that led up and over a tumble of rocks, away from the bustle of the square. After a few minutes of climbing and walking, she found herself alone on a small trail between two jagged cliffs. Looking high above her, she could see elaborate windows carved just below the flat tops of the cliffs, and she wondered how they had built scaffolding to reach such heights. Then she smiled as a thought struck her. "They probably lowered themselves on ropes from the top of the cliff, and carved that way," she murmured.

She continued to follow the trail as it twisted and turned through the rocks. Everywhere she saw evidence of other habitations, and finally, as she topped a steep rise, she found herself looking over a jumble of rock cliffs, tumbling in and out of one another, rising in clusters and rows. As far as her eye could detect, there were dark patches in the stone that indicated rooms or doors or tombs. She was not foolish, and she knew she had come far beyond the ordinary perimeters of the tourists' view of Petra.

Around her was a sense of enormous desolation and neglect. Somehow she knew these ruins had never been studied or mapped, and that the area she was in was of little interest to anyone. She stood studying the lifeless ruins for a moment longer. No living thing stirred, but her sharp eyes saw something on the traces of a trail that twisted up through the straggling rock. She squinted in the sunlight at the dark stains, curious as to what they were. "Oh!" she exclaimed, and then laughed at her misplaced interest. "Horse droppings—how fascinating." She turned to go back and rejoin the others, dismissing the observation with an ironic shrug and said, "I doubt they are prehistoric." It wasn't until much later that she thought she should have wondered what horses would be doing so far back in the ruins, a considerable distance from the area where tourists ever ventured.

When Leslie climbed back over the cliffs and hurried down the trail to the square, Michelle Green caught sight of her and came running to scold her. "Where have you been, Leslie? We have been so concerned about you. The rest of the group is on its way back to the bus; we must hurry or we'll be late getting to the border!"

Leslie flushed. "I'm sorry, Michelle. I got separated, and I couldn't seem to find you."

"Well, no problem," Michelle said, obviously still a little annoyed, but relieved to have located Leslie. "There are still a few more stragglers, so fortunately you haven't delayed us."

The two women walked over to the treasury, where some of the teenagers from the bus were mounting their horses for the run back. "Do you have your two dollars?" Michelle called to them. Leslie could have sworn one of the runners gave Michelle a murderous look, and she guessed he could speak English and was furious at the way the tour guides controlled the price.

The man next to her came over with a brilliant smile. He was holding the reins of a small-boned black Arabian with slender legs and restless hooves. The Arabian came very close to her, and she could smell his breath, heavy with spice. He was shorter than she was, and his hand was small and dirty as he held it up to her and whispered, "Eight bucks." He rubbed his fingers and thumb together and placed his smiling face very close. "Very fast, very easy." His eyes indicated his horse. "Eight bucks."

Leslie was at a loss, and she looked around uncomfortably for someone to come help her. She only had two dollars left in her pocket after paying the other runner. The square was rapidly emptying, and Michelle Green was busy a few yards away dispatching the last of the youngsters.

"I only have two dollars," Leslie said helplessly. The man's eyes registered disgust, and before Leslie could react he spit at her feet and turned away with a growl. For a moment Leslie was alone, standing dwarfed by the enormous pillars of the treasury building, and the strangeness and menacing unfamiliarity of the land overwhelmed her. As she glanced despairingly around the square, her eyes caught a glimpse of a strange sight. She saw the white stallion on which she had ridden into Petra. Beside it stood her runner, still unsmiling, but he was talking. The person to whom he was talking was hidden in the shadow of one of the rock doorways. It was only a brief moment, then he turned and led his horse quickly toward the treasury. As Leslie continued to stare at the doorway, a man came out into the sunlight of the square. It was Hal Johnson. He was carrying a camera slung around his neck, and he was wearing aviator-style sunglasses.

What would Hal have to say to an Arab runner? she wondered. *Can the man speak English? How else could Hal speak to him—or was he just trying to get his picture? If so, why didn't he take the shot now, with the man and his brilliant white horse posed in front of the treasury? That would be a shot worth saving.* But Hal seemed to have lost all interest in the man. He was standing gazing past the square into the ruins where Leslie had been exploring earlier, and he seemed to be frowning. Impatiently he jerked off his sunglasses, put them in his pocket, and picked up the binoculars, which were slung around his neck along with the camera. He trained the binoculars on the surrounding cliffs of Petra, and with meticulous care, he slowly made a comprehensive perusal of the city, rotating in a semi-circle, as though he did not want to miss one detail before he left this extraordinary site. The binoculars swept the scene, and Leslie continued to watch in fascination as the binoculars moved slowly along the outer reaches of the cliffs across the sides of the square. It was a second before she realized the binoculars had come half-circle, and that Hal had trained them on the treasury building directly above Leslie. Deliberately, he continued his perusal of the rock facade, and as he lowered the binoculars, he ceased moving.

With a shock, Leslie realized the binoculars were trained directly on her. Hal Johnson, across the square, was staring through his binoculars at Leslie staring at him. Even though she knew it was ridiculous, for one awful moment, she felt as though they were looking into each others' eyes, even though all she could see was the man standing far from her and the two blind lenses of the binoculars pointing her way. Embarrassed, she dropped her gaze and walked to Michelle. "Do you have a horse for me?" she asked.

"Why don't you and Nick ride back together?" Michelle suggested. "I'll go over and hurry Mr. Johnson along. I think we are the last of our group." Nick stepped out of the shadowed main room of the treasury building.

"It's cooler in the shade," he remarked with his pleasant accent. "Shall we go?" He gestured toward the white stallion again, and reluctantly, Leslie mounted it; then Nick climbed on the small black horse of the Arab who had demanded the eight dollars. With a shout the runners were off. Nick remained behind her as the runners and horses, eager to return to the cooler air and comfort of their compound, moved swiftly up the defile.

"Did you enjoy your visit to Petra, Mrs. Brinton?" Nick called over the clatter of the horses' hooves and the clank of the harness.

"Yes!" Leslie shouted back, her voice echoing in the canyon. "But it seems so lifeless. I wonder if it was ever a . . . you know . . . a happy place. I mean, I wonder if it was ever . . . " she struggled for a word to express what she meant, "comfortable. I guess that's the word."

Nick laughed a short, harsh laugh that rang against the rock walls. "Ha! That is such an American word—*comfortable*. That word has no meaning here. Life is never comfortable in a

land like this. It is harsh and uncompromising, like the rocks
and the sand and the sun itself."

She was angered by his answer, because she knew it was
true, and she felt like a fool. "I don't know why I talk to him,"
she muttered to herself. "He is such an impossible man. To all
the others he is too nice, as fawning as a gigolo, and then he
treats me with such contempt and impatience." Without thinking, Leslie clenched her knees and touched the sides of the
horse with her heels. It was a reflex reaction. She had momen-
tarily forgotten that she was not riding alone, that her horse
was being handled by its runner. With instant response, the
white stallion sprang forward and began to gallop. In fury the
Arab looked up at her and flung out a curse, but the white
stallion, tired of the restriction of the hand on his bridle, shook
his head and continued to run with the Arab owner clinging
to his harness and shouting commands. Just as Leslie was sure
the charging horse would break away altogether, the Arab
pulled hard on the bit, and the horse, caught between training
and desire, reared up and came to a nervous standstill, its
hooves beating a staccato on the stony path. Leslie had remained
seated, but her face was white.

"I'm so sorry," she murmured, "I wasn't thinking. I am so
sorry." The Arab continued to glare at her furiously, and Nick's
horse came up beside her. Nick jumped out of his saddle and
hurried over to her.

"Are you all right?" he asked.

"Yes," she whispered, "I hope neither this man nor his
horse were hurt."

"You little fool," Nick hissed, his voice shaking with relief
and anger. "Am I going to spend the next two weeks rescuing
you? Won't you try to keep your head about you?" He reached
up his arms and lifted her, light as a feather, out of the saddle.
"We can walk the rest of the way back. It's only about half a
mile. I think our friend may have trouble settling his horse."

Nick turned to the Arabs and spoke to them in their language for a moment. He reached into his pocket and took out
his wallet. Wordlessly, Leslie observed that he gave them each

a five-dollar bill. The two men mounted their horses and, with high cries, galloped down the trail.

"Thank you," Leslie said. "I only have two dollars. I'll pay back the rest when we get to the bus."

"Fine," Nick said shortly. She looked at him in the shadows of the rocky gorge. He was handsome, she had to admit it, and even with his dark unreadable eyes, it was odd, but she felt no fear of him. The only thing she feared was his magnetic, overpowering masculinity, which seemed to leap out at her, threatening to destroy her carefully built reserves and smash her guarded indifference. For a moment they stood quietly on the empty trail, the motes of dust hovering in the filtered sunlight, and in the silence of the rock shelter, she found herself staring at Nick's full, strong mouth, unsmiling now beneath the neat, dark mustache. He took a step toward her, and she caught her breath. Just then, they heard the sound of voices and horses, and they looked up to see Michelle Green and Hal Johnson riding around the twist of the gorge toward them.

"We'd better hurry," Nick said matter-of-factly. "We'll be the last ones to arrive." Without another word, he took her elbow and guided her quickly along the rocky path. Michelle and Hal called to them as they passed, and Leslie hurried breathlessly trying to keep up with Nick's stiff pace so they would not keep the bus waiting.

A few minutes later, tired, dirty, and breathless, Leslie climbed onto the bus and collapsed gratefully onto the comfortable seat in the air-conditioned coolness. She slept through the next two hours. She awakened for the brief stop on Mount Pisgah, from which she observed Jericho, like a green lily pad set in the brown plains of Israel, and the Dead Sea sparkling like a sapphire far to the southwest. She dozed again and late in the afternoon was awakened by Michelle, who told her they were approaching the Allenby Bridge and would be passing through customs in a few minutes. Leslie woke up, freshened herself with a moist towelette, and prepared to face the tedium of waiting, which invariably attended the crossing of a guarded border.

Chapter Five

The Allenby Bridge was a disappointment. Far above the winding, muddy Jordan River was the ruin of an old and narrow metal bridge. The bridge was twisted and rusted, as though some giant hand had grasped it, crumpled it, and flung it back down upon the banks to dim with time and age. It was such a little ruined thing to have endured for so long as the symbol of a mighty conflict.

The passage through Jordan customs was largely a matter of formality. Young soldiers boarded the bus and walked down the aisles quickly checking passports. They spoke to Nick for a few moments, asking standard questions, and then they spoke for a few moments in Arabic in comfortable friendly raillery. The border guards knew both Nick and Sam, and the whole procedure was routine. The bus then drove slowly into the neutral strip of land between the two countries, proceeded for a hundred yards, and stopped before a wooden-framed building flanked by bunkers and several small wooden barracks.

The area in front of the building was filled with passengers from two other tour buses. The buses were parked in front of the building along with several military trucks, some passenger vehicles, and three or four produce trucks. The last vehicle in the lineup was a truck filled with open boxes of oranges. The fruit was glorious: large, perfectly round, and brilliant in color. The fruit had much the same effect on the tourists waiting in the hot, dusty courtyard as the sight of water would have had on a castaway. Leslie, too, found her mouth watering as she climbed stiffly out of her seat. Suddenly she felt an overwhelming thirst, and her mind became occupied with fantasies of the sweet juice flowing into her mouth.

"What's the holdup?" Nick asked one of the young Israeli soldiers who was standing casually at guard in the crowded yard.

"The peace commission is coming to Jerusalem this week, so security is doubled," the young man answered in unaccented English.

"Well, why don't you let me go over and see if we can buy some oranges for these people? They'll start passing out on you in this heat."

For a moment the young soldier looked doubtful, but finally he nodded, and Nick went over to the truck with the load of oranges. In a moment, he was back, and standing on the front of the bus so that he could be seen, he called over the hum of conversation in the courtyard, "If any of you are thirsty or hungry, the people in the truck have agreed to sell you oranges. They will bring some boxes over, and you can buy them."

A burly young fellow stepped out of the truck and a smaller fellow climbed out after him. They went to the back of the truck, unhooked the guard panel, and pulled three boxes off their cargo. They carried the boxes over to the courtyard and announced the oranges would be twenty-five cents each.

The hot, hungry tourists converged on the salesmen, and they began to do a lively business. In the meantime, the customs officials continued to cram as many people as possible into the crowded anteroom of the customs building. Leslie found her suitcase and stood patiently in line, eating a delicious Jaffa orange. The fragrance and flavor of the fruit was intense, and it made Leslie feel this was the first real orange she had ever eaten.

At last she found herself at the head of the line in the courtyard, and when the customs officers opened the door and beckoned the next group to come in, Nick and Sam shepherded their bus group through the door. Leslie found herself squashed against a peeling, wooden wall, waiting in another line to have her papers checked and stamped. Both Sam and Nick were handled quickly and informally. In their position, they crossed the border several times a month. Their papers offered special transport, so the customs officials simply glanced over them and sent them into the next room. Both men, instead of suit-cases, carried a case that looked like a large attaché case. This they took with them into the adjoining room where the lug-gage was checked. By the time Leslie had her papers processed and had moved into the second room, she saw Nick and Sam talking to another young guard while the tedious business of checking suitcases went on.

Glancing at the men's attaché cases, she saw they were already sealed with the customs certificate, which meant they had cleared inspection. The room was hot and noisy. Each hand-carried piece of luggage, suitcase, purse, paper bag, and camera case was being checked. It was tedious, boring work, and Leslie thought she would suffocate in the closed, noisy room. When the tourists finished with all their checks, they passed through to a door at the far end of the room, cleared their papers with the guard stationed there, and returned to the bus.

Nick stood restlessly leaning against the rough wall, bored and impatient. Finally, he signalled to one of the customs men and pointed to a sign that said "No Smoking." Nick shrugged ruefully, and the official pointed to the exit door. With a grin and a nod, Nick picked up his bag and walked out the door.

If that isn't just like him, Leslie thought. *He's going out there to relax in the fresh air while the rest of us are suffocating in here. I hope he chokes on his cigarette.* A few minutes later, Leslie's bag was searched. The clearance sticker was placed on it, and thank-ful for the respite, she hurried out the exit door. A young guard took her bag and placed it on the bus. Another guard checked her passport to make sure it was properly stamped and sug-gested she board the bus.

"May I stay outside and walk for a few moments?" she asked. "I'm stiff from sitting."

The soldier informed her that she could if she remained within the compound on the same side of the building. Disso-lutely, she strolled through the small area back toward the cus-toms building and idly walked along the barbed-wire fence, which outlined the back part of the customs house. Sam came out of a side door and called to the young guard on duty by the back of the building. The guard turned and walked over to speak to Sam, and for a moment, the stretch of fence on the Israeli side of the safe compound was left unguarded. In that brief second, Leslie saw Nick step away from the wall where he had apparently been leaning, enjoying his cigarette. Swiftly, Nick walked to the fence that separated the Jordanian area from those who had already passed customs on the Israeli side, and she saw a hand pass an orange to Nick through the closed, wire gate. It all happened so swiftly and naturally that Leslie thought nothing of it. She was about to turn and go back around the building to speak to Sam and ask him how soon they would be leaving when she felt something sharp and hard press into her back.

"Do not make a sound," a voice said, "or you are a dead woman. I knew those sharp eyes of yours would get you into trouble." It all happened so fast, Leslie did not even have time to be afraid. Her mind was numb with bewilderment and shock. Powerful hands grabbed her arms and propelled her toward the barbed-wire fence and gate.

Nick looked up in astonishment as she came parallel to him. Hands were over her mouth, but her eyes questioned him frantically. The voice behind her gave a terse command. "Diversion Two, Nick. Now!" Nick moved wordlessly past her and around to the side of the building where Sam and the guard were still talking. She saw him raise both of his hands as though he were stretching, but something in his deliberate motions made her know it was a prearranged signal. Almost immediately, she heard angry shouting and people running. There was laughter and a confusion of tongues, and guards and soldiers began running toward the front of the building. In that moment of uproar, she felt herself thrust through the back gate, back over to the Jordanian side, and in a second, she was pushed and rushed through the milling crowd. Soldiers were shouting, trying to maintain order, while busloads of tourists tired and hot from their long wait were running to pick up dozens of oranges that had apparently been spilled from the top boxes of the loaded truck. The driver of the truck and his helpers were shouting and scolding, but the tourists continued to load their pockets and purses with the golden fruit. Leslie thought surely someone would notice her, but the cruel voice whispering in her ear kept informing her that silence was her only protection. Although she could feel a knife cutting through her thin shirt and into the skin of her back, she supposed she was being held in such a way that she must appear to others like the man's wife or sweetheart with his arms around her protectively.

By now, Leslie's initial shock had worn off, but her mind was still in turmoil, and the pain of the knife piercing her back told her whoever was carrying her meant business. Fear made her knees weak, and she thought she would not have been able to call out even if anyone could have heard her in the general uproar. Everything was happening so quickly, faces and sounds seemed to blur. The next thing she knew, she was surrounded by men dressed as laborers, who closed off all sight of the crowd and rushed her to the back of the orange truck. Swiftly, one of them pulled out an orange crate. Inside was a dark cavity. One of the men grabbed her, and within a second the brief opening was closed again with orange crates. Leslie lay panting in the sudden darkness, the smell of the man's stale perspiration and the sweet smell of the oranges mingling with her fear.

She opened her mouth to scream, but she felt the cold point of steel at her throat. "One sound and you are dead," a menacing voice whispered. She felt her arm grabbed roughly and the sharp jab of a needle. She twisted away from the pain, but the man held her arm tightly, and slowly she began to slip into unconsciousness. As she fell forward, her face struck the floorboards of the truck, and just before she blacked out, her eye caught a glimmer of light from a crack between two orange crates. There on the ground beside the truck, she could clearly see one white, patent-leather shoe. She didn't know if she were dreaming or not, but she thought she heard the deep voice of

Hal Johnson speaking to the truck driver. "Here, I'll help you repack these oranges. Bad luck to have lost so many."

It was the fleas biting that awakened her. They were biting her ankles, and each bite was like a red-hot dot of fire. She opened her eyes and lay quietly, taking quiet assessment of her body. Her ankles burned and itched where the fleas swarmed, her back ached where the knife had penetrated the skin, her arms felt bruised and stiff, and her head ached with the dull aftereffects of whatever drug had been used on her.

She did not move. Her body was heavy with pain, and she felt nauseous and dizzy. With determined effort, she tried to breathe deeply, to force herself into action, and as she did so she became aware of the stench around her. She was lying in semi-darkness on a pile of dark blankets, and around her were the smells of animals, soured milk, cooking odors, and stale humanity. She was hot and sticky, and her nausea made her perspire more. The fleas went mad, and in a spasm of discomfort she sat up, brushing her arms and ankles furiously, trying to rid herself of the bloodthirsty insects. Panting, she looked at her surroundings. It was gloomy and dark, but her eyes soon became accustomed to the darkness, and she could see that she was inside a tent. The shape of the tent was sagging and irregular, and the heat of the sun beat down upon the dark enclosure and made it an oven. Hanging on the walls were goatskin containers, cooking utensils, and soiled robes. At the far side of the tent, a woman dressed in black was seated on a filthy carpet, spooning food from a horn bowl into the mouths of three half-naked children. Cradled on the woman's crossed legs was a tiny infant lying listlessly and silently while the mother fed the others.

Leslie watched the domestic scene with a growing sense of puzzlement. The woman had not even looked up when Leslie moved. She seemed to have no interest in what Leslie did. The children, too, appeared unaware of her and continued to sit quietly eating the food that their mother spooned into their mouths.

Was there no guard? Leslie wondered. Where was she, and why had she been left unattended and untied? Nothing made sense. Leslie stiffly rose to her feet. Every bone and muscle in her body protested, and for an awful moment she thought she was going to throw up, but the wave of nausea passed, and after a few moments of standing, her head cleared and she felt a little better. The woman did glance up at her now with dark, unreadable eyes, but then she turned her attention back to the children, with no gesture of interest or recognition of Leslie at all.

Still puzzled, but with hope springing, Leslie moved toward the flap of the tent. If they intended to keep her prisoner, surely they would do something to prevent her from reaching the opening. There was still no reaction by the woman, although now the children had turned around and were staring at her with frank curiosity. Leslie inched toward the gap, hardly knowing what to expect. She placed her hand on the goatskin cloth and pushed it outward and upward, but still no one moved, and Leslie prepared to step out of the tent. It was then that she realized she was barefoot, and she quickly looked back at the pile of rags where she had been lying to see if her shoes were there. They were nowhere to be seen, and Leslie, fearing that someone might still try to stop her, stepped quickly out of the tent.

There was no guard outside the tent either. She was standing under an awning flap, which provided a modest shade from the beating sun. It seemed to be around noon, because the sun was directly overhead, and Leslie knew she must have been unconscious through the night. Where had they brought her— and why? What was this place? She was baffled, frightened, and desperate. But at least it seemed she was free. There was no one to stop her but that frail woman and her children. Leslie looked out across the expanse of the desert. The sun was mercilessly bright, and the wasteland of sand and rocky hills stretched on either side, but in front of her, about a mile distant, she could see the highway. Even as she stood in the tent doorway, she discerned the dust trail of a vehicle driving along the road.

Only a mile! She could run it in less than ten minutes. With a jolt of hope she sprang forward, and as she left the shaded square of the awning, her feet struck the desert sand. It was like running on hot coals. She gritted her teeth and forced her legs to continue to move, but the heat increased and the intensity of the pain became unbearable. As the soles of her feet burned, the feel of rocks and thorns piercing them was excruciating. Still, she forced herself to continue. Finally her feet would no longer respond, and she stumbled and fell headlong on the burning sand. Panting under the deadly sun, Leslie lay on the merciless desert floor. She could feel the hungry air absorbing the moisture from her body, and her fair skin blazed and cracked in the relentless heat. She tried to raise herself, but there was no strength left in her arms, and her wounded feet refused to move. *I shall simply dry up and blow away,* she thought, and almost giggled at the crazy picture in her mind. How long she lay there she didn't know. She was unconscious for part of the time, because at intervals her mind was filled with images of waterfalls and green grass. Then she would again become aware of the sun, like an orange pinwheel in her closed eyes, and the constant burning of the desert against her aching skin.

She woke to a sharp pain and a harsh voice. "Stupeed woman!" growled a man's voice, and someone slapped her face again. She squinted up against the sun and saw a large, shaggy man with a graying beard and weathered face. He was dressed in the dark robes of a Bedouin.

"Eef you die, I weel not get pay," he growled at her. Leslie's tongue was swollen, and her lips were cracked and bleeding.

"Water," she whispered. "Please . . . " But she could say no more and looked up at him with desperate eyes. The man reached for the goatskin bladder strung around his shoulder and squirted a fine stream of water into her mouth. The water was stale and bitter, but she thought she had never felt anything so delicious. Slowly, a thin stream at a time, the man let her drink, and she began to feel better. Her breathing became easier, and the blessed moisture eased her sunburned lips. As soon as she began to breathe better, the man stood up and roughly grasped her arm and pulled her to her feet. As her burned and tender feet touched the sand, she let out a moan and the Bedouin looked at her with fury.

Leslie crumpled onto the desert again. "I can't walk," she groaned. As she looked around her, she was amazed to see what a short distance she had come from the tent. She understood why it had been unnecessary to tie her or guard her. The desert made a perfect prison, more cruel and efficient than iron bars or stone walls. The mile or two to the highway might as well be a hundred when one had no shoes. For the first time, Leslie felt the full horror of her situation, and the ghastly part was that she had no idea who had kidnapped her, or why. All she knew was that she was abandoned, hopeless, and imprisoned.

The Bedouin grabbed her by the shoulders and hauled her unceremoniously up over his own shoulder. Her sore, bruised body screamed in protest as he walked with jolting steps back to the tent and threw her onto the shaded square beneath the awning at the entrance. The woman and the three children stood in the doorway stolidly looking at her. The woman's dark veil covered her head and face so that only her expressionless eyes were visible. The man shouted a few words to the woman in Arabic and then turned and strode back across the desert. In the distance, Leslie could see a small flock of sheep and goats foraging on a small patch of scrub in the shadow of a low hill. The man was going back to shepherding.

After he left, the children shyly inched out of the tent and came over to where Leslie was lying. They squatted beside her and regarded her with their beautiful, liquid eyes. Tentatively, she smiled at the one who crouched nearest. The boy looked startled, and then he returned her smile with a huge grin that almost split his face. He turned to the other children and began to chatter excitedly. The other children laughed and came closer to Leslie's face, watching her intently. She continued to smile. The mother remained in the doorway, her eyes unchanging in their expression, but intent.

Painfully, Leslie pulled herself up into a sitting position and bent to look at her injured feet. The skin was red and tender and marked with cuts and bruises. The children also looked at her feet, and then the oldest boy stood up and ran into the tent. In a moment, he returned with a small bowl of rancid grease. Without a word, he handed it to Leslie and pointed at her feet. Touched by his kind gesture, Leslie scooped up some of the evil-smelling lard and gently rubbed it on her foot. Amazingly, she felt a soothing relief, and she eagerly continued to apply the ointment until her feet were covered. The pain had abated considerably, and she felt an enormous gratitude to the children. The mother had watched without reaction and stepped out of the tent and sat down under the awning with her back against the tent wall in the deepest shade.

The baby lay listlessly across the mother's lap, and Leslie, looking at the child, was horrified to see flies swarming around the baby's face, lighting on eyes that were swollen shut and matted with infection. Leslie was a scientist, a biologist, but she had done a great deal of work in the medical field and recognized that the baby was suffering from a severe case of conjunctivitis. The disease was a simple one, and very common, but left untreated it could impair the sight and health of the child. Besides, the flies swarming around the area of the infection could cause terrible damage to the tender eye tissue.

Leslie stood up and limped over to the mother. Crouching beside the baby, she began to murmur to the infant, hoping to soothe and disarm the mother enough to let her handle the baby. How could she communicate with this woman and make her trust her enough to allow her to show the mother how to tend the illness?

"Oh, you darling baby," Leslie crooned, smiling and clucking at the infant with the universal sounds of love and affection. The mother watched her carefully, but without fear. Leslie continued the loving sounds, and looking at the mother, indicated that she wanted to hold the baby. The mother did not react, so Leslie cautiously reached out and put her arms around the little body. The mother did not stop her, as Leslie lifted the baby over onto her own lap.

The Bedouin woman was watching with fierce intensity, so Leslie did nothing but hold the baby gently, continuing to murmur quietly. All the while, Leslie was examining the infant's eyes, and she knew her diagnosis was correct and that the baby could, and must, be helped.

Frantically, Leslie wondered how she could communicate with the woman and gestured to the other three children, and they clustered around her and the baby. Without thinking, she began to sing "Hush little baby, don't say a word . . . " The old song, sweet and monotonous, lay lightly on the desert air, and the children listened, entranced. Their fresh, inno-cent faces pierced Leslie's heart, and the memory of singing the song to her own little boy filled her mind. Tears spilled from her eyes, and she bowed her head and wept over the baby. She felt a hand on her arm, and looking up, she saw the Bedouin woman. The veil had been dropped, and the mother's face, surprisingly young, was turned toward her in concern and understanding. In a flash of insight, Leslie knew what she must communicate to this woman. She was not just a scientist, but a mother too. For the next half hour the two women struggled with gestures and pantomime, and finally they were satisfied. Leslie felt that the mother understood Leslie could show her how to help her baby, and she sensed the young Bedouin mother was ready to allow her to try.

"Water," Leslie indicated by simulating the process of drink-ing. The oldest child responded immediately and ran into the tent, bringing back the skin of water. With similar gestures, and the responsiveness of the children, Leslie soon had a small fire going and water boiling in an old dented pot. After the water had boiled, Leslie permitted it to cool in the shade. The only disinfectant she could imagine in these primitive condi-tions was alcohol. She discovered the Bedouins had a wine made from fermented dates. The alcohol content was high, and she put a few drops of the wine in the cooled water. Fortunately, she discovered a clean handkerchief left in her jeans. She dipped the hanky into the sterile mixture and gently began to cleanse the baby's eyes of all foreign matter. It was slow, painstaking work and had to be done very carefully. The mother watched intently, and the children gathered in a semicircle, their heads almost touching, as they watched every move of Leslie's tender hands. Once or twice the baby whimpered, and the mother's eyes narrowed, but she allowed Leslie to continue until the eyes were completely cleaned. With the sticky pus removed, the baby was able to open her eyes a little, and though the small eyes were still red and sore, the baby had begun to look better. The point that needed to be made to the mother was that the discharge must not be allowed to accumulate. The eyes needed to be gently washed every two or three hours.

Another problem was keeping the hanky as sterile as possible, but Leslie came up with the obvious solution. The sun was a disinfectant itself, and she stuck a small stick into the sand and hung the hanky to dry in the full heat of the sun. An hour later, she repeated the process of washing the baby's eyes. Later in the afternoon, when the eyes needed to be tended again, Leslie began to wash them, but the mother came over and took the baby from her arms. Tentatively, the mother reached for the hanky in the boiling water, and looking at Leslie to be sure she was doing it correctly, she began to cleanse the baby's eyes herself. Leslie watched and smiled, nodding encouragement. When the mother finished and hung the hanky on the stick to dry, the two women knelt by the child, who was lying on a cloth in the shade, her little feet kicking. Her eyes looked much better, freed of the irritation of the stinging flies, and she cooed and smiled. The Bedouin woman looked into Leslie's eyes for a long moment. She did not smile or speak, but for a moment, there was a bond of warmth and understanding between the two women that needed no words.

The sun was getting lower, and suddenly the woman and children burst into a flurry of excited action. The fire was stirred and rice was placed on it to boil. Meat and dried dates were chopped and mixed together. A bowl of almonds and a bowl of something that looked like sour milk, or yogurt, was placed beside it. Soon Leslie heard the bleat of sheep and goats and the sound of their tiny hooves as they skittered over the barren ground. The Bedouin shepherd rounded the tent, his face dark and furious. He spoke angrily to the woman and children, and they scurried into the tent as he sat down under the awning. The woman waited beside the tent flap, on her knees to serve her husband. He grabbed the wine flask and poured himself a cup of the powerful drink, which he downed in one quick gesture. As he put the cup down, his glance fell upon Leslie, who was still sitting beside the tent. His voice rose in fury, and his wife hurried out of the tent and grasped Leslie's arm tightly, pulling her into the tent. With frantic gestures, the woman indicated the heap of blankets in the corner of the tent where Leslie had been lying when she had awakened in the morning. It was clear she was expected to go back to the corner of the tent and remain there. Remembering the fleas, Leslie hesitated to go, but she knew if she refused, the woman would be in trouble, so she quickly moved back into the dark corner.

Throughout the evening, she remained in the shadows as she listened to the rough and limited conversation of the Bedouin family. The children climbed into the tent soon after dark and quietly clustered in the far corner and fell asleep. From her dark corner, Leslie watched as the Bedouin mother washed the baby's eyes secretively in the tent, while the father remained outside. Leslie could smell a sweet tobacco drifting from where the man sat by the tent front. The family acted as though she did not exist, and suddenly she had a wrenching feeling, because in a way, she did not exist. There was no one to miss her, no one who would shout an alarm or even notice she was gone. Who had brought her to this wilderness, and how long would she remain? She searched frantically in her mind for some kind of answer that would make sense. Perhaps for the rest of her life, she would be a prisoner, chattel to these mysterious desert people. She had wanted so desperately to become invisible so life could not hurt her anymore, and now she had her wish. She had done a good job of becoming invisible—too good. By cutting off all human relationships, she had doomed herself to be overlooked in this terrible time of need. Her life had become so useless and unnoticeable, who would report her absence or trouble to look for her?

Suddenly a flaming desire rose in her. She wanted to live! And by all that was holy, she intended to. She was not about to let these mysterious, cruel people rob her of the opportunity to feel, to touch, to experience, to grow, and to serve. Even here, in this wretched prison, she had felt the joy of helping a baby, the satisfaction of touching a mother's heart, the pleasure of children's smiles. She thanked God; she was ready to begin again! And she would not let this second chance be snatched from her. Determination and courage rose in her like a tide, and she sat in the corner, frantically trying to think through all she knew.

Obviously, she had been taken prisoner because of something that had happened at the border. But what? She couldn't imagine. Carefully, she went over in her mind the events at the customs station. She remembered eating the orange, having her papers and bags checked—nothing there. The bus, she had avoided boarding the bus and had walked down by the barbed-wire barrier. It had to be Nick, something to do with Nick. She remembered how he had left the customs room to have a smoke, leaning against the back of the building. He hadn't seen her as she walked toward him. Sam . . . Sam had deliberately distracted the guard. That was it! And the orange! She remembered now! She had seen a hand with an orange reach through the gate that separated the unscreened passengers in the Jordanian courtyard from the Israeli compound where the cleared passengers boarded the bus. The orange . . . but what could that mean?

She remembered many things: the man's voice in her ear, the knife at her back, Nick raising his arms and then the oranges spilling, the men spiriting her into the truck, and the needle—

then nothing. But wait, something more . . . the white shoes—
Hal Johnson?

None of it made any sense to her. Surely someone would
search for her. Not Nick, surely, not if he were part of the plot.
What about Michelle Green? But maybe she was part of it too,
if Nick was. If Susan knew, Susan would move a continent to
find her, but Susan wouldn't know she was missing for at least
two weeks when the tour returned to California, and by then
perhaps no one could find her. The very thought made her
shudder.

She closed her eyes for a moment and thought about Susan.
Dr. Susan Westerly, doctor of philosophy and comparative religions at the university where Leslie taught. Susan alone had
been undeterred by Leslie's aloofness and her desire to be left
alone. Leslie had met Susan one day at the indoor track. A
small brunette with curly hair, a round dimpled face, and a
plump body, Susan spent her days in a good-natured struggle
to keep her shape. On the day they had met, Susan had fallen
into stride with Leslie as Leslie was finishing the final laps of
her daily workout.

"I have given up the battle," Susan had declared merrily as
she ran, uninvited, beside Leslie. "I simply love food too much.
I will never get into shape by dieting, so I've decided exercise is
my only hope." In spite of herself, Leslie had smiled. There
was something irresistible about Susan's high spirits. Leslie had
known who Susan was since it was a small college and Susan
enjoyed a reputation as one of the more popular teachers. The
two women finished the lap together, and as they ran, Leslie
could see that Susan had no understanding of the principles of
exercise or body toning.

"You're not breathing correctly," Leslie said, not wanting
to continue the conversation, but feeling, in spite of herself, a
certain pity and exasperation for the puffing woman beside her.
"You shouldn't start right out running fast, either. You should
start with warm-ups."

"Warm-ups," Susan groaned breathlessly, "believe me, I'm
warm."

That was how their friendship began. Of course, in the beginning, Leslie had no intention of it becoming a friendship, she simply could not stand to see Susan have trouble with her exercise program. In the next few weeks, Leslie had taught Susan the correct principles of fitness and had shown her the techniques for building a realistic program. After three weeks, Susan was running smoothly on the indoor track, her endurance considerably increased, her appearance already beginning to be more svelte.

They ran together frequently, and Susan, always talking, gradually drew Leslie out. Then one day as they walked around the track while cooling down, with towels around their necks and perspiration matting their hair, Susan asked bluntly, "Why do you shut the world out, Leslie? Don't you have any family—or someone you feel close to?"

The question was asked with such a sweet, natural concern that Leslie found herself pouring out the story of Adam and Kerry to Susan. It was the first time she had spoken of the accident since coming to the university, and as she talked, she began to cry, and finally she sobbed incoherently while Susan led her over to a bench and sat beside her with her arms around her until Leslie quieted.

"Three years ago?" Susan asked, and Leslie nodded. Susan's dark intelligent eyes searched Leslie's. "Don't you think it is time for you to resolve it?"

"What do you mean?" Leslie sat up, bristling defensively. "You don't resolve something like this. You just live with it. What choice do you have?"

"No," Susan replied, "you can't live with it. It will destroy you if you try to. You have to resolve it, Leslie. You have to come to some understanding emotionally, philosophically, and spiritually, and if you don't work that through, then you are not living, you are just going through the motions."

Leslie had been furious. *What does this meddling woman know about anything?* she had thought angrily. Everyone else, when they learned of her tragedy, had at least had the courtesy to express sympathy and change the subject, but here was this woman continuing the conversation, probing, asking her questions, trying to force her to think about the unthinkable. Why did she have anything to do with such a busybody?

"I know this is making you angry," Susan said equably, "and I'm sorry. The easy thing for both of us would be for me to stop right now. But Leslie, I have spent my life studying the nature of mankind and the meanings of life and death, and I know everyone, in order to live fully, must search out their own answers. You have to find some means for hope, some basis on which to build your own life in the years to come."

"I have!" Leslie shouted and turned on her heel and left the gymnasium. At the door of the locker rooms, she had turned and glared at Susan, who was still sitting on the bench. "I only want to be left alone. Do you understand?"

That evening as Leslie sat in her austere apartment eating a tuna-fish salad and grading examinations, the doorbell rang. At the door stood Susan, her usually smiling face serious and contrite.

"I'm sorry about this afternoon, Leslie. May I come in?"

Leslie, too, felt sorry for the scene between them, and she invited Susan into her home. That evening was the beginning of many discussions. Some of them were painful, some of them were irritating, and many of them were beautiful and healing. Susan led Leslie carefully through the things Leslie had felt during the days following the accident. She encouraged Leslie to talk about the joys of her married life and the love she felt for her husband and son. Finally, Leslie dared to talk about the black despair of the unknown. She told Susan how agonizing it was never to have seen the bodies of Adam or Kerry, to only have the memory of them living. She told of the urgency she felt to know they were still in existence somewhere, not vanished forever, but somewhere waiting for her, knowing her, caring about her.

Susan smiled and nodded her head. "Of course," she said with the quiet satisfaction of someone who has run a long course and finally arrived at the end. "That is what you must find out—your answer to that question."

"But there is no answer," Leslie protested. "That is why I don't want to think about it anymore. Why beat myself against a locked door, why pin my hopes—my very sanity—on something that can never be known for certain?"

"But you have just said the word, Leslie," Susan had replied. "The word isn't *know*, it is *hope*. The method isn't intellect, it is faith."

"I am a scientist, not a philosopher," Leslie responded flatly.

"Yes. But first of all, you are a woman, a mortal being, and as I believe, a spiritual being. I promise you there are things to be known in this life by other evidences than just the five senses. I am not a philosopher either, Leslie, because all a philosopher adds to the five senses is the gift of reason."

"Then what are you?" Leslie asked.

"A Christian," Susan responded, slowly, judiciously. "I think that would best describe what I am. You see, I add one more thing to the process of knowing, and that is the discernment of the Spirit."

"Faith is for children," Leslie replied. "I don't think I can return to the simplistic beliefs my mother taught me. The Church was her life, but she never tried to evaluate or question the validity of any of its concepts."

"What church?" Susan asked.

"The Mormon church is what it's called. I haven't been involved with it for years."

"Oh, Leslie, I knew we had something in common!" Susan exclaimed, throwing her arms around her friend. "It's my church too! I promise you, if you'll search, if you'll try, it holds the answers to all your questions. Please give it a chance, Leslie."

"I'll think about it," Leslie said hesitantly. "But I promise you, Susan, no matter how strong your belief is, I will have to find valid answers for myself. I can't be mollified by myths or possibilities or Pollyannish solutions. I won't be content with a sop."

"Blessed are they which hunger and thirst for they shall be filled," Susan murmured with an irrepressible smile.

Together they had begun a perusal of the scriptures, and although Leslie was far from convinced of the value of their studies and often chaffed at the experience, intellectually she still had to admire Susan's knowledge and background. As a friend, she was drawn to the zest of Susan's spiritual beliefs.

One evening, as they concluded the book of John, Susan turned to Leslie. "I am going to the Holy Land for a two-week tour this summer. Please come with me."

Leslie was taken aback by the request. "No," she said shortly. "I do not like traveling."

"How do you know?" Susan countered. "You haven't even tried it."

Suddenly the pressure of Susan's expectations was too much for Leslie, and she stood up in exasperation. "Look, Susan. I've enjoyed studying with you, and I admire and respect you, but it isn't going to work. I'm no closer to an understanding of myself, or life, or death, or whatever . . . and I'm tired of thinking about it. I just want to stop—here—now! No more! We can continue being friends, but you have to know that I feel I can never know whether any of this," Leslie said, pointing to the Bible, "is real—and I never will. So let's drop it, shall we?"

But Susan was undeterred. "Leslie! I know, maybe you're right, but if you'll just give it one more chance, I promise you that I'll let up on you. We'll never talk about it again."

Leslie began to protest, but Susan interrupted. "Look, you're a scientist, and you know that when you want to find the answer to a scientific problem, you begin at the source, and you gather every available piece of data before you come to a conclusion. Well, as a spiritual scientist, you've studied the evidence, now why won't you come with me to the geographic source, just to see for yourself. If you don't find any answers, if you don't feel anything, then I promise you I'll never bring it up again. Come with me please, Leslie. At least it will make the summer go faster."

The last sentence was an afterthought, but it was the sentence that had convinced Leslie to go on the trip, because the summer loomed long and empty before her. Leslie allowed

Susan to sign her up for the tour of Israel, and she watched as Susan's excitement mounted through the spring. For Susan, this was to be the trip of a lifetime.

The day before the plane was to leave, Susan had been biking over to Leslie's to bring some last minute items to be packed. On the way, a convertible driven by teenagers on their way to the beach ran into Susan and threw her up onto the curb, breaking her shoulder and cracking her hip. In traction, her face tight with pain, Susan spent an hour begging Leslie to go to Israel without her, and finally, out of loyalty and pity, Leslie had agreed to go through with the trip.

Susan had wanted Leslie to find the reality of Christ and his resurrection—his victory over death—in this ancient land. Well, thus far, Leslie had not found any of those things, but she had found the desire to live, and maybe in a way that was another kind of victory over death. .

Her thoughts returning to the present, Leslie realized that the Bedouin woman had crept across the tent to where she lay and was pushing a crust of thick bread into Leslie's hand. She then gave Leslie a drink from a cup. It was water mixed with goat's milk, and Leslie felt her thirst and hunger abate. Then Leslie heard a rustle of garments and saw the woman reaching into the breast of her robe. The woman took something out and reached for Leslie's hand, carefully closing it around the object. It was a small knife. Leslie could feel a smooth handle and a short, sharp blade. Without a word, the woman moved away from Leslie back to the other side of the tent, and moments later, her husband came in, grunted a few words, and walked over and lay down beside his wife.

It was dark and silent, and it occurred to Leslie that during the night the desert would not be hot. She decided she would wait until she was sure everyone was asleep and then she would escape. Perhaps she could take some rags to wrap around her feet. Hope burned brightly as she lay making her plans. From the other side of the tent, she heard a grunt and the rustling of someone moving heavily. In a moment, her face was illuminated briefly by a flashlight. She was blinded by the light, but she knew it was the Bedouin. He shut off the light and in the darkness, she could sense him kneeling beside her, his rough hands fumbling to find her. She shrank back from his touch, feeling for the knife, which she had wrapped in a rag and hidden in her pocket. His hand grazed her face, but it did not linger; instead he reached for her shoulder and flipped her over onto her stomach. He felt for her wrists, and when she struggled, he sat on her and pulled her arms painfully behind her. She felt him fumbling and heard him cursing in Arabic as he pulled a rope around her wrists and tied it with vicious tightness. She began kicking her legs, but to no avail. He knelt on her knees, and the pain was excruciating as he tied her ankles together in the same brutal way. Then, still in darkness, the man groped back to his own side of the tent, and she heard him grunt and cough as he resumed his place. In despair, she turned her head on the rough bedding and wept.

Chapter Six

As tired as Leslie was, she could not sleep, so she was alert when the sounds of men's voices and the crunch of heavy boots walking toward the tent shattered the night's stillness. The Bedouin grumbled and rose from his place, and she heard him knock over a heavy utensil as he moved to the tent opening and lifted the flap. The night was bright with moonlight, and she could see brilliant stars dotting the sky through the opening. Men's voices whispered, and she heard the clink of coins. Minutes later, a flashlight was trained on her. She turned to face it, but again, it was flashed in her eyes so she could not see who was holding it. Hands seized her, and she was lifted and carried. For a moment she struggled, but the ropes on her arms and feet cut into her, and she gave up the battle, knowing it was hopeless. As the men carried her out into the night air, she saw the hands of one of them reaching into a small case, and in another second in the moonlight, she saw the flash of a needle.

"No!" she screamed. "Not again! What are you doing? Why are you here? What do you want from me?" While she was screaming, the hands held her immobile, and then she felt the needle plunge into her arm and again blackness descended.

This time, it was still night when she awakened. She was lying on a stone floor in total darkness, and she was shivering with cold. Her hands and feet were still bound. The sunburn on her arms and face burned, but her body was trembling with shock and chill. Her empty stomach churned. She pressed her fiery cheeks to the cold stone and wondered if this was how her life was going to end. Somewhere she could hear voices, and she knew she was not alone. As she became accustomed to the dark, she could make out the dim outline of a square doorway, and beyond that the shadows of men moving in another dark room. Presently she heard the sound of a match and the crackle of kindling as it blazed. Through the door, she could see the men hunched down around a fire, and she could see smoke rising. Conversation was desultory, and the men moved back and forth as if bored and waiting. From the distance, she heard the jingle of a harness and the sharp sound of a horse's whinny, and she knew instantly where she was. "Petra," she breathed.

The men rose and walked out of the room. Moments later, three or four men returned, and one was speaking Arabic in a subdued but powerful voice.

Even though the words were in a different language, she would know that voice anywhere! It was Hal Johnson. She could not see him as he spoke, but one of the other men came into sight, and as she saw him through the doorway, she started with surprise. It was the runner with the white stallion, who had led her into Petra the day before. Apparently, he and Hal were arguing. The man gestured toward the room where Leslie was lying and drew a large knife out of his waistband and shook it at the darkened room. Hal Johnson replied with a sharp command, and the man, resentfully, put the knife back in his waistband and strode out of sight.

Seconds later, she heard running feet, and someone came bursting into the room in a great hurry. Her ears, sharpened by fear and cold, picked up every possible sound, but the voice she heard was indistinct. Apparently the newcomer was standing at the far side of the room. Gradually the voices moved toward the fire, and she could hear them better. With a shock, she recognized Nick's voice. Nick *was* in on this too! No wonder she had sensed he was a phony. *What was their business,* she wondered, *white slavery?* No, surely not, or they would not have allowed her to be physically damaged. Why? She wanted to scream at Nick. She hated him! Hated the way he deliberately courted trust and friendship and then betrayed it so viciously and without feeling. Whoever these men were, she knew she must abandon all hope of kindness. Nick and Hal were speaking in English, and when Leslie heard what they were talking about, she understood that they did not want the other men to know what they were saying.

"Have you questioned her yet?" Nick said, obviously furious. "I think you were crazy to grab her. She didn't know anything! If you'd let her alone, I could have convinced her I was only hungry for an orange—"

"Don't be a fool." Hal's voice cut across Nick's fury. "Nothing—you understand me—nothing is going to stand in my way now that we are this close to the end. One stupid young woman—rude, undisciplined—how do we know who she is or what she is? Every time I have turned around these past two days, she was watching me. Do you think for a minute she is what she seems to be? I don't. I do not think it was coincidence that she was watching you at the border. I have not trusted her from the start. There is something suspicious about her behavior."

"Hamji," Nick's voice was conciliatory, "you're letting the pressure get to you. I tell you, she is nothing but an innocent tourist, and who knows what is going to happen when they discover her missing? You may have blown our whole plan!"

Hal gave a short laugh. "Who's to discover her missing? You told Michelle Green she was feeling ill and had decided to rent a car, drive to Jerusalem, and fly straight home, didn't you? No one on the tour even knew the woman. She kept to herself."

There was a moment of silence. Leslie realized Hal had pegged her accurately. No one would be concerned that she was missing—even if they noticed.

"Hal, I was hoping I wouldn't have to tell you this," Nick said intensely. The men's voices came closer to her, and Leslie saw through the doorway that Nick had led Hal toward the opening to her cell. He put his arm across Hal's shoulder, and they turned their backs to the fire and away from the other men so their faces were toward Leslie's room. "Hal," Nick said in a voice barely above a whisper, which Leslie could hear distinctly because of the position in which he stood. "This woman will probably be missed almost immediately. Do you know who she is?"

"No," Hal said impatiently. "I have just finished telling you, I am suspicious of her, but I don't know who she is."

"Think," Nick said intensely. "What is her name?"

Hal raised his head and looked into Nick's eyes. "Mrs. Brinton," he said slowly. "Leslie Brinton." He raised his eyebrows impatiently, questioningly. "What of it?"

"And the name of the senior senator from Washington, who will be the chief American observer at the peace talks?" Nick prodded.

"Jeremy Brinton," Hal whispered. "Senator Brinton. So, are you implying a connection between this scrawny nobody and—"

"Not implying," Nick continued. "She was married to his nephew. It's a close family. She planned this trip to coincide with the peace visit. She was going to phone the senator in Washington tomorrow to report on her observations and to arrange a visit in Jerusalem with him when he arrives there at the end of the week."

Hal grabbed Nick's shirt collar in fury. "How do you know all this?" he demanded, and even in the shadowed light of the room, Leslie could see that Hal's face was dark with rage. "Tell me! How do you know?"

Nick brushed Hal's hand from his shirt and stood calmly. "Mrs. Brinton told me when we walked back from Petra. She asked me to arrange the phone call in Jericho. Do you know what is going to happen if Senator Brinton doesn't get that phone call tomorrow, or even worse, if she is found dead back in Jordan after she had been cleared through customs into Israel? The Americans will immediately know something is fishy, and the blame will come right back to the Palestinians. Don't you see? They'll relocate the Jerusalem meetings, and we'll lose our chance. Your grand scheme will become just another aborted act of Palestinian terrorism, and you'll bring it all crashing down because of this one woman. Mrs. Brinton's death in Jordan, or her disappearance, will eliminate the chance for any international commission meeting in this area. They'll go somewhere safer."

Hal Johnson looked like a trapped man. He wagged his head from side to side, searching for a way out. "We could leave her body here . . . they'd never find it—or we could bury it in the desert."

"No—tomorrow, as soon as she fails to make the phone call, they'll assume she's missing and launch an international search. This country will be swarming with intelligence personnel, and someone is bound to remember something they saw at the border and put two-and-two together: the orange crate, the young woman wandering down the back fence, you going through customs *twice* because you 'got confused about which bus you were riding.' It won't stand up to much scrutiny, Hamji. We can't afford to have her die in Jordan, not this close to the end."

"What do you suggest?" Hal asked fiercely.

"Look, I've got a plan, and it might just work. The important thing is to get back over the border into Israel, and then make her death look like an unfortunate accident on the right side of the border." Leslie thought she detected Hal Johnson relax when he realized Nick was not against killing her, but just wanted it done believably. Nevertheless, Leslie sensed a wariness between the two men.

"I got myself assigned to another tour bus," Nick continued. "Sam and I left the other tour group in Jericho with a relief team and crossed back over the border to pick up a new group of tourists in Amman. The bus will be in Aqaba tonight and in Petra tomorrow. I can get some phony papers for the girl. We'll drug her, put her on the new bus, and say she was with another tour group until she became sick, so we're taking her across to Israel to send her home. As soon as we get across the border, we'll take her off the bus in Jericho and arrange a fatal car accident on her drive to the airport in Jerusalem. I know it's patchy, but it's the best we can do."

There was silence as Hal weighed what Nick had said, then a third man joined the group. Leslie recognized the owner of the white stallion again. The men continued to speak English and Leslie realized the Arab horseman knew the language perfectly. He spoke it without accent and with American ease.

In quick, terse sentences, Hal explained to the newcomer the things that Nick had said, as well as Nick's plan for getting Leslie back over the border where she could be "accidentally" killed. In the shadowed light of the cavelike room, the Arab's face seemed even more harsh and cruel than Leslie had remembered. His eyes seemed to penetrate the darkness of the room in which she lay, and she felt he knew she was conscious and listening. In a harsh voice, he responded, "I think Nick is right. If she disappears altogether or if her body is found in Jordan, it can only cause an international investigation. We cannot afford that right now. She must die in Israel in a logical way so no questions will be asked."

"I'm glad you agree, Ahmud," Nick said, his voice tinged with irony, and Leslie sensed the two men either disliked or distrusted one another.

"I only agree with the principle," Ahmud answered coldly. "I think you are very sloppy with the details. If you sedate her so heavily that she cannot move or speak to anyone on the bus, the other tourists will become uncomfortable, suspicious, and overly curious. The less conspicuous she is, the better."

"Of course!" Hal exclaimed. "But how else can we transport her across the border? We don't have time to develop a method of concealment."

"She does not need to be concealed, only controlled," Ahmud answered. "I will ride along with her as her attentive husband. She will look ill, but not unconscious. The other passengers will be concerned, but not alarmed."

"No!" Nick rapped out the single syllable like a shotgun. "There is no need for you to come. I will handle this. It's my operation."

Ahmud turned and faced Nick, his eyes flashing. "You have more important things to handle. Have you forgotten? How dare you come back over the border to Jordan in the first place. You knew what your mission was, and now you have placed everything in jeopardy!"

With cold intensity, Nick returned Ahmud's furious stare. "It was not I who placed us in jeopardy; the unfortunate kidnapping of this woman did that. We have to wait three days until I deliver the Star, and any alarm in those three days could destroy everything. We cannot afford to bungle getting rid of Mrs. Brinton."

"You are an arrogant, stupid man," Ahmud said. "You already have your assignment. We could have handled this situation without you. You have no right to be here—it is dangerous!"

"Yes," Hal said, turning to Nick, his voice cold with suspicion. "Why did you return when everything was depending on you?"

"Because," Nick replied evenly, "I, and I alone, knew of the danger you were in with Mrs. Brinton. I knew you would plan to kill her, not knowing who she was or the disaster of that action. I had to warn you."

For a moment Hal stood looking reflectively at Nick. Then he nodded slightly, acknowledging Nick's explanation. "And the Star? What has become of it?"

"Safe," Nick replied. "Safe and across the border in Israel. Don't worry. I'm doing my part, and I'm here to see you don't ruin it on this end with any more foolish actions."

Ahmud hissed with anger at the insult, but said nothing.

Hal's voice cut across the darkness. "Ahmud is right, Nick. The girl must be escorted onto the bus, and he is the one to do it. The loving couple will board the bus tomorrow, while you are in Petra. If anyone asks, you will explain they were on another tour that planned to spend several days in Jordan, and the girl was too ill to continue. The less explanation, the better. They will sit quietly and lovingly in the back of the bus. You can arrange papers?"

"Yes," Nick said, his disapproval of the plan showing in the tight line of his jaw. "I tell you, it is unnecessary for Ahmud to come. Sam and I can handle it."

"Enough!" Hal said sharply. "The plan is set. Ahmud will need American clothes and a close shave—sunglasses as well. As for the girl, someone will need to clean her up, and she will need presentable clothes. Can you arrange it, Nick?"

"I already thought of it," Nick replied, indicating his attaché case.

"Then see to it," Hal said shortly, "and hurry. You should get back to Aqaba as quickly as possible."

Nick crept into the dark stone room where Leslie lay. She was still shivering, and her hands and feet were numb and lifeless from the tight bonds that held her. As Nick approached her, she shrank from his touch, and her eyes glared at him in the darkness. "Don't touch me," she whispered fiercely. "I would rather you kill me now. Why prolong this torture?"

"Sh-h-h," Nick warned, so softly that she could scarcely hear. "They are listening. Pretend you are still drugged."

"Now, my girl," he said in a louder, bright tone, "let's make you presentable. What? Not ready to cooperate? Well, I don't have much time, so one way or another the job will be done."

Nick turned a flashlight on, and as she closed her eyes against the brightness, he searched her body with the beam and winced. "What have they done to you," he whispered. Swiftly, he reached over and untied the ropes that bound her wrists and ankles. Then, with his strong hands, he began to gently massage her hands and feet. As the circulation was restored, she moaned with agony, and her shivering became more intense. "I can't do anything for you here," he whispered. "Listen to me. I'm going to have you taken to Aqaba to be cleaned up, then you'll be taken back across the border. But you've got to trust me. No matter what I say or do, go along with it. Do you get that?"

"Why?" she began in protest, but he put his hand over her mouth. "Sh-h-h," he whispered fiercely. "You've got to trust me. Use your head, our lives depend on it!"

He got up from his crouching position and went to the doorway. "Hamji!" he called to Hal Johnson. "What on earth have you done to this woman? I can't possibly make her presentable here! We'll have to take her to the hotel in Aqaba. We can board her on the bus there. That's more believable anyway."

Moments later, Hal Johnson and the menacing Arab named Ahmud came to the cell door. Leslie, stunned and confused by all that had happened, lay on the rock floor, unmoving. The two men stood in the doorway and shone flashlights on her. "Right," Hal said. "You'd better get going right now. Ahmud can go with you and get ready for the trip as well. You can take her out on the horses with you." Hal stepped into the room and came over and squatted by Leslie. She raised her eyes weakly, and he looked at her with a smile of malice. "I guess right now you *are* my little lady," he said mockingly.

Her mouth was bruised and sore, and she was so weak she could barely speak, but she returned his look, and mustering all her strength, she replied, "Never. No matter what you do with me." Her defiance cracked Hamji's icy control, and his face suffused with anger. He reached out and slapped her with the back of his hand. Before he could hit her again, Nick caught his arm.

"Not again, Hal. It's going to be hard enough to fix her up as it is."

With an expression of disgust, Hal dismissed her and sprang to his feet. "Get her out of here," he growled. In an instant, Ahmud was beside her and Leslie once again felt the needle in her arm. As she slipped into unconsciousness, she heard Nick saying coldly, "That wasn't necessary, Ahmud. You're going to kill her with that stuff."

The men were arguing when Leslie woke up. She was warm and the shivering had stopped. Somehow, even before she opened her eyes, she knew she was in a bed, probably in the hotel in Aqaba. The cool sheets and soft mattress were like a balm to her bruised and aching body. She could have gone back to sleep were it not for the harsh and intrusive voices.

"I know you are supposed to be her husband, Ahmud, but that's tomorrow."

"Hamji has given me the responsibility of guarding her and supervising her disposal." The voice of Ahmud was sharp and menacing.

"No," Nick replied, calmly authoritative. "I am in charge. All you are to do is act the part of the husband on the bus ride, so she doesn't do anything foolish."

"You take too much on yourself, Nephti." Ahmud's voice was angry and bitter. "There is no place for personal ambition in our cause. There is also no place for personal feelings. Something about you and this woman does not seem right to me. I myself will prepare her for the bus."

Frightened, Leslie opened her eyes. The men were sitting across from one another at a small table by the draped window. Nick leaped out of his chair and grabbed Ahmud by the front of his shirt. With a powerful thrust, he pushed the man backward and pinned him to the wall. Then Nick brought his face very close to Ahmud's, and in a voice of hushed power, he whispered, "Ahmud, if you go one step near her, I'll kill you. You speak of personal ambition—it is you, not I, who is thinking of himself. Do I make myself clear?"

There was murder in Ahmud's eyes, but he did not fight. "The only reason I do not kill you now, Nephti, is because the sound of fighting might alert the hotel. We will finish the work of this week, and once it is completed, you and I will settle our score."

Nick did not release the Arab. "Then you will go to your own room and get yourself ready for tomorrow, and leave me to guard and prepare Mrs. Brinton?" he demanded.

"Yes," Ahmud answered, but the word sounded more like a curse than a reply. Slowly, Nick released his grip, and Ahmud, without a word or a glance in the direction of the bed, walked to the door. As he reached it, he turned back to Nick. "And why should you be any more trustworthy than I am with a helpless woman?" he asked, his eyes black with contempt.

"Because," Nick responded with a grin, "when you deal with hundreds of tourists, you get to know that one woman is the same as another—this one is nothing special."

Ahmud yanked open the door and left the room. Nick hurried over and sat on the bed. "He will not leave us alone for long," he whispered. "We must hurry. Can you move?"

Leslie tried to raise herself to a sitting position, and Nick put his arm behind her back for support. She pulled away from his arm and slumped forward. With her head down, she supported herself on her elbows, gasping, trying to regain her strength.

"The dizziness and weakness will pass," Nick murmured. "I have some chicken broth and orange juice here. I want you to try to eat. It's imperative for you to get strong as fast as possible."

"What is going on?" Leslie began to cry. "You tell me to trust you, and yet you are planning to kill me. I don't even know why I'm here. What are you trying to do with me?" Confusion and terror racked her, and her voice was strained.

"We can't talk now," Nick whispered. "Here, eat as much as you can. I am going into the bathroom to run the bath water."

He placed a tray on her lap and propped her up with a pillow. She sipped the broth and juice and listened to the sound of water splashing into the tub. She wondered if she could make it to the door by herself, but almost instantly, Nick reappeared.

He glanced at her tray and saw she had eaten. "Good," he muttered. "I'll give you more later. Now, let me look at you." He pulled the covers back and stared at her in the dim light of the lamp. Her hands and feet were filthy with blood and dirt. Her face was sunburned, her lips were cracked, and her hair was matted.

"It's a good thing you were wearing jeans," Nick observed, "or it would have been a lot worse. Do you think you can manage to bathe and dress by yourself?" Leslie nodded her head and pushed herself out of bed. Nick grabbed her around the waist before she collapsed to the floor.

"Let me help you, at least until you feel stronger."

"Get your hands off me," she whispered hoarsely, pulling away from him and walking shakily toward the door.

He grabbed her roughly and held her close to him, whispering fiercely, "Don't you understand, there's no time for nonsense. I don't know how long I can keep Ahmud under control. You must do as I tell you." She opened her mouth and tried to scream, but all that would come out was a croak. He put his hand over her mouth tightly. "If you bring him back into the room, it will be on your own head," Nick said, his face close to hers, his eyes glittering with anger. "I lied for you. Doesn't that tell you something?"

She twisted her head away from his grip and faced him in rage and terror. "Yes," she replied, her voice trembling, "it tells me that you were worried they'd kill me in their own way, and you had to convince them your way was right. You're using me in some kind of power play, using me as a pawn. Ahmud was right, you are ambitious and arrogant, but I won't let you kill me without a struggle. I won't be some meek lamb, a worthless nobody you can throw away like a piece of trash." She was breathing deeply, and her anger had forced adrenaline through her system. She could feel herself growing stronger. Nick could sense it too, and he smiled arrogantly.

"Think what you will. I insist you go in and bathe now," his eyes narrowing. "And if you try any tricks, I will come in and drown you."

Abruptly, he released his hold on Leslie, and she almost fell. With pride, she pulled herself upright and painfully walked to the bathroom.

The tub was filled, and Leslie turned the faucet off. Slowly she began to peel off the filthy clothes in which she had been kidnapped. Every bone and muscle in her body ached and burned. Slowly, she lowered her body into the water. At first, she felt nothing but pain, but gradually she felt the soothing warmth begin to cleanse her wounds. After a minute or two, she began to soap herself carefully. Her arms were almost black from the sun. She could feel her ribs, and her whole body seemed shriveled.

As she washed, her eyes searched the room for some mode of escape. "I can't think," she agonized, her mind still fogged by the drugs.

"Are you hurrying in there?" Nick's voice hissed.

"I'm almost finished," she answered. Quickly she shampooed her hair, pulled herself out of the tub, and began using the towel. Her feet felt better, and she could stand without wavering. On the towel rack, Leslie observed clean clothes with a blouse and wraparound skirt. She dressed, pulling the shirt over her head, wrapped her wet hair in a towel, and then tied the skirt around her.

For the first time, she looked at herself in the mirror. Her face was dark with sunburn, and there was a bruise on one cheek. Her lips were red and swollen, and her eyes looked enormous in her thin face. There was a glass by the sink; she filled it with water and drank slowly. "Will I ever get enough to drink again?" she wondered.

As she unwound the towel and began to brush her hair, Nick knocked on the door. "Done?" he asked.

"Almost," she replied, but the door opened anyway. Leslie whirled. "How dare you?" she spat at him. "You had no right to come in! You are no better than Ahmud."

Nick grabbed her wrist and held it tightly; his eyes were stone-cold. "Don't ever say that to me again," he said, his voice like steel. "Anything else, but not that."

The menace in his eyes frightened her, and she stepped back from him. He threw her arm down with disgust. "Finish what you are doing. I brought you some makeup, and you can wear dark glasses tomorrow, so you should look presentable. Do something with your hair." She began to towel the thick blonde mass, and while she worked, he stood watching her and began speaking in a soft intense voice.

"We won't have much longer together. It's almost dawn, and Ahmud will be back here expecting you to be ready, so listen to me. Do not try to resist him in any way. Be quiet and cooperative until we cross the border and arrive in Jericho. Your life depends on remembering this. Don't do anything! Do you understand? Don't try to be brave or clever. Just follow orders."

"Why?" she flashed. "So that your little scheme will be successful, and you can look like the great mastermind? If I find a way to escape, I will do it."

Her defiance was as bright as a flame, and Nick came over to her and started to shake her. "Don't!" he ordered her. "You must do as I say. Trust me . . . we must—"

The doorknob rattled, and there was the sound of a key in the lock. "Ahmud," Nick whispered. "Get into bed and act like you are sleeping—quickly."

Not knowing why she obeyed, Leslie moved out of the bathroom and climbed back into the bed. She pulled the sheet over herself and closed her eyes just as the door opened as far as the chain would allow.

"Nephti," Ahmud's voice was soft and fierce. "Open this door at once!"

"Sh-h-h," Nick said, going to the door and unlatching the chain. "She's fallen asleep. You want her to look as good as possible tomorrow, don't you? We don't want any awkward questions on the bus."

Ahmud looked at Leslie's form suspiciously, but he did not attempt to waken her. Instead, the two men resumed their seats by the window and sat silent and wary through the hours of dawn.

Leslie and Ahmud boarded the bus while most of the passengers were still at breakfast. Nick had dressed her feet with an antiseptic cream before putting thick tennis stockings and soft tennis shoes on them. She found that she could walk painlessly, and her strength was returning rapidly. Ahmud was dressed in slacks, a sport shirt, and sunglasses. He had shaved and looked very American. As Leslie walked beside Ahmud, she pretended to be very weak and dizzy. He walked with one arm around her shoulder and his other arm locked in her arm closest to him. To an onlooker, it appeared that he was merely supporting his sick wife, but hidden from view was a small syringe he held pressed against her. Before they left the hotel room, Ahmud had informed her that the syringe contained a drug that caused instant death and was untraceable. The diagnosis of her death would be a simple heart attack.

"I do not wish to use it," he had said. "There will be too many witnesses, and it will involve a lot of time, reports, questions—things we do not desire. But you may be assured, I will not hesitate to use it if you make so much as one false move. Do I make myself clear?" Leslie had nodded numbly.

Now, she and Ahmud were seated near the back of the bus, and he held her tenderly, with a gentle, loving look on his face. *They are all actors,* Leslie thought angrily. As they sat together, Ahmud's free hand began to gently pat her.

"Oh, my poor little wife," he whispered into her ear, his voice heavy with irony. She felt sick to her stomach with aversion and despair.

A few passengers were beginning to board the bus, and one or two looked inquiringly at the new couple. Leslie steeled herself against the disgust she felt at Ahmud's touch and whispered through gritted teeth, "You will really attract attention if you are seen making passes at your sick wife." Ahmud looked at her, his face so close to hers that she could see the pupils of his eyes contract. Hatred filled his eyes, and he smiled at her cruelly.

"Don't worry, my dear wife. I will treat you as you deserve," he hissed. Leslie shuddered.

Nick walked to the back of the bus. He looked fresh and professional, every inch the charming tour guide. "Well, Mr. and Mrs. Hopewell," he said with heartiness, "if there is anything we can do to make your trip more comfortable, please let us know. This evening you will be in Jerusalem, Mrs. Hopewell, and your flight back to New York is being arranged."

"Thank you very much," Ahmud replied formally. "All my wife needs is rest and quiet. It was good of you to let us join your bus today."

As Nick turned to walk back up the aisle, a passenger stopped him and whispered, looking back at Leslie and Ahmud with curious eyes. Nick explained that the Hopewells had been with another tour group that was going to spend several more days in Jordan, but Mrs. Hopewell had become ill and needed to return to New York.

The news spread through the bus and Leslie could hear murmurs of "The poor woman," "What a shame," "Probably the food or the sun," and "What a wonderful, solicitous husband." The flurry soon died down, and the bus was underway.

Leslie sat next to the window, thinking desperately. She had grown used to her terror. It was lodged inside her like a cold, dead weight, but her mind was clear, and she could feel the fire of determination burning within her. She did not want to die, and if she could think of any way to escape, she would do it. Realistically, she knew that as long as Ahmud sat beside her with the deadly needle, she was within seconds of death. The risk of any precipitous move was too great for the moment.

As for Nick, she didn't trust him anymore than she did Ahmud. After all, it was Nick who had betrayed her into being kidnapped. It was he who had given the signal to have the oranges spilled as a diversion so that she could be abducted. It was he who had developed a plan for her death so that it would go uninvestigated. As for the lie he had told Hal Johnson in Petra about her being related to Senator Brinton, Leslie felt that it was not something he had done in order to save her. He had done it, she was certain, as part of a power struggle with Ahmud. She sensed it was important to each of these men to further their own position with Hal Johnson by being the one who resolved the difficult problem Leslie represented. She felt her death would be a stepping stone for one of them, and Nick was anxious to remove her from Ahmud, so that he himself could move up that step. As she thought about her situation, her terror began to mount again. She felt her mind racing frantically and her breathing becoming shallow. She was barely able to stifle the urge to scream for help.

With a shuddering breath, she brought herself under control. *I can't go on thinking,* she decided, *or I will go mad.* With icy calm, she decided she must do nothing for the moment but wait, watch, and pray—then an unexpected opportunity would present itself. *And when it does,* she told herself with resolve, *I will be ready for it.*

The day passed slowly. The long miles of the King's Highway rolled past. Once or twice, solicitous passengers came back to ask how she was feeling. Ahmud murmured, "She seems to be a little stronger. I think she is going to be fine if she can get some rest."

At the gorge in Petra, Leslie felt a thrill of fear as she thought about all the passengers leaving the bus to ride into the ancient city. She panicked at the thought of being left alone with Ahmud. As the tourists hurried off the bus, Sam got out of his driver's seat and walked to where they were sitting. "I thought I might keep you company," he said. "As a matter of fact, Mr. Hopewell, if you want to go see the city, I would be happy to keep an eye on Mrs. Hopewell for you."

A murderous glint flashed into Ahmud's eye, but he masked it with quick ease. "No, thank you, driver," he said. "Mrs. Hopewell is too ill for me to leave her." Sam shrugged his shoulders and turned away, but his eye caught Leslie's, and she could have sworn that he winked at her.

Maybe Sam could help me, she thought with a flash of hope, but then her spirits plummeted as she remembered that Nick and Sam were partners. There was no one she could trust.

Fortunately, several elderly ladies who were on the bus decided the trip into the stone city would be too arduous for them, and they remained on the bus, much to Ahmud's concealed fury. In the drowsy heat of the afternoon, with flies buzzing at the windows, Leslie nodded and finally slipped into a light doze.

When she awakened, the bus was speeding through the fields and orchards near the border of Israel. She recognized

that very soon they would recross the border, and in a brief
time, she would be driving into the city of Jericho.

Instantly, she was alert. The awful thought occurred to her
that she might have only an hour or two of life left, and again
she felt a burning desire to live rise up in her with a force she
could hardly measure.

The border crossing went without a hitch. Her forged papers
in the name of Ellen Hopewell were very good, and they were
accepted without hesitation. The bus drove out of the military
zone of the customs buildings and down the narrow road that
led to the lush oasis of Jericho. As they drove into the city,
Leslie saw the streets were lined with orange trees, date palms,
oleander, and exotic foliage that bloomed with flowers and
fruit. Vegetable stands, fruit stands, and riotous flowers were
everywhere. The bus drove directly to the site of Old Jericho.

The excavation site of the ancient city was on a hillside on
the outskirts of the town, directly across from the Spring of
Elisha, which had provided the oasis of Jericho with abundant
water for three millennia, and which had caused this city of
the desert to blossom like a rose. About half a mile from the
tells, or hills, in which the historic excavations were being done,
Leslie could see a plain at the foot of a tall mountain that was
covered by small, square cement huts. Each hut was identical,
and the buildings covered several acres, row upon row, like a
vast cemetery of small, square tombs. It was an oppressive sight.
The huge compound was enclosed in a tall, wire fence.

Nick picked up the microphone. "We are at the tell of
Jericho," he announced. "I will be leaving the tour here. Your
new guide is waiting at the top of the excavation site and will
continue with you for the next ten days. You are about to see
the excavation of the walls of Jericho, which are probably the
very walls that Joshua brought tumbling down. You will also
see the remains of an ancient watchtower, which is thought to
be the oldest known structure on earth. To the right of the
tells upon which the excavations are taking place, you will see
a large vacant refugee camp. This was one of the Palestinian
displacement camps in which Arabs were placed at the time of

the partition of Palestine. It is deserted now, but at one time it housed thousands of Palestinians who had been evicted . . . I mean . . . relocated from their homes." Nick's voice remained coolly informative, but Leslie wondered why no one protested the obvious bias of his words. Something about the oppressive aura of the deserted refugee camp made her shudder.

She was in Jericho, and the bus had stopped. Leslie wondered what Ahmud's plan was. How was he planning to get her off the bus? How would he arrange for the car rental? Would he simply decide that it was all too complicated and give her the fatal injection immediately? Now that they were across the border, her body would be found in the right country. She stiffened with fear, and as she looked up at Ahmud, she sensed his deep-seated hatred. It frightened her more than the thought of death.

Nick strode toward them as the passengers rustled in their seats preparing to go out to view the ruins of Jericho. "How are you feeling now, Mrs. Hopewell?" he asked loudly. Before Ahmud could answer, Leslie spoke up.

"Much, much better, thank you!" she exclaimed strongly. Her eyes sought Nick's desperately. Better to die neatly and cleanly at the hands of Nick than to chance being taken alone by Ahmud. Throughout the journey, Ahmud had been switching the deadly needle from hand to hand. At present, he was holding it in his right hand and had his left arm around Leslie's shoulders and his right hand tucked in the crook of her elbow.

"Good for you!" Nick exclaimed exuberantly. Then, without warning, he reached down and grabbed Ahmud's right hand and began to shake it, smiling delightedly. "Congratulations, Mr. Hopewell," he said cheerfully. "It looks like you've done a great job of doctoring." As soon as Leslie saw what Nick was doing, she sprang from her seat and squeezed past Ahmud's feet to stand in the aisle. She alone could tell the silent power struggle going on between the men as they continued to shake hands, each face masking enormous physical strain as they struggled for control of the syringe. Leslie could see the rigid muscles in their hands and fingers curling like vises.

Fortunately, no one else was watching closely. The other passengers were busily preparing to leave the bus.

Suddenly, the small syringe fell to the ground, and before anyone could see, Nick's foot slammed down, crushing it. Just then, Sam opened the bus door, and the tourists surged along the aisle toward it. In the general commotion, Leslie saw Nick kick the crushed syringe under a seat.

Ahmud was on his feet, his face still smiling courteously, but his eyes red with rage. "My wife and I will go rent the car to Jerusalem now," he said.

"It's too far for you to walk," Nick replied. "My driver, Sam, will be glad to take you in the bus as soon as the passengers are cleared. He needs to pick up the new driver at the car-rental office anyway. Why don't you let Mrs. Hopewell stay here with us to see the ruins of Jericho? She seems better, and the air might do her good."

"No!" Ahmud shouted, and the sound of his voice was like the report of a rifle. Several heads turned, and some of the departing passengers stared at him with surprise. He struggled to smile. "She is not well enough," he added with an air of solicitude.

Leslie knew this was her one chance. "I'm feeling much better, darling," she replied sweetly. "I have had an excellent rest this afternoon. Perhaps I could stay with Mrs. Hansen." Mrs. Hansen was one of the elderly women who had remained in the bus at Petra and had been very concerned about Leslie.

"Of course, dear," Mrs. Hansen responded as she put on her straw sun hat. "I'll take very good care of you. You must see something of the Holy Land before you go home. Oh, do say yes, Mr. Hopewell. She is looking ever so much better."

"That settles it, then," Nick said rapidly, not waiting for Ahmud's reply. "You can go over to the car-rental place and be back in a few minutes. The tour authorities have arranged for your car so it should be waiting for you."

Ahmud threw such a look of hatred at Nick that Leslie knew he would have killed him on the spot if there had not been so many witnesses. Nick quietly moved Leslie and Mrs.

Hansen up the aisle in front of him, putting his body between Leslie and Ahmud. As Leslie stepped out of the bus and breathed the late afternoon air, she felt hopeful for the first time.

A moment later, she realized it might be as difficult to get away from the grandmotherly concern of Mrs. Hansen as it had been to get away from Ahmud. With a show of courteous concern, Nick attached himself to the two women and accompanied them as they walked with the other tourists toward the ruins. It was a steep climb and soon Mrs. Hansen was puffing. Seeing her chance, Leslie turned to Nick. "I think I'm walking a little too fast for Mrs. Hansen, Nick. Perhaps you should escort her up the path at her pace, and I'll go on ahead so that I can hear what the guide is telling the group. Then I can share the information with you, Mrs. Hansen," she said, turning to Mrs. Hansen and patting her arm.

Without waiting for Nick's reply, Leslie turned and hurried up the path toward the tourists clustered at the top. She rapidly threaded her way through the group. They were standing at the top of the dig looking down into a deep hole where the watchtower, stone walls, and other ancient remnants of Jericho were being unearthed. On the far side of the group, she quickly surveyed the terrain and saw she was standing on the top of one of a series of smooth, low-lying hills on a sloping plain that led to the foot of the Mount of Temptation. The mountain itself, imposing and rugged, lay some distance to the west. It was part of a long chain of jagged peaks that divided the valley of the Jordan River from the high, mountainous plateaus of Judea, where Jerusalem, Bethlehem, and Hebron were situated.

The hills around Old Jericho were bare of foliage. But because they were rocky and irregular, Leslie thought they would offer adequate cover if she could get to them. She knew she only had a few minutes before Nick would reach her or Ahmud would return. Her only alternative would be to try to ask someone for help, but could she trust anyone? The passengers would probably think she was crazy, and in the ensuing incident, she was sure Nick or Ahmud would find some way to recapture

her. The safest thing was to get away. In a flash, she slipped
from the crowd and swiftly walked along a faint path leading
down the far side of the tell.

In a moment, Leslie was out of the sight of the tourists and
into a small ravine that ran away from the low hill. She began
to run along the valley, glancing back up the path to see if
anyone was coming over the top of the hill in pursuit. Seeing
no one, she turned abruptly to the left and darted behind an
outcropping of rocks. She was on the face of a hill that twisted
away from a view of the excavation site, and she began to climb
around it, hiding in rocks and depressions. Finally, the path
dipped down again, and she saw another ravine with a third
hill running parallel to it.

She went to the new slope and began struggling up the faint
path that led to the summit. As she paused for a rest behind
some rocks, she glanced backward. From her higher vantage
point, she could clearly see the site of Old Jericho, with the
tourists still clustered around the guide. They looked small,
colorful, and far away. In the background, she could see the
tour bus. Sam must have returned. Fear spurred her on, and
she began to scramble rapidly up the slope, her anxious feet
dislodging pebbles as she climbed. Surmounting the top of the
steep hill, she began a rapid descent down the opposite side,
slipping and sliding over the rough clay and gravel. Below her
lay another valley with some scrub bushes, and on the other
side were three low-lying hills. Beyond that was the immense
expanse of the empty refugee camp, with its hundreds of empty
one-room dwellings.

It was growing late in the afternoon, and the sun was already
touching the rims of the mountains. The ravines between the
little hills were dark pools of purple shadow. With swift determination, Leslie entered the last ravine and tackled the final
ridge. If she could reach the refugee camp, she could hide for
the night, and in the morning, perhaps a solution would present
itself.

By now, she was panting with exertion, but she crested the
last hill. In the gathering twilight, she began to run across the

stretch of open ground between the foot of the hill and the fence that enclosed the gray rows of deserted huts. She ran rapidly, her feet almost silent, but her breathing was hoarse and ragged. As she neared the fence with its signs written in Hebrew and English warning that the area was restricted, she heard the ominous sound of racing footsteps behind her. Involuntarily, she looked over her shoulder and saw the figures of two men dashing toward her. She looked for a place to hide, but nothing presented itself, so in desperation, she sprinted toward the wire fencing and began to tug frantically at the twisted wires, not even noticing the scratches and gashes the sharp barbs made on her hands and arms. In a few moments, the men were upon her. She fought like a wildcat until they pinned her to the ground. She heard Nick's voice.

"Will you use your head for once," Nick growled angrily. "How can I help you if you keep fighting me?"

"Help me!" she shrieked, spitting out sand and gravel as her face was pushed into the ground. "Help you kill me, you mean."

"Okay," Nick said. "There's no time to convince you; we'll play it your way. Pull out the gun, Sam, and let's get going."

"Right," she heard Sam reply.

So he is in on it too, Leslie thought.

"All right, Mrs. Brinton," Sam's voice ordered coldly, "I've got a gun trained at your head. Either you get up and come with us quietly, or I'll blow it off." Wearily, Leslie pulled herself to her feet.

"Quickly," Nick hissed. He yanked an opening in the wire, and Sam pushed her toward it. "Move like your life depends on it—because it does," he said to her as she squeezed through the fence. Nick and Sam followed, and then Nick grabbed her arm and began racing with her through the deserted refugee camp. Sam was following silently and swiftly behind them with the gun trained on her. Nick zigzagged through the streets with a sure sense of direction, holding her as they ran low so they could not be seen from level ground. At one point, he paused, and Sam stayed with Leslie while Nick ran down a side street to reconnoiter. In a moment he was back. "There's a car speeding down the road," he reported. "Did Ahmud get help?"

"Two of Hal's men were waiting with the rented car," Sam answered.

"Then there'll be three of them searching. That triples their chance of success." Nick's voice was tight. "We'll have to be prepared to move out."

They continued running through the streets lined with hundreds of square, empty stone and cement hovels. To Leslie, the experience had taken on a nightmarish quality as though she were running down one unending street, always the same and yet always stretching beyond sight. Finally, deep within the recesses of the old camp, on a street that looked like all the others, they stopped, and Nick pulled her into one of the little huts. Inside was a small, square room with a single, glassless window and an old wooden door. The walls of the hut were sandstone, and the floor was stone as well.

"Made it," Nick breathed and sat down in the far corner. "Take a seat, Mrs. Brinton," he added, with mock courtesy. With a flourish of his hand, he indicated the dirt-covered floor. Leslie, tired and discouraged, sat down slowly in the opposite corner, and Sam stood to one side of the window, his gun still trained on Leslie, but his eyes searching the surrounding area in the fading light.

"I think they have parked the car on the road," Sam said. "They're so angry, they're getting careless. They know where we are though, and they'll search these houses one by one until they find us."

"What are our chances of getting out of here unseen?" Nick asked.

"Not good," Sam answered. "The streets may seem like a giant maze, but they are laid out in a neat, square pattern, so they can search them very efficiently. Until it is dark, we can't break cover. The risk of being seen is too great. It will take them a long time to get up this far. I think our best bet is to wait until nightfall."

"Okay, then," Nick answered. "This is your territory. We'll wait."

Leslie sat in the corner like a trapped animal, her eyes searching the two men, fear and exhaustion plain on her pale face. Suddenly, Nick stood up and went over to her. She raised her arm and cowered, and he reached down and gently moved the arm away from her face. "Are you ready to listen," he asked, "or do we have to keep up this nonsense with the gun?"

She felt defeated and weary. "Do whatever you like," she replied listlessly.

Nick sat beside her, but didn't touch her. "You've really complicated our lives, Leslie," he said with a rueful smile. "Do you know that?"

"I've complicated your lives?" she retorted in a bitter whisper. "What do you think you have done to mine?"

Nick said nothing, only shook his head. "It was your own fault," he said. "You refused to behave like a good little tourist. You have no gift for the herd instinct."

"What is this all about?" Leslie asked, her frustration and exhaustion evident in her voice. "What reason could anyone have for wanting to kill me? What is this important plan I've fouled up—and how?" Her voice was rising.

"Sh-h-h," Nick warned. "Sounds carry in these empty streets." Sam stood alert by the window, his eyes and ears straining.

"You see, my girl," Nick whispered, "this week the International Peace Commission is meeting in Jerusalem. It's the first time Israeli, Arab, and western nations have met together. History is being made: the first possibility of workable compromises in the Middle East. If this group makes so much as one statement on which they all agree—even if they just make it through the week without someone walking out—then they will have succeeded." Nick's voice was filled with quiet fervor.

"I can understand that," Leslie said impatiently. "But what does this have to do with me? Why have you kidnapped me? Why am I running for my life?"

"There are factions on all sides who don't want these meetings to succeed. There are fanatical groups who will stop at nothing to prevent any peace that involves compromise. Hal's group is one of the oldest and most rabid of the terrorist groups. They make the Shi'ites look like children. Hal and Ahmud and their gang are not only determined to prevent the peace commissioners from succeeding, they are determined to blow them to smithereens, including your supposed relative, Senator Brinton."

Leslie's face showed her shock. "But how?" she stammered. "And what on earth does this have to do with me?"

In answer, Nick signalled for silence and glanced over at Sam, who was still keeping his vigil by the window. "Any sign of them?" Nick whispered.

Sam shook his head. "They're still at the far end of the camp," he replied. "It should be dark in another half hour or so, and we can get out of here." Nick nodded and turned back to Leslie.

Leslie shook her head, and tears of frustration formed in her eyes. "I don't understand any of this," she murmured tiredly. "Who are you and why am I here?"

"Think, Leslie," Nick said quietly. "You know why you're here."

She was silent for a moment, thinking through the events of her capture one more time. "The orange," she murmured at last, in a dead tone of recognition. "It has to have something to do with the orange I saw somebody hand to you through the border fence. That's it, isn't it? But why all this fuss over an illegal orange?"

"Smart girl," Nick prodded. He turned from her and began scraping at a stone in the far corner of the floor. Within moments, he raised the stone tile, reached his hand into a cavity beneath it, and pulled something out. He handed an orange over to Leslie, and she examined the fruit. It was large, soft and over-ripe, but it felt unaccountably heavy. She placed her thumbs in the indentation at the top, and the orange split in her hands. There, shining in the dusky room, filling the torn orange with glorious color, was an enormous ruby. Leslie gasped at its beauty.

"The Chaldean Star," Nick said.

"Sh-h-h," Sam hissed, and silence fell in the hut. It was late evening now, and the sky was almost dark. In the quiet they could hear the sound of swift feet, dislodged pebbles, whispered commands, and the thud of doors being thrown open.

"They're closer than I thought," Sam said, frowning. "Possibly only a few streets away, and it's still too light to risk going out in the open."

Leslie's heart began to pound as the sounds of the search grew closer. Ahmud and his men were calling back and forth to one another. Only a few more streets were left, and the terrorists sensed the chase getting warmer. There was a feeling of frenzy in the clamor of their search.

Slowly Nick picked up the jacket he had been carrying. It was a dark green military-style jacket with deep pockets. From one pocket, he drew a small revolver. Then he pulled a chamois cloth from another pocket, cleaned the ruby, and wrapped it carefully. He put on the jacket, and suddenly he looked very much like one of the young military civilians who walked the streets of Israel. Dropping the wrapped jewel into one of the pockets, he zipped the pocket closed and buttoned the flap over it. Leslie stood up in the corner, and Nick went to stand by the door. Both he and Sam held their guns in readiness. A sound came that chilled Leslie to the core.

"Nick!" It was Ahmud's voice, cutting through the graying light of evening. "We're going to find you. Give us the girl, and I won't tell Hal you helped her escape. You can go on to Jerusalem and deliver the ruby like you're supposed to. Don't be an idiot! Why risk everything just so you can get the credit for disposing of her. Let me have her, and you get on with what needs to be done."

Nick said nothing, but in the gathering gloom Leslie saw him smile and shake his head. "Fat chance," he mouthed to Sam.

Now Ahmud's voice rose with a feverish tone. "I'll kill you, Nick! You won't get away with this! I'll kill you all!"

Leslie caught her breath in terror. Ahmud's voice sounded very close. Frantically, she searched the room for something to use as a weapon. Nick reached into one of the pockets of his military jacket and held up an object. She recognized the knife the Bedouin woman had given her. He nodded to her and threw it carefully. She caught it and felt a stirring of resolution as she touched the small, sharp blade. Ahmud would not take her without a fight.

The tension in the hut grew unbearable as the sounds of men's feet and slamming doors filled the street just below them. Sam raised his gun and aimed it through the window. Just as his trigger finger tightened, a deep voice called from far down the camp. "Halt!" In the small hut, the three of them listened to the sound of booted feet running. Sam pressed his head closer to the window and cautiously looked out.

"Hands up!" an authoritative voice shouted, and Leslie heard the heavy clank of rifles being shifted.

Another man's voice, very close to their window, ordered Ahmud and his two friends to place their hands against a wall. "Do you speak English? Do not move or we will shoot!" The voice was cold and military.

Ahmud's voice was so near to them it sounded as though he were in the same room. "Officer," he exclaimed, sounding innocent and surprised. "We were only sightseeing. We haven't done anything wrong, have we?"

"Can't you read?" the harsh voice inquired. "Just because you are American does not give you immunity from our laws. I would advise you when you are a guest in another country to be very careful to observe local restrictions."

Another voice, even more authoritative, spoke up angrily. "What are you doing in this restricted area?"

Ahmud laughed an apologetic chuckle. "My name is Adam Hopewell," he said. "I am visiting for a few days in Israel from Chicago. These two men are friends of mine who live in Jerusalem. They were showing me the old city of Jericho, and I expressed an interest in this refugee camp. I'm sorry. They encouraged me not to come, but I was curious. I had no idea it would be a serious offense. After all, what harm can there be in looking around?"

The owner of the second voice was not placated. "This is clearly posted and obviously restricted. I cannot imagine why you find it interesting. Perhaps we should go to headquarters and discuss this further."

There was a sound of retreat, and as the voices began to recede, Leslie heard Ahmud protesting, "You will find I am a simple tourist. I crossed the border today and sent my wife on to Jerusalem. She was not feeling well. You may check the records."

Nick, Sam, and Leslie stood as still as statues until the sound of footsteps died away. For several minutes afterward, they dared not move. In the distance, they could hear the roar of a heavy military truck starting up and driving away. Then silence. Suddenly, Leslie's knees turned to water, and she sank wordlessly to the ground. Nick stepped over beside her. "Are you all right?"

"Yes," she whispered. "Do you think they have gone?"

"As far as we can see," Nick replied. "I think, however, the Israelis are suspicious and may come back to investigate further. We can't stay longer. Can you walk?"

"Of course," she answered. "I'll do anything to get out of here. This is the most oppressive place I have ever seen."

A look of pain crossed Sam's usually cheerful face. "Yes," he said, "oppressive is a good word for it." There was such anguish in his voice that she reached up and touched his face. To her surprise, she felt tears on his cheeks.

"My mother died here," he said quietly. "This hut was my childhood home."

Chapter Seven

They stumbled through the darkness for several hours. Finally, a full moon arose, and it became bright enough to move quickly. Leslie grew so tired that her feet refused to obey her will, and she stumbled. When she stumbled and fell a second time, Nick picked her up and supported her.

"She can't go on, Sam. Isn't there somewhere we can stop and rest?" Nick asked. They had crossed the sloping plain and entered the canyons and valleys of the mountain range. Sam told Nick to wait with Leslie. He left them for several minutes, and when he returned, he whispered urgently, "There are some caves in the mountains. I think I have found one that is well-concealed. Perhaps we could be safe there for a few hours."

Wearily, the three picked their way through the steep canyons and scrambled up a rough slope. Behind a sharp outcropping of rock, they entered a deep crevasse in the mountainside, and following the defile, they moved slowly upward. Suddenly their way seemed blocked by huge rocks, one on top of the other. Sam led the way across the boulders and showed them a narrow opening. "Here," Sam whispered, and they clambered into the blackness of the cave. It was small, dusty, and very dark. With a groan of weariness, Leslie collapsed. Nick pulled her next to him, and Sam moved around to her other side. In the cramped darkness, the three fell asleep almost instantly on the hard-rock floor.

Leslie woke once to the sound of voices. Sam was whispering to Nick, "I'm sorry I slept. I'll keep watch for an hour and then call you. We can't stay long. Put your jacket over her to keep her warm."

"Right," Nick replied. "The police probably let Ahmud go almost immediately, and he'll be back on the trail. I'd give anything to know where he is right now—and how much he knows."

"Right-o," Sam said and moved to the front of the cave.

Leslie slept again, not waking until Nick shook her gently. "Time to go," he murmured.

The three fugitives moved to the front of the cave in the gray light of early dawn and looked out over the wilderness. They were high in the mountains that ran north and south between the valley of Jordan and the plains of Judea. Twisting across the landscape, they could see the narrow highway leading from Jericho winding through the canyons and passes of the mountains and out the other side to the rugged terrain and rocky hills of Judea where Jerusalem, Bethlehem, and Hebron lay.

The road looked like a narrow ribbon below them. As they studied the view, they saw a trail of dust coming from the direction of Jericho. It was a car moving at high speed, and as it drew nearer and passed on the road far below, they could hear the roar of its powerful engine in the dry, rarefied air. Sam watched through a small pair of binoculars. "It's Ahmud's car," Sam whispered. "I'm sure of it. It's the car he picked up when I drove him to the rental station."

"Are you absolutely sure?" Nick asked.

"Absolutely," Sam replied.

"Then the Israelis did release him," Nick replied. "But why isn't he looking for us? Maybe he left his men to search for our trail while he goes on to Jerusalem." Nick's brow was creased in a thoughtful frown.

"No!" Sam exclaimed. "I'm sure that I saw all three men in the car."

"That doesn't make sense," Nick said. "He can't let me get away with the Star, unless . . . unless he still believes I'm loyal to Hal, still believes I'm committed to the cause, and that I only want the girl for my own purposes. If he thinks it's only the girl I'm trying to keep him from, that I still intend to deliver the Star, then he can afford to wait."

"He isn't waiting," Sam exclaimed with sudden comprehension. "Don't you see? If he still believes you're continuing your part of the mission, even though you've taken Leslie with you, he knows he doesn't have to look for you. You'll come to him."

"Of course," Nick said. "He's headed for Hebron to wait for me there."

"Hebron!" Leslie exclaimed. "What has that got to do with anything? Why can't we just go to the authorities? Warn the peace commission today—right now. You'll be a hero. Whatever you've done, whatever your involvement, for the sake of mankind you must give up the ruby. We'll be protected, and this madness will be over!"

"No, Leslie, we can't do that," Nick's voice was quietly intense.

"Can't," Leslie hissed. "Won't, is more like it. I don't know what kind of game you're playing. I don't even know whose side you're on. Maybe you want the peace commission blown to kingdom come—I don't know. You certainly have evil friends, and you're involved in terrible things." Leslie shuddered and shook her head in tired bewilderment. "But, for some strange reason, I'm not afraid of you. I feel that you—" She broke off the sentence, and her eyes clouded over with weariness and confusion. "I just don't understand. I don't understand any of this."

Sam glanced over his shoulder. "Tell her, Nick," he said, his soft voice like a command. "Tell her. She deserves the truth."

Nick sighed in resignation and turned to Leslie. "Listen," he said curtly. "Listen, and don't interrupt or ask questions. I'll tell you only as much as you need to know, and no more. If this operation is blown, and it very well could be because of your interference—"

"What interference!" Leslie exploded indignantly. "I didn't do anything."

"All right," Nick conceded grudgingly. "Your unwitting blunder, then."

Leslie opened her mouth to protest again, but seeing Nick's face, she decided to remain silent.

"Months and maybe even years of planning, as well as the lives of many people—possibly even the peace of the earth— could be in jeopardy."

Leslie's face registered disbelief, and Nick frowned.

"This isn't just the assassination of an International Peace Commission, serious and disruptive as that would be," he said soberly. "It is much more than that."

"You mean Hal and his few terrorists are that powerful?" Leslie asked in a disbelieving voice.

Again Nick frowned at her interruption. "In today's world, it is possible for a lone man to be as powerful as an army. Think of three terrorists holding an airliner hostage, making the strongest nation in the world—your country—dance to their tune. Think of Anwar Sadat, calm and confident on the reviewing stand one minute and dead on the ground the next, the hopes and dreams for reconciliation in the Middle East lying with him. Determined, fanatic men who care nothing for their own lives can rock the foundations of civilization if they are well-armed and well-placed."

"That's true," Leslie conceded. "Think of Kennedy and one lone gunman." She thought for another moment. "True, but even when great men are tragically killed, the world manages to go on."

"Yes," Nick agreed. "Even if everyone in the peace commission was assassinated—even, as you say, when your own president was assassinated—the world goes on. But, suppose it were not a man who was destroyed, but a whole city, especially a strategic one. What if a man, or group of men, could get their hands on an atomic weapon and could aim it at Washington, D.C., or Moscow, or . . . Jerusalem? What then?"

Suddenly Leslie was frightened, as though she were looking over the edge of some dark and fearsome chasm, and she drew back from the fears that were forming in her mind.

"What has all this to do with me and you and the ruby?" she asked hesitantly.

Sam saw her fear, and he changed the subject abruptly, as though to give her a moment to absorb some of the things Nick had said.

"Do you know anything about rubies, Leslie?" Sam asked, interrupting Nick in a quiet conversational tone.

Leslie shook her head. "Give me the ruby, Nick," Sam said, and when Nick handed it to him, Sam held it up in the clear light coming through the mouth of the cave. A shaft of color as red as blood slashed across the floor of the cave.

"When the earth was formed, there were probably less than a dozen crystals in the entire crust that were as large and as perfect as this. Such gems are priceless and as rare as a great mountain. They are one of a kind, and they cannot be duplicated, replaced, or equalled. The Koh-i-Noor and the Cullinan diamonds, for example, are priceless.

"Rubies are among the rarest of gems, but large rubies, especially ones that have the color of pigeon's blood, are the rarest of all. Imagine this, Leslie—three carats is considered a large pigeon-blood crystal, yet this ruby that I am holding has the finest coloring possible and is almost five hundred carats—five hundred! Can you even begin to imagine its value? Five hundred carats in a single crystal, almost the exact size of the diamond in the sceptre of the Queen of England, but a ruby, not a diamond. This particular stone is perhaps the rarest gem in the world."

Leslie gasped, "Where did it come from?"

Sam gave a humorless laugh and shrugged, "The mists of time."

Nick took the ruby from Sam, put it back in his pocket, and explained, "No one is sure where it came from originally. It's very ancient, and its existence has always been shrouded in mystery and legend. As a matter of fact, it wasn't until I opened the orange and saw it with my own eyes that I was sure it existed. Add to its value in rarity and size the legend that it once belonged to Abraham. He supposedly seized it from a pagan idol in Ur of Chaldea as he fled from the priests of darkness. Some believe he kept it as a symbol of the triumph of light over darkness, good over evil. Because of that, rubies have come to symbolize peace, love, and happiness.

"Whatever the truth of its beginning, this ruby almost certainly did come originally from the antiquarian gem craftsmen of early Mesopotamia. Its ancient cut and the historic references to its existence through the centuries indicate great age. Some say Abraham kept the ruby and passed it on to one of his sons. Others say it was given by Abraham to the King of Salem, Melchizedek, who wore it in a bracelet as a symbol of office. Who knows? Legends swirl around the stone like smoke. For decades, its whereabouts have been unknown, but it was believed to be in the private collection of an Arab prince. There are many such men in many countries of the Middle East, wealthy beyond belief, with private inherited treasures of enormous antiquity.

"Needless to say, the thought that the treasured ruby of Abraham, the Chaldean Star, was owned by Abraham's Arabic descendents was tangible proof to some that Abraham did indeed consider Ishmael and not Isaac to be his rightful heir. The Chaldean Star, as you can see, has the possibility of symbolic worth, as well as vast monetary value."

"So," Leslie exclaimed. "The Star, being small and relatively easy to smuggle across a border, is a way of transferring millions of dollars into Israel. It also is something of a symbolic triumph if it ends up in the possession of the Israelis."

For the first time, Nick smiled at her. "You are bright," he said admiringly. "Hal was right when he figured you were not safe with even a scrap of information. You can't fault the man's instincts for survival."

"Ahmud's either," Sam said with a bitter grin. "He's smelled something funny, and he isn't going to let any of us out of his clutch."

"I'll deal with Ahmud," Nick said grimly.

"But you could still get help," Leslie pleaded. "Get the police to go to Hebron to round up Ahmud and his men. Turn the ruby over to the authorities—"

"Leslie, we're not after Hal, Ahmud, or their band of terrorists. As dangerous as they are, they're identifiable and known enemies. The man we're after is infinitely more dangerous, and we have no idea who he is."

"What did you mean when you said the target was not the peace commission?" Leslie asked.

"The real target is Old Jerusalem," Nick answered gravely. "The peace commission is meeting within its walls, and they will be destroyed too—along with the entire city. The sacred and symbolic site of three great religions—Judaism, Christianity, and Islam—will be destroyed, obliterated. The whole world will be left wondering who and why: blaming one another; becoming filled with distrust, anger, and fear; nation against nation; religion against religion. There will be reprisals, fury, and hell unleashed—the beginning of Armageddon."

Leslie's face was white. "How?" she gasped.

"An atomic missile fired from a desert silo. Years ago, someone infiltrated the highest ranks of the Israeli military machine. We don't know who he is. He has left no trail, no clues, no pattern of behavior. He is an anarchist because he seems to support no single cause. His only predictability is his unpredictability. We only know that through the years the most sensitive things that could go wrong have frequently done so. The intelligence department has become convinced these leaks and malfunctions are all linked to one highly placed source. But this had only been speculation until Sam and I were able to infiltrate one of the terrorist organizations, finally landing in Hal's elite. For the first time, we have received confirmation that someone in high Israeli circles—we still don't know who: soldier, politician, scientist—is cooperating with the terrorists.

"Hamji, or Hal as he is now called, was somehow contacted by this unknown man who claimed he could hold the city of Jerusalem hostage or even destroy it, whichever Hamji desired. The man's price was unnegotiable—the Chaldean Star, the ruby of Abraham. I don't even want to know how Hamji obtained the ruby. His connections are very powerful, and he is ruthless. He lives with one fanatic determination, to wipe Israel off the map.

"Hamji trusts me and has chosen me as the courier to make the final delivery of the ruby. Once the Star is delivered, the city of Jerusalem will be destroyed. No one will claim credit. Rumors will circulate. Chaos will reign."

"Jerusalem . . . " Leslie's voice was a ragged whisper.

"Our information is that the traitor has managed to steal or duplicate a computer chip that links to Israel's atomic missiles. He has programmed the release of one of these low-level missiles with an altered flight plan and has aimed it directly at Jerusalem. As soon as we deliver the ruby to him, he will turn the key, and within seconds, a city that has survived four thousand years of turmoil will be reduced to dust, and with it, the hopes of world peace will be in ashes too."

"What will the man do if the ruby is not delivered?"

"We don't know," Nick said. "But my feeling is, he will destroy the city anyway for his own purposes. We will never have another chance to discover who he is, so I have to play out this hand until Friday when I make the delivery. I've got to remain free from Ahmud so I can be at the rendezvous and find out who the traitor is."

"Hebron?" Leslie asked. "Is that where you deliver the Star?"

"No. I have to go to Hebron to meet Hal's contact: the man who's setting up the final meeting. The go-between will tell me where and when I'm to give the ruby to the man who's waiting for it. This man in Hebron is just a courier. He does not know who his boss is either. No one knows. I have to go to Hebron in order to finish my mission, and Ahmud knows it. He'll be waiting for us, and we'll be sitting ducks."

"All he really wants is me," Leslie asserted. "I'm not afraid. If it's the only way you can stop this unknown madman from destroying Jerusalem, then I'm willing to go. Give me back to Ahmud if it will leave you free to complete your mission."

Nick turned and looked at her steadily, his eyes glowing with open admiration. "You would, wouldn't you?" he said softly. "But it wouldn't do any good. I'm sure once Ahmud finds us he will simply kill all three of us, take the ruby, and complete the mission himself. His action would look very plausible to Hal. Ahmud has wanted to be Hal's right-hand man for years, and now I've provided him with an opportunity I don't think he'll pass up," Nick said.

"Then what are we going to do?" Leslie asked. "You'll have to go to the authorities."

"Authority—that's it! Sam, did you hear what she said? That's our answer! We'll call Levi!"

Sam looked contemplative. "Break radio silence?" he asked warily.

"Look, Sam, this is our last assignment, no matter what. If we haven't blown our cover by now, it's so thin it'll never be of any use. Levi would be the first to agree. Can you make it back to the radio and get a message out within the next hour?"

Sam looked across the terrain to the refugee village far in the distance. "Maybe an hour and a half," he said. "The place is probably under increased surveillance since last night—should be quite interesting."

Nick laughed. "Send this message to Levi: Code Red Alert. Send helicopter immediately. Disguise as military maneuver. Pick up Sam behind Jericho excavation, Project Star."

"Got it," Sam said. "What's the plan?"

"Levi will pick you up. Then bring the helicopter here to the flat area at the base of the mountain. Leslie and I will be waiting. The essential thing is to get to Hebron before Ahmud, so he can't intercept the rendezvous message. Once we know the place and time for the exchange of the Star, we lie low until the meeting is to take place. If we beat Ahmud to Hebron, the rest should be a piece of cake."

"I never did like cake," Sam replied. The two men looked at each other, smiling, and then they embraced before Sam was off like a mountain goat. Leslie thought she had never seen a human being move so swiftly and surefootedly. He seemed to know instinctively how to blend with the landscape, and it was a moment before she realized he had vanished from sight.

Her eyes could not find him anywhere in the shadowy stretches of mountains and plains.

"We'll wait," Nick said, "and pray it's only an hour. Our margin for error is very slim." Leslie watched Nick's face as he looked downward where the unseen Sam must be racing across empty fields towards the desolation of the refugee camp. Nick's face, though impassive, nonetheless seemed filled with deep concern.

"You really care about Sam, don't you?" Leslie asked.

"He's my brother," Nick said simply.

"Your brother! But you look so different."

"Well, my half brother really," Nick replied. "My mother died when I was born. My father went to London to complete his education, and while he was there, he met a beautiful Arab Jewess named Saria. They fell in love, and she bore a son. When they returned to Israel, they were unprepared for the feelings of bitterness between the Arabs and the Israelis. Saria couldn't bear the way her own people were treated. She was an emotional, idealistic woman, torn between her loyalties as a Jew and an Arab. She finally left my father and married a Palestinian liberation fighter. He was killed, and she was taken to the camp you have seen.

"My father searched for her for years, but records were badly kept. It was not until he befriended a man of power in the government that he was able to locate information about where Saria and the child were being held.

"I was eight years old at the time, and I will never forget the day we went to the camp. All those huts were filled with people." Nick paused, and put his hands over his eyes as though to wipe away the memory. "I remember my father saying, 'These are our brothers and sisters. It is right we should have a homeland, but what a price we are paying—our immortal souls.'

"We found Sam that day. He was only two years younger than I, but half my size. He looked like he was all eyes, but he was proud and quick and bright. My father held out his arms and said, 'My son.' It is the only time in my life I have seen my father cry. We learned that Saria had died the year before.

"We took Sam home with us, and my father simply introduced him as his son, born in London. Nobody ever really
questioned that Sam was a Jew, an Israeli, and we grew up
together. I was the biggest, but Sam was the quickest and the
bravest. We made an unbeatable team." Nick smiled at the
distant memory.

"Why do you both speak with an English accent?"

"When we reached the age for boarding school, our father
sent us off to London and the Continent. That's where we
were educated. Father remained in Israel because of his business interests, but he told us he did not want us to live here,
ever. He felt if Sam's true origin were ever known that it would
destroy him like it had destroyed his mother. My father hates
politics. He has nothing to do with it, and he wanted us to
wipe it out of our lives too."

Leslie said, "Then you are a Jew and Sam passes as one,
and you are working for the Israelis."

"Things are not always as they appear," Nick said. "Sam
watched what prejudice, suspicion, and division could do to
human lives as he grew up in the refugee camp. My father
watched what prejudice could do to love when Saria left him,
and I watched the family I loved living in deceit and fear because
of ancient hatreds. We are all children of Abraham and yet we
have been at each others' throats for untold centuries. Where
did the tradition begin that Arab and Jew could not live together
in peace and brotherhood? I love Sam with all my heart. There
is no Arab or Jew in us, only brotherliness. Father Abraham
understood brotherly love. He knew the secret of bringing his
children together, but look what we have done. We have torn
the fabric apart.

"Sam and I were determined, and we made a pact in blood
when we were boys, to spend our lives serving the cause of just
boundaries and lasting peace. Before that can happen, we must
rid ourselves of the fanatic factions who want nothing but
blood and hatred. We work for the Israeli counterintelligence
to serve this one cause." Nick paused and said apologetically,
"It's not often when I get out the soapbox anymore."

"And this man you are calling—Levi?"

"He's our control agent. He is the only man who knows we are working for the Israelis. Everyone else believes us to be Arab agents."

Just then the silence of the morning was shattered by a distant sound, like a dull explosion. Startled, Leslie and Nick saw through the golden light of the desert a cloud of fire and smoke rising up from an explosion in the center of the refugee camp.

"Sam," Nick whispered, sinking back silently on the stones.

Leslie said nothing for a moment, then asked in a small voice, "What are we going to do?"

"Wait," Nick replied.

Time dragged, and the sun began to climb in the cloudless sky. Leslie realized she was very thirsty, but said nothing and continued to sit just inside the cave where the shade was cool.

After what seemed an endless interval, Leslie decided she would have to speak to Nick again. They could not stay here indefinitely. Gathering her courage, she raised her hand to touch his sleeve, but she heard a sound high above them. Squinting in the sunlight, she looked up to see three military helicopters rocketing through the sky. They fanned out across the plains below, and two of the machines landed, letting out young soldiers dressed for army maneuvers. The third helicopter flew farther, and they saw it perching near the refugee village. In a few minutes, it was airborne again.

"Come on!" Nick exclaimed and grabbed her arm. "We haven't got a minute to lose!" Then he looked up at the sky and the approaching helicopter and said to himself with a ring of triumph, "I should have known he'd make it."

They scurried down the side of the mountain, Leslie sliding more than she walked, and soon they were hurrying down the ravine that led to the open field. Within minutes, the helicopter landed, the sand and dust blowing in every direction. Nick grabbed her arm, and they raced under the spinning blades and were hauled up through the open doors. Immediately the chopper took off, and Leslie and Nick crawled to the opposite side of the machine where parachutes and gear were piled. Sam was sitting across from them, smiling. There was another man, short and powerful, with graying hair and a dark, handsome face.

"Levi!" Nick exclaimed, and reached over to shake the man's hand affectionately. "You are a welcome sight." Then he turned to Sam and said, "And so are you—what happened?"

"I don't know," Sam said, "but I think we have company. Our friend from America, Tappin, must be close on our tail. I got into the camp all right, unearthed the radio, and sent the message. As I was waiting for acknowledgment, I checked the window. There were quite a few people around this morning, mostly military types and a couple of men who looked like Israeli intelligence. But suddenly I noticed a chap who looked decidedly like an American tourist. After last night, that just didn't ring right, so I didn't wait for acknowledgment, I got out of there. Two minutes later, the place blew up. I think he thought I was still in there."

"So did we," Nick yelled over the roar of the engine. "You lead a charmed life, my brother."

Levi cleared his throat impatiently. "If one of you would be so good as to tell me what we are doing, I would appreciate it. We are desperately searching for a way to save the city of Jerusalem, and you two are sitting here in a commandeered helicopter congratulating yourselves."

"Sorry, Levi," Nick said. "We had to have some rapid transportation, and we couldn't think of any other way to get it than to call you."

"Who is Tappin, and who is this young woman?" Levi asked, glaring at Leslie.

"It's a long story, Levi, but if you'll head for Hebron, we'll explain it to you. Tappin is an American counterintelligence agent who has caught wind that something big is happening with Hamji, so he is hot on our trail."

As the helicopter changed course for Hebron, Nick and Sam began to explain the events of the last two days while

Levi continued to glare at Leslie. "Well," he said to Leslie, "you certainly have a knack for creating complications. What is this going to mean to Project Star, Nick? Do you think we should simply withhold the ruby now and forget about trying to catch the traitor? A lot is at stake and if anything should go wrong, it would be a terrible thing. If the traitor isn't paid, perhaps that could save the city."

"Even if it worked this one time," Nick replied, "it won't be enough. If he's as important and powerful as we think he is, he doesn't need a Hal Johnson, or anybody else. He doesn't even need the ruby. We have to stop him forever, and this may be our one chance."

Levi looked dubious. "What are your chances of bringing this off successfully now?" he asked. "Hal couldn't possibly trust you anymore since you have taken the girl."

"I think Ahmud and Hal are convinced I've stolen Leslie because I want to get rid of her in my own way. They think I'm power hungry. If I keep to the rest of my orders, get my instructions in Hebron and meet the rendezvous in Jerusalem, I don't think Hal will suspect me of anything more than foolhardiness. Ahmud hates me, of course, but not because he doesn't trust me, because I'm competition and he wants me eliminated." Nick continued, "This is my idea. I think I should send Sam to get the message in Hebron. He'll tell Hal's men that I'm with the girl. I'm lying low to protect the ruby, and I'm using the girl to stave off boredom. Sam will assure them I'm going to kill Leslie as soon as I get to Jerusalem. Ahmud is just twisted enough to believe a story like that. Leslie and I will wait for Sam in Ephron Square in Hebron. Once Sam has the information, he'll signal us and we'll be in Jerusalem by nightfall if you can arrange transportation."

"Why don't you let me take the girl?" Levi asked. "I can keep her in protective custody until this is all over."

"Too risky," Nick replied. "If Ahmud or Hal catches up to us, I have to have her with me, or a body on record somewhere, and there's no time to arrange that. As long as Leslie is with me, I'm believable. If I can't produce her, they'll never let me keep the ruby and will kill me themselves. But they aren't going to catch us."

"All right," Levi agreed, "you know these people better than I do. When you get to Jerusalem tomorrow, meet me at Station Blue at three o'clock in the afternoon. I will arrange for disguises and a safe house where you can wait until the Friday rendezvous. Good luck!"

The helicopter began its descent into a field on the edge of Hebron. "This is Potter's Field," said Levi. "If you return here, there will be a car waiting for you over by the stone wall. Good luck. Tomorrow at Station Blue."

The three descended from the helicopter and ran to the shelter of the stone wall. A few yards into the field was an old sheep pen and donkey stable. They ran, crouching, into the dilapidated shed. It was filled with moldy hay and the dry scent of long-ago animals. Levi had thrust a knapsack into their hands as they left the helicopter. It contained a change of clothes.

Sam pulled on a pair of dark, cheap slacks and a worn, clean sportshirt. There was also a comb and brush, and he cleaned himself up. When he finished pomading his hair, he looked like any one of the hundreds of Arab vendors who thronged the square of Hebron in front of the enormous church that housed the tomb of Rachel and marked the graves of Abraham and Sarah.

"If Ahmud has any of his men watching us, they will be looking for three, or possibly two. They will not be watching for one," Nick whispered. "You must allay any suspicions Hal's contact man might have when I do not show up. He will probably know about Leslie, and you must be careful to talk about the situation openly, with just the right touch of suggestive humor. They'll be angry because I am so frivolous, but they have grown used to that about me.

"The important thing is that you get the man to pass the message on to you before Ahmud gets there. The go-between has orders to repeat the message only once, so if you are given it, he will not repeat it to anyone—including Ahmud. You are to meet the messenger before noon in the shop of Omar the plate painter. It is a little shop on the street that runs to the right of the square. It's two doorways down and is always crowded with tourists buying hand-painted plates. A man wearing a red shirt will approach you and say, 'Your plate is ready, I have it in the back.'

"You are to reply, 'Are you sure it is the Star design? I want nothing else.' Then he will take you into the back room and will repeat the information once, and once only. He will tell you the place and the time for the meeting in Jerusalem. Have you got that?"

"Yes," Sam replied. "How will I get word to you?"

"We'll mingle in the crowds around the square. When you come out of the shop, walk over to the square. If there is any problem, drop the plate, and I will figure out a way to speak to you. Afterward, we will meet here at Potter's Field. If there's trouble, I'll go on to Jerusalem, and you'll have to get word to me there."

"Done," Sam whispered and was gone in a second.

"Now," Nick said to Leslie, "I have a change of clothes for myself, but nothing for you. What are we going to do? Perhaps you should stay here while I go into Hebron."

"Remember, you told Levi as long as I am with you, you are still believable. You can't afford to go on without me," Leslie answered.

Nick was pulling on a madras sport coat. In it he was transformed into a prosperous tourist. He reached into the bag and pulled out shaving equipment and began to shave very closely, trimming his mustache off. The result made him look older and more American. Lastly, he pulled a pair of heavy sunglasses out of the bag. There was also a camera case into which he inserted his gun.

"I wouldn't recognize you," Leslie exclaimed.

"Well, Ahmud will if he gets a close look, but in that crowd of tourists, he probably won't single me out. You, however, are another matter, what with that blonde hair and those filthy clothes."

Leslie looked around desperately. "Isn't there anything else in that bag of Levi's?" she asked. He pulled out another pair of sunglasses. "For Sam, I guess," Nick shrugged.

"Wait a minute!" Leslie exclaimed. "Sam and I are about the same size. Let me see . . . " She grabbed up the slacks that Sam had been wearing. They were a light brown chino. "I have an idea—give me your razor." Nick handed her the razor, and she carefully cut the legs off the slacks. Then she took the white shirt that Sam had been wearing and cut the sleeves. "Turn your head!" she commanded Nick.

He heard the rustling and snapping and zipping as she dressed. "All right," she said, "turn around and see what you think." He turned around, and there she was dressed in a pair of long bermuda shorts with rolled cuffs and a neatly tailored white shirt with rolled short sleeves. She had ripped the red lining out of the wraparound skirt she had been wearing and had tied it around her head in a tight turban that covered her hair and looked neat and stylish. For a final touch she put on the other pair of dark glasses. She looked like a tourist dressed neatly for a day of sightseeing.

"I can't believe it!" Nick exclaimed. "I think it will work."

Nick knew the city of Hebron well, and they were lucky because on one of the side streets they met two other American couples who were exploring on their own. They walked back to the square in their company. As the group of them entered the central square of Hebron, Leslie was taken aback by the crowds of people thronging the area. There were dozens of Arab hawkers selling painted plates, wooden beads, headdresses, lace, olive-wood carvings, and artifacts of every description. There were at least five tour buses parked in the square, spilling out brightly dressed tourist groups who milled among the citizens of Hebron. She was awed by the majestic proportions of the square and the brooding fortresslike church that towered above it.

It was close to noon and activity was at its height. Leslie and Nick were careful to remain in the thick of the tourists, drifting from group to group but always managing to remain in sight of the little street leading off to the right of the square.

Shortly after noon, they caught sight of the slender, jaunty figure of Sam walking down the side street toward the square, carrying one of the hand-painted plates that were a popular tourist item. On either side of Sam was an Arab dressed in dark slacks and short-sleeved shirts. Suddenly, Sam seemed to stumble, and one of the men walking beside him reached out a hand to steady him. Sam did not fall, but the plate he was carrying flew out of his hands and broke on the stones of the street. The man said something to Sam, and Sam, after scanning the square with his eyes, shrugged and walked back in the direction from which they had come. The Arabs remained close beside him, one on each side.

Swiftly, Nick left Leslie's side and threaded his way through the crowd. None of the tourists had paid any attention to the accident, and the broken plate remained on the street. "Someone is going to cut themselves on this," Nick said nonchalantly. He kicked at the broken pieces, his eyes assessing if anyone was watching. Then he quickly stooped and picked up the broken plate. "I wonder where a trash can is," he said to a tourist standing near him.

"Are you kidding," the man answered. "In this berg, they don't have litter baskets." The man laughed at his joke, and Nick shrugged and stuck the broken pieces in his pocket, then moved back to Leslie's side.

"Let's get out of here," he murmured. They hurried across the square just as another tour bus entered and parked. Behind the bus, they saw Ahmud's car. For a breathless moment, they remained pressed in a darkened doorway and watched while Ahmud and two other men sprang out of the car and ran up the street where Sam had disappeared.

"Come on," Nick whispered. "No time to lose. They mustn't catch us in Hebron—not before I stash the Star." They threaded through the back streets of Hebron and slipped out through a side gate in the wall. They climbed downward through steep grape arbors to the rocky plains below Hebron, where goats and sheep were grazing. Finally, they came back to Potter's Field and the little stable where they had changed clothes that morning.

"Get down," Nick whispered urgently, indicating a spot behind the haystack in the old shed. They both crawled into the cover of the dry, musty hay and buried themselves behind its shelter. For a while, they remained as still as the dust motes in the air, listening for any sounds of pursuit in the golden afternoon, but silence filled the tiny hut. It was so quiet; Leslie could hear the rustle of rodents and the distant bleating of goats and sheep.

"What about Sam?" she finally whispered, her voice trembling with unshed tears. "Shouldn't we go back to help him?"

"No," Nick answered fiercely. Then she heard him take a long, shuddering breath. When he spoke again, his voice was more controlled. "He's safe as long as they don't catch us—or get their hands on the Star."

She realized what it had cost him to leave Hebron and to lie in hiding with her, knowing Sam was in danger. "It's all because of me, isn't it?" she murmured. "You left Sam in Hebron with those awful men because you needed to stay with me. I know how much Sam means to you . . . I'm so sorry."

For the first time since the whole ordeal began, she felt herself overcome with despair and grief. She bent her head and began to cry silently. Nick brushed aside the hay between them and grabbed her roughly by the shoulders.

"Stop it!" he commanded, shaking her angrily. "You don't understand anything, not anything at all." She pulled away from his hands, glaring. "Look," he said in a reasonable tone, as though he were talking to a child, "as long as I'm with you, Hal can go on believing this whole incident is just a private quarrel between Ahmud and me over a beautiful blonde. After all, I'm not the first man to fall crazy in love with a woman and still do his job. Hal loves me like a son and trusts me as well, so it will take some pretty hard evidence to convince him that I'm trying to double-cross him. He's being cautious, though, and that's why they're keeping Sam."

"And Ahmud?" Leslie asked. "Does he still need convincing?"

Nick gave a short laugh. "Ahmud's hated me since the first day I joined the terrorist group. I am his rival. He's a sadist, a fanatic, and he's ambitious. That's a bad combination in an enemy. Ahmud will kill me the first minute he sees me and ask questions afterwards. Hal knows that Ahmud's insane, but he has used Ahmud's madness effectively. Ahmud has been Hal's persuader and executioner as well as his personal bodyguard."

Leslie watched Nick's face and saw in his eyes the memory of horrors she could not even imagine. Then slowly, his look changed into one of deep concentration. Almost to himself, he continued, "Even Hal fears Ahmud's lust for killing. He won't dare use Ahmud in a situation that requires patience and negotiation. If Ahmud kills me, or if someone proves I'm disloyal, then Hal will have to break cover and deliver the Star himself, and he doesn't want to do that. For certain, they'll give Sam the right information for me about where and when to deliver the ruby. But—they'll be watching every move he makes and after Sam and I rendezvous in Jerusalem, they can watch me too. That's what they're counting on."

"If Ahmud doesn't find you first. Then there won't be any rendezvous anywhere, with Sam or anyone," Leslie added.

Nick turned to her with a mirthless smile and said, "For a dumb blonde, you catch on quick. Of course, Ahmud doesn't know for certain we even came to Hebron. Maybe we sent Sam by himself."

Leslie shook her head. "He knows you too well, and he knows wherever Sam goes, you go. If Sam made it to Hebron, Ahmud's about eighty percent sure you're here, too."

Nick laughed softly. "Touché!"

The afternoon heat in the little shed became oppressive. Leslie took the scarf from her head and unbuttoned the top of her blouse, patting at the perspiration running down her neck. She leaned back on her elbows and shook her heavy hair loose. "What do we do now," she asked, "stay here and roast quietly?"

Through half-closed eyes, Nick looked at her. He didn't say a word, but she sensed the intensity of his gaze, and for a brief second, they were simply a man and a woman alone together in a close, private world. The golden dust from the hay hung in the air between them, and he saw her fine, beautiful face, which only a day before had been self-enclosed and almost lifeless. In the furnace of terror, courage, and outrage, she had come alive, and she seemed to glow with vitality and determination.

He wanted to touch her face, to catch her flame and let it burn in him as well. He had lived a double life for so long and had played so many parts, becoming callous to danger and all other emotions, the fire had gone out for him. All that was left in him was ice-cold conviction and the hard, bare bones of his mission. For a brief instant, he wanted to feel the fire of emotion again, the warmth of love and caring. His hand moved toward her, and as he bent his head to kiss her, his eye caught a small flash of light through the cracks between the boards of the hut.

His body responded like a whipcord, and in a single motion, he was pressed against the wall, his eyes searching the landscape through a large crack between the slats. The city of Hebron sat like a crown on the hill that rose out of the valley floor. Potter's Field was at the foot of the mountain, and the single road to Hebron ran past the field and then began its serpentine climb up to the walled city. As far as Nick's limited view could see, the road was almost untraveled. A tour bus and one or two cars were winding their way toward the city, but aside from that, the road was deserted in the stunning heat of the afternoon. Even the city seemed to be slumbering in the lazy heat. Nick's shoulders relaxed, and he prepared to return to the hay when the flash of light stabbed across his eyes again.

This time he was sure. Someone was standing on the wall of the city, watching the roads and the valley below with binoculars. As the binoculars swept Potter's Field, the angle of the sun caught them, making the lenses gleam like a mirror.

He went back and crouched beside Leslie. "We haven't got long," Nick whispered. "Someone is watching the area and has probably already figured out that this shed is the only cover for miles. Ahmud's bound to come and check it out."

"What will we do?" Leslie asked.

"We can't get out of the shed. If we try to cross the field, we'd be sitting ducks for that guy with the binoculars, but we're sitting ducks for Ahmud if we stay. There is simply no place to hide."

"The hay," Leslie suggested hopefully.

Nick laughed. "They'd never guess," he said sarcastically.

"Then what can we do?" Leslie asked. "We can't sit here and wait for them to come get us—and the Star. There are too many lives at stake. We have to get out of here. You hide in the hay, and I'll wait for Ahmud. Maybe I can distract him so that he won't check out the hut. I'll tell him I'm waiting for Sam, that you have already gone to Jerusalem." Leslie rattled on desperately.

Nick put his hand over her mouth. "Stop. There's no time for dramatic nonsense. Ahmud won't waste his time searching through the shed anyway. He'll probably just set the thing on fire. That's his style—direct and thorough."

"Nick . . . " Leslie's eyes were fierce. "I won't die like a sitting duck. I want to fight."

"Fire!" Nick exclaimed. "That's it. Quick, Leslie, look out the crack. Is there any traffic on the road?"

Leslie ran and squeezed against the boards so that her eye could peer out of the crack that looked toward the road. "There's a tour bus coming down the road from Hebron. It's moving very slowly. There's a motorcycle—no, two motorcycles—and one of them has just passed the bus." Nick moved quickly to the other side of the hut and scanned the road for traffic coming from Jerusalem. All he could see was an ancient Mercedes truck limping down the road. The windows were gone and were replaced with flapping canvas, and the back was filled with several older children. The mother and father appeared to have two or three smaller children clinging to them. The mother's head was wrapped in a black scarf, Arab fashion, and the children were dark and Arabic in appearance. Apparently, the truck had a flat tire. It was wobbling down the road, and the father appeared to be wrestling with the steering wheel.

"The more the merrier," Nick murmured.

"What are you talking about, Nick?" Leslie whispered. "I'm frightened. The second motorcycle has passed the bus, and they are at the bottom of the hill and coming up the road at the side of the field."

Her voice was urgent as she watched the two motorcycles approach in a blaze of dust. The two riders were wearing helmets and goggles. Leslie didn't know if it was her imagination or not, but the rider of the first motorcycle, stiff and upright, looked like Ahmud. She knew Nick was right. He would stop at nothing to get rid of Nick, to secure the ruby for himself.

The motorcycles had stopped at the far edge of the field, and the two men leaped the stone wall and began walking toward the shed. Goats and sheep blocked their way, but they pushed through the flock in a straight line. Leslie was sure now that the first one was Ahmud. Another shaft of light reminded her that someone with binoculars was watching everything from the heights of Hebron.

"How much time?" Nick asked.

"Maybe two minutes," Leslie whispered. The men were slowing their walk and looking off to the other side of the field. Leslie could hear the sound of children's voices and a woman's voice, shrill and whining, screeching across the open field. Leslie could not see what Nick could.

The ramshackle truck had finally pulled to a coughing halt at the side of the road, and the woman and children had piled out and were running across the field toward the two men from the motorcycles. The woman was calling in Arabic, "Please, sir, help us!"

Ahmud motioned the woman away, but the children, as eager as puppies, gathered around the men and impeded their progress. Their voices chorused as they begged for a ride on the motorcycle.

In a furious motion, Ahmud tore off his goggles and helmet and looked into the woman's eyes with fury. "Leave us alone, you poor excuse for a camel."

The woman, undeterred, placed herself in front of him and began to screech. Leslie saw Ahmud roughly thrust the woman aside. His face was black with anger.

"The tour bus is nearing the field," Leslie whispered.

Nick had moved from his position by the crack in the wall and was standing near the hay. "Leslie," he said in a low voice, "I am going to set fire to this shed. We must try to stay in the building, no matter how hot it becomes, until the tour bus stops and the tourists come running. Then try to run out as far from Ahmud's range of vision as possible, mingle with the tourists, and head for the bus."

Leslie understood instantly, and she nodded her head. "The bus is by the wall," she whispered. Nick threw a lighter on the floor and smashed the cheap, plastic case with his heel. He struck a match and threw it on the leaking fluid. With a whoosh, flames leaped up, and the dry hay caught like tinder. In a moment, the rotted wood of the ceiling was blazing, and sparks and smoke were leaping into the bright afternoon sky. The tour bus rolled to a halt, and the driver jumped out, followed by excited tourists who ran across the field with their cameras clicking. Leslie stood in the far corner of the shed, hiding in one of the makeshift stalls, watching as the roaring, hungry fire devoured the weathered wood. She felt the roar of the air as it fed the flames, and the heat seared her face and arms. Suddenly, Nick was in front of her, shielding her from the desperate heat with his safari jacket. He held her tightly against him and pressed her against the one untouched corner. He was gasping for air, and perspiration was streaking down his face.

"Just another second or two," he whispered, his voice harsh with pain. "If we can wait until they're a little closer." The tourists were pounding across the fields in an untidy formation, one or two of the men leading the others. The Arab woman and her children were standing transfixed in front of the shed, the glowing flames reflected in their jet black eyes. Ahmud and his henchman had stepped back a few yards, watching intently.

A center post gave way, and part of the roof collapsed. The resulting rush of fresh air added impetus to the inferno, and the heat intensified. Leslie watched over Nick's shoulder as the flames began to devour the manger in which they stood. "We can't wait any longer," she whispered. She placed her arm around Nick and felt the back of his shirt. The shirt was so hot, she wondered why it had not burst into flames.

"Now," Nick croaked, and they edged toward a break in the shed. The roof above them was dropping flaming brands, and the timbers of the front opening creaked and crackled in the heat. As unobtrusively as possible, they slipped through an opening and covered the few feet between them and the gaping tourists.

Leslie slipped behind a heavy man who was clicking away happily with a camera, his face pouring perspiration from the heat of the fire. She then moved past him to a woman who was searching in her bag for her sunglasses. The woman was carrying a shopping bag and a purse, as well as her shoulder case. "Here," Leslie said easily, "let me hold these for you while you look."

"Thank you, dear," the woman said, and handed her the heavy shoulder bag and her packages. Leslie held the bags in her arms so they obscured her face, and she peered between them to see if she could locate Ahmud and the other terrorist. They had obviously observed something, because they had abandoned their position apart from the rest of the crowd, and they were moving through the milling tourists, staring carefully at their faces. Leslie's heart sank. She looked wistfully across the field to where the tourist bus and the rattletrap truck lay waiting. It seemed so cruel after all they had been through to have a haven so close and yet so unattainable.

The bus driver blew a whistle. "Ladies and gentlemen," he called, "we have a schedule to maintain. If we want to get to Jerusalem before dark, we must leave immediately."

The bus driver and the tour guide set off at a rapid pace, and the tourists hurried after them. Leslie saw Nick moving swiftly next to the heavy man with the camera.

"I'll carry these bags back to the bus for you," Leslie said to the woman.

"How nice of you, my dear," the lady replied. "They are heavy, and apparently we must hurry. I appreciate the help."

They set off at a brisk pace, surrounded by several other women and teenagers. Leslie saw Ahmud moving toward her group. She felt as though her breath was being squeezed out of her. At least he didn't know what she was wearing, so he would have to see her face before he could be sure who she was. She held the bags closer and murmured to her companion, "Perhaps we should hurry a little more. I hate to have the tour guide mad at me."

"I know," the woman agreed conspiratorially. "He really is short-tempered, isn't he?"

The children from the stranded family were having a merry time. They were weaving in and out among the tourists, touching the pretty fabric of their clothes, staring at binoculars and cameras, and asking for gum in a very charming way. The mother was going from passenger to passenger asking for help and gesturing to the truck where her husband continued to work desperately on the engine. The hood was raised, and he had taken no part in all of the excitement.

Just as Leslie thought that Ahmud would surely get to her before she could get to the bus, two things happened. As Ahmud stepped into the group of tourists surrounding Leslie, one of the teenage boys in the group saw the helmet and goggles in Ahmud's hand. "Hey, man, are you the guy with the motorcycle that passed us up on the mountain? Man! You must have been going sixty miles per hour down that crazy switchback road. What kind of a bike is she, anyway, to handle like that?"

Ahmud said nothing, but his face was menacing, and he hissed through his teeth at the boy.

A woman walking beside the boy stepped over in front of Ahmud. "Now you listen here, young man! You've no call to

be rude to Marty here. He was just trying to tell you how much
he likes your machine. You go roaring around on that thing
endangering life and limb, not just your own, but everybody
else's, and then a young boy asks you a simple question and
you act as though . . . "

Leslie did not stay to hear; she continued walking swiftly
toward the bus. She was almost certain she could make it now,
and she prayed that Nick was already on it, although she had
not seen him get aboard.

Suddenly her way was blocked by the noisy Arab woman.
She was still holding her baby, who seemed to be sleeping peace-
fully and who looked perfectly healthy. The woman let out a
string of Arabic words in a shrill voice. "Please," Leslie whispered desperately. "Please let me pass. I must get on the bus."
She took a step forward, but the woman grabbed the bag she
was holding in front of her face as though she would take it
away. Leslie clung to it. "No!" she said sharply.

The Arab woman looked angry and put her face very close
to Leslie's and began cursing her in a quiet, menacing tone.
Leslie was so desperate to get away from the woman that for a
moment she did not realize the woman was speaking very softly
in broken English. "Go around the bus, and get under the floorboards of the truck."

Leslie just looked at the woman, stunned and uncomprehend-
ing. The woman's face still kept its angry look, and she threw
the package back into Leslie's face. She hissed another few curse
words and then softly, under her breath, she whispered, "Levi."

Levi—Nick's Israeli control agent. Should she trust this
woman? What if it was a trap? Leslie's mind was frantic with
questions and fear. There was no time to make a decision and
the word *Levi* seemed like a life raft, so she clung to it.

Most of the tourists had arrived back at the bus and were
standing in a crowd trying to reenter the narrow door one at a
time. In the confusion, Leslie could see Ahmud pressing his
way forward, and with sudden determination, she handed the
parcels back to the woman and squeezed through the mass of
people by the bus door. She walked around the front end of

the vehicle, and when she saw Ahmud mount the steps to enter the bus, she ran swiftly down the far side, well below the view of the windows. She dashed across the few feet between the bus and the stalled truck and threw herself under the truck bed. The father, working on the engine, acted as though he had not seen her, but he moved his position so that his feet and legs were directly in front of her, screening her from the vision of anyone on the bus. Lying on her stomach, she slowly inched backward until she was under the back of the truck bed. *Now what*, she wondered. She sat up and curled herself on the inside of the heavy wheel so she could not be seen by a vehicle passing on the road, but she was still visible to anyone coming down the road toward the truck or going the opposite way, so it was not safe cover.

The truck owner slammed down the hood of the truck and hit it three times with his fist. Instantly she heard a voice. "Leslie, are you there?"

"Nick," she almost whimpered with relief. "Where are you?" She looked around in wonderment. The voice seemed to be coming from above her. Suddenly a metal panel slid open above her, and Nick's hand reached down and pulled her toward him.

"Quickly," he said. "It's a false bottom. Climb in."

She squeezed through the opening and rolled into the narrow space. "It's really only made for one, but we should fit," Nick whispered. He held her close, pulled a hydraulic lever, and the panel slid back into place. In a moment there was a loud thumping and bumping as children's feet scurried across the truck bed. They heard the heavy rear gate clang into place.

Relief, as poignant as fear, made Leslie giddy. "I wish I could see Ahmud's face when he realizes he's taking a ride on that tour bus without us," she giggled. "Did you know this truck was from Levi?"

"No," Nick said ruefully, "not until the woman told me. It's pretty good cover when Levi can even fool his own agent."

"That woman's really something, isn't she? I mean the way she stopped Ahmud in the field and got our message to us. She was risking her life, but she never broke character once."

They heard the tour bus go roaring by, and then all was silent. For a few minutes they listened to the sounds of the family: the children shouting and singing. The man and the woman apparently were having a domestic quarrel.

"Something's wrong," Nick whispered. "Why didn't we leave after the tour bus was out of sight?" They strained their ears for clues. Suddenly they heard the high-powered grind of a motorcycle engine starting. "The other man," Nick murmured. "He didn't get on the bus." The motorcycle drew even with the truck, and the driver put it into idle. They could hear his voice speaking Arabic to the driver and the driver answering. The woman's voice occasionally interrupted, shrill and angry. "She's demanding that the man stay and help them change the flat tire," Nick translated softly. "He is saying that he has no time, but wants to know if they have seen anything of a man and woman on the road today? Did they see anything unusual about the shed?"

"'Yes, you fool,' the woman is answering. 'I saw it catch fire from heaven in the broad daylight under a clear sky. It is obviously a sign that you are cursed for not helping a poor, unfortunate family with sick children who must get home by dark.'"

"That should do it," Nick whispered, and apparently he was right, because the motorcycle started and drove away, but before they could breathe a sigh of relief, they heard the sound of it returning. Without a word, Nick reached back and pulled the lever and the panel opened soundlessly. "As soon as I'm on the ground, close the panel," he whispered. Then he took her hand and pressed something into it. He dropped from sight, and Leslie obediently pulled the panel closed. Lying in numb and silent horror she realized it was the Star that he had placed in her hand. Leslie thought to herself, *He must believe that something is terribly wrong and that his life is in danger.*

Nick crouched silently in the shadow of the truck's wheel. The man had stopped his motorcycle and had thrown it on the side of the road. He spoke to the man and woman in Arabic. "Get out of the truck with your hands up, or I will start shooting the children." From under the truck, all Nick could see were feet and legs. The woman was quiet for the first time, and Nick watched as her feet dragged her to the side of the road, the man following. His feet were also slow and reluctant. The younger children clung to the woman's skirts.

Ahmud's henchman must have pointed his gun at the older children in the truck. Nick heard him shout, "You too!" and they ran across the truck floor and jumped down onto the road. Nick watched as their young feet and bare legs, as thin as sticks, walked past him.

As the oldest child slid out of the truck, Nick heard a soft thud. The boy had dropped a large and heavy wrench on the soft dirt of the road just a foot from Nick's hand. The terrorist was swearing at the children, trying to hurry them up. Nick saw all of the feet in a cluster, and in front of them, he saw the black legs of the terrorist's slacks and the heavy motorcycle boots underneath.

"Now," the terrorist said, "you will tell me the truth. What is this? Where did it come from? Who are you?"

Nick had no idea what the object was that Ahmud's man had discovered, but he knew it must be incriminating, and he also knew that the agents were vulnerable because of the presence of the children. How awful if they had to choose between the lives of these children and the lives of the whole city of Jerusalem. It was inhuman to have to make such choices.

There was the sound of a savage blow, followed by another, and Nick watched as the agent who had acted as the father fell to the ground, his nose apparently broken and blood flowing onto the ground. He was unconscious, but the terrorist gave him a brutal kick in the ribs.

"Now!" the terrorist advanced on the woman. "I will take the baby, and I will give you until I count to twenty. If you have not told me all that you know about the man and the woman, I will shoot the baby, and every ten seconds after that I will shoot another of the children."

He took the baby from the woman's arms, and Nick saw the woman's feet move toward the terrorist, then he heard a harsh laugh. "If any of you move anything except your mouth, I will shoot the baby before I count at all."

The woman's feet became motionless. The man's vicious voice began counting. "One, two, three . . . "

Nick moved from behind the wheel and pressed against the far side of the truck. Silently, he glided past the old rust panels. His only chance was if the terrorist was so intent on watching the family group that he did not turn around. The slightest movement, the slightest flicker, and the killer would see Nick before he could reach him. What if the children gave him away? They would see him as soon as he came to the front of the truck. If one of the children so much as focused his eyes on him, the terrorist would be bound to notice the direction of the child's eyes and turn around. It seemed hopeless to Nick, but he had to try.

He rounded the truck and saw the terrorist standing with his back to the truck, the woman and children in front of him, and the baby dangling from his powerful hand with the gun trained at its head. The baby began to cry, screaming and twisting in the rough grip, and the harsh voice continued its countdown. "Fourteen, fifteen . . . "

Nick could not believe it! He knew the children had seen him, and yet not one of them looked at him. They kept their eyes trained on the baby. It was still a long shot. He had to cross at least two yards of dirt and loose gravel, praying that no sound, movement, or shadow would betray him before he could smash the skull of the gunman—and he had only five seconds to do it.

"Don't!" screamed the oldest boy in Arabic. "Shoot me first! Not the baby!" He was crying, and the wail of his voice was high and keen. The baby renewed its squirming and screaming. The rest of the group remained still.

The gunman turned to the teenage boy in fury. "I'll kill you both if you don't shut up!" he shouted, and aimed the pistol at the boy's head.

It was a perfect diversion. In two leaps, Nick covered the distance, and before the gunman could whirl around, Nick brought the heavy wrench crashing down. However, some last minute warning had reached the man's reflexes, and he moved aside enough so that the wrench hit him full on the shoulder instead of the head. He dropped the baby, and the baby rolled into the soft grass at the side of the road, but the man still clung to his revolver. Stunned by pain, the henchman none-theless twisted rapidly and slashed at Nick's head with his heavy gun. Nick reached up and grabbed the wrist of the killer's gun hand. The powerful Arab grabbed Nick's wrist above the hand that held the wrench. Nick could feel the man's power-ful grip numbing the strength of his fingers, and he did not think he could continue to hold the heavy tool. With the speed of light, two of the children broke away from the group and threw their arms around the terrorist's legs. The oldest boy dashed over and grabbed the wrench from Nick's nerveless grip. Now Nick and the terrorist were both grappling for the pistol with two hands. Suddenly the gunman let out a scream and kicked violently. The child on his leg had sunk his teeth deep into the calf. Nick felt the man's grip on the gun loosen for a moment, and taking advantage of the weakening, he pulled the man's hand down and then jerked it up. The motion was violent and the terrorist's finger jerked against the trigger. There was a violent explosion, and the last thing Nick remem-bered seeing was the gunman's astonished expression as a red flower of blood blossomed on his white shirt. Just then, the teenaged boy brought the wrench down, missing the falling terrorist and hitting Nick by accident.

When Nick came back to full consciousness, he was lying in the back of the rattling truck. It was dark, and the sky above him looked like black velvet spangled with diamonds. His body was lying on the rough boards of the truck, but his head was cradled in something soft and comfortable, and he could feel a gentle soothing motion on the side of his face. He reached up and touched a slender hand. "Leslie," he murmured.

"Yes," she answered. "You were wonderful. The children told me all about it."

"They were wonderful," he answered.

"They're dropping us off outside Jerusalem. We'll need to go in on foot. Are you up to it? They don't know if our friend with the binoculars saw the truck, and they don't want to take a chance that there is someone on the lookout for it in Jerusalem. We need to get off in a few minutes."

Nick tried to sit up and pinwheels of pain danced behind his eyes. Leslie's gentle hand on his forehead restrained him. "Don't get up yet," she said soothingly. "Give yourself as long as possible."

"What I still don't get," he said, after a few moments of companionable silence, "is what made Ahmud's buddy suspect the truck. I thought their cover was perfect."

"It was your shirt. The woman told me that when the man drove away on his motorcycle, he noticed a piece of white cloth lying behind the truck. He came back to investigate. When he grabbed the cloth, he saw that it had been scorched by the fire. He knew none of the people in the truck had been near enough to the fire to get their shirt burned . . . so . . . "

"How's the driver?"

"The woman's driving. The man has a broken nose, but the bleeding has stopped. I think he may have some internal injuries too. We didn't dare put you back in the hidden compartment; we were afraid you might die there." Leslie's voice choked, and she fell silent. He reached up his hand and felt her face. Tears were streaming down her cheeks. Headache or no headache, Nick knew what he had to do.

He sat up and took her in his arms. He could feel her body shaking with quiet sobs, and then her firm, slender arms were around him, and her tired, tear-stained, beautiful face was lifted up, shining in the moonlight toward him. With all the emotion that still lived in his tired, disillusioned heart, he bent and kissed her.

In the darkness, he heard the murmur of children's voices and a tiny giggle. Suddenly, he and Leslie were laughing too. It was a refreshing, cleansing laughter that reached out to the weary children clustered against the wall of the old truck. The children joined in, at first cautiously, and then as the contagious laughter spread, they abandoned themselves to the wonderful merriment. In the relief of danger past, they shouted their laughter to the stars.

Almost as quickly as the laughing began, it died away. Leslie and Nick sat side by side against the back of the cab. The children shifted into more comfortable positions and tried to sleep.

"What did they do with the man and the motorcycle?" Nick asked.

"They put them on the truck. They're over there," Leslie shuddered. She pointed to a dark canvas-covered mound on the far side. "The woman assured me that by morning the truck, the man, and motorcycle will have vanished without a trace."

"Yes," Nick nodded. "Levi is very thorough."

"Don't you think we should thank these people? They've been so brave. Who do you think they are? Will we see them again?"

Nick said, "Don't ask any questions. They don't know who we are, and we don't know anything about them. In this business, the greatest wisdom is to know nothing. That way you can't give anyone away."

"Oh," Leslie said in a small, sad voice. "I know you're right, but it seems so cruel." The truck stopped on a dark patch of road. Ahead of them they could see the sky lit by the growing metropolis of New Jerusalem, and before it, on the brow of a mountain, they could see the dull gleam of a large golden dome and the dark shadow of a stone wall.

"Old Jerusalem," Nick said, pointing to the cloistered city. "We come like thieves in the night."

The truck rattled away, and Leslie and Nick were alone in the rich darkness. Leslie shivered in the chill of the night wind, and Nick put his arm around her.

"Well, old girl, we'd best get on with it," he said, his Oxford accent very pronounced.

She reached for his hand and firmly pressed the giant ruby back into it. "Thank you for entrusting the Star to me, but I'm most thankful you're here for me to give it back to you. Two more days is all we have . . . can we do it, Nick?"

"Come on," he said, beginning to trudge up the steep road without answering her question. "We've got a long way to walk before daylight. How would you like to sleep on the Mount of Olives tonight?"

Chapter Eight

The truck had dropped them in the hills above Bethany. They followed a footpath lined with crushed white gravel that gleamed clearly in the moonlight. "You know what path this is, don't you, Leslie?" Nick asked.

"Of course I don't," she answered shortly. "I don't even know where I am."

"You are walking on the path from Bethany to Jerusalem. We are walking toward the back of the Mount of Olives."

"Bethany . . . " Leslie mulled the name in her mind. "Isn't that where the Savior stayed during the last week of his life?"

"Right," Nick answered. "As a tour guide, I would like to point out that this road may have been the one he used during his triumphant entry. If you'll stoop down and pick up some of the gravel, you may find small square pieces." The gravel was almost chalk white, and the moon was high. Leslie picked up a handful of stones as they walked along and put them close to her eyes so she could examine them in the dark. Two of the pieces of gravel were chiseled into small cubes.

"Those are pieces of rock from the original paved road the Romans built in the time of Christ."

Leslie's hand closed over the square rocks, and she held them against her like a talisman. "Incredible," she whispered.

"He may have walked on those very stones you are holding." Nick verbalized her thought, and she turned to him with shining eyes, then walked on in silence.

An hour before dawn, they reached the crest of the Mount of Olives. A modern hotel dominated the top of the steep hill. Few lights were on, and a drowsy doorman slumped at the entrance under the dimly lighted marquee. Nick and Leslie stood in the dark shadows under a grove of olive trees. No one appeared to be watching, so they broke cover to run across the wide avenue in front of the hotel. They climbed over a stone frontage wall that ran along the side of the road and let themselves down onto the steep slope of the mountain. Below them, like a river of darkness, ran the deep Valley of Kidron, and on the other side of the valley rose Mount Moriah, a black shadow against the predawn sky.

"They are excavating a park for a monument on the face of the Mount of Olives," Nick whispered. "We can probably find a place to hide there and sleep for one or two hours."

He took her hand and moved swiftly along the paths and through the groves of trees on the steep slopes of the hill. Leslie stumbled and fell several times. Branches scratched her face and tore at her clothes and exhaustion washed over her.

"How much farther?" she gasped.

Nick pointed ahead, and she saw the outline of a bulldozer and other heavy machinery clustered together.

"The Mormons are building a monument to Orson Hyde," Nick said, "although I don't know who on earth Orson Hyde is." He laughed.

"He was a Mormon leader who dedicated the Holy Land to the gathering of Israel about a hundred and fifty years ago," Leslie said slowly. "I remember that from my youth." Nick gave her a surprised glance and continued to move swiftly. He pulled Leslie toward a scaffolding, and they lowered themselves into it and squeezed between the boards. There was the scent of freshly turned earth, and somewhere in the night, jasmine or ginger blossoms had opened their moist richness and drenched the still, cool air with sweetness. For a moment, Leslie leaned against the boards, her aching legs stretched out against the cool earth, and her tiredness roared into every nook and cranny of her mind and body. Sleep became a tyrant that would not be denied.

"We should be safe here, at least until morning," Nick whispered. "This is the pedestal of the statue."

"Do you think his dream will ever come true?" Leslie asked.

"I don't know," Nick said. In her last moments of consciousness, she heard him sigh. "So many people love this land, and yet it's as though mankind has been trying to destroy it since the world began. If we don't find out who's betraying us, this time they might succeed."

Giddy with sleep, she mumbled, "For each man kills the thing he loves—"

She was gone, snoring a little in her exhaustion, but Nick sat awake, strangely alerted by the quotation she had begun. The words gave him an odd feeling, as though there were something in their thought that had significance, but his mind was too tired, or the thought was too elusive for him to grasp. "If we destroy the things we love, then the destroyer is also the lover . . . " he mused. In his grogginess, Nick slumped down and set the small alarm on his wristwatch. As he, too, drifted toward sleep, his mind finished the quotation, " . . . each man kills the thing he loves . . . the brave man with a sword, the coward with a kiss."

The sun struggled up to the height of Mount Moriah, and its shining fingers touched the golden Dome of the Rock. The glorious mosque burst into shining rays that gleamed, dazzling and triumphant, against the sky. It sat like a jewel against the gray stone of the ancient walled city of Jerusalem. Across the valley, the Mount of Olives was still in shadow.

Nick's watch alarm buzzed, and he awoke abruptly, instantly alert. Leslie slept on beside him, so tired the sound had not penetrated her deep slumber. He looked at her in the pale light that filtered through the scaffolding. She was curled up on the soft dirt, her arm curved under her golden hair like a pillow. Her face was streaked with dust, but her fair skin glowed and his heart ached with tenderness.

As one would stoop gently and naturally to wake a sleeping child, he bent and kissed her. Her eyes opened, and she stared at him without moving. There was no fear or surprise in her expression, and without speaking, she lifted her hand and placed it in his. "Is it time to go?" she asked.

"Time to plan," Nick replied. "They'll be watching Sam, of course, so I can't meet him at our prearranged location."

"Why not?" Leslie asked.

"Because it is our 'safe' spot. It's where Levi communicates with us. It would be too risky to let Ahmud and his thugs know where it is. They might see something or find something that would reveal our relationship to Levi. I can't blow that location. It's the only place where Levi knows to reach me."

"Then what can you do, Nick?" Leslie asked in near panic. "You have to rendezvous with Sam to find out where to meet the Israeli traitor. Sam's the only one who knows where and when the meeting is. Everything hinges on him. You'll have to take the chance of blowing your contact point. This terrible thing has to be stopped. Somewhere out there," she looked up into the spotless blue sky, "is a great destructive weapon and a madman—and the ruby you are carrying will lead you to them. There is no safety anymore, no place to hide. Some faceless unknown man is using Hal and his terrorists, the United States' weapons, and Israeli know-how, and he is going to bring it all crashing down on the world like a hammer, or a great malevolent fist, aimed at the very center of man's faith." She looked across at the ancient city of Jerusalem, still slumbering in the quiet daybreak.

"The city must have looked just like that two thousand years ago—except for the golden dome, which would have been Herod's temple then. It's as though time has had no impact on it, and men of faith, like Orson Hyde, have seen it as the spawning ground of truth. Perhaps God is a little closer to man in this spot. This is the place where truth resides—if it resides anywhere. So many people need this place of faith, a place to find themselves again—" her voice broke.

Nick knelt beside her. "You are tired. It makes your thinking and your emotions sloppy." His voice was tough and harsh. "Don't think about what can happen or what has happened. All you can afford to think about is what needs to be done now. Don't you understand? Sam came out into the square in Hebron to give us a message. We've got to figure out what the message was. I know he gave us a clue or a signal—something to tell me where to meet him. Think! We haven't any time to waste. Think back about everything you saw him do."

"He came out with the two men on either side," Nick continued, struggling to recall.

"Yes," Leslie said, slowly visualizing Sam in her mind. "He acted like he wasn't worried or even looking for anyone. He walked very naturally."

"M-m-m, yes," Nick agreed, "almost like he didn't know they were going to detain him—but he knew. He must have known. Otherwise, he wouldn't have broken the plate."

"The plate!" they both exclaimed together. Nick had slept using the safari jacket for a pillow. He grabbed it up from the ground and opened the pocket into which he had buttoned the broken pieces of the plate. They smoothed a spot on the earth in front of them and began to put the plate together like a puzzle.

The plate was typical of the tourist souvenirs sold in Hebron. It was cheap pottery, dinner-sized, with a bright-colored, free-style geometric design painted on it. The souvenir plates were painted by hand in Arab workshops and the patterns were varied and gaudy. This particular pattern consisted of wavy blue lines in concentric circles, with a star in the center radiating lines to the outer circumference. There were circles, flowers, and dots interspersed.

"Do you think Sam chose this plate from all the others?" Leslie asked.

"I'm sure he did," Nick said, staring at the design with a frown of intense concentration. "He had plenty of time in the shop."

"Well, he couldn't have chosen it with good taste," Leslie said. "It is the ugliest thing I ever saw. But then, I guess men don't have an eye for this sort of thing."

"Not Sam!" Nick said hotly. "He is one of the most artistically gifted men I 've ever . . . you're right! Sam would have hated this design. He chose it deliberately . . . " Nick stared at the plate, his brow furrowed in an anguish of thought. "What is it, Sam?" he whispered, intently looking at the plate. "Why this one?"

"Look!" Leslie said. "Apparently they draw the design in pencil first, and they didn't finish this." She pointed to two faint pencil marks curved over the waving blue lines.

"Here," Nick said, picking up the piece of plate with the pencil lines. "Let me see that." When he removed the section of the plate, the waving blue lines didn't look like a circle any longer, but seemed to run straight, and over them curved the two pencil marks. Nick stared at it for a minute, then thrust it in front of Leslie. "What does it look like to you?" he asked.

"Well," Leslie said slowly, "if it were Indian picture language, or hieroglyphics, I would say it was a stream of water under an arch—that is, if you count the pencil marks as part of the picture."

"Exactly!" Nick said with a triumphant laugh. "Exactly! The Arab craftsmen didn't make those pencil marks over the water, Sam did. It isn't an arch, but a tunnel—Hezekiah's Tunnel. That's where he wants us to meet. It's the only running water in Jerusalem, that's why he chose this plate with the wavy blue lines."

"Oh, Nick!" Leslie exclaimed. "How can you be sure?"

"I'm as sure as it is possible to be. I'll assume the same rendezvous time—eight o'clock tonight. I'll go—"

"We'll go," Leslie interrupted. "If Hal is there too, and I'm still with you, then everything you have done will make sense. If I'm not there, Hal will assume you've turned renegade, and that will be the end of you and Sam and any hope of saving the city."

Without a word, Nick put his arms around her and drew her close to him. He held her fiercely as the early morning sun filtered into the dusty silence beneath the scaffolding. "Someday, if we get out of this alive, I want to tell you . . . " His voice trailed off, and he kissed her hair and gently released her.

"We've got to get out of here," he said. "The workmen will be arriving soon." He stood up and peered out between the boards, scanning the ragged olive orchards, twisting roads, and barren patches of the Mount of Olives. Down below, at the bottom of the steep hillside, he could see the twisting road that followed the Valley of Kidron, then turned abruptly to wind its way up Mount Moriah to the southern gates of the walled city of Jerusalem. The eastern wall, which faced him, had no roads leading to it. He could see the square arch of the magnificent East Gate, and below it spread a barren hillside. No paths or roads led to the unused gate.

As he watched the road below, he could see an occasional car winding its way toward the old city. No motor vehicles could enter the walled city near the oldest section, and the streets were too narrow and winding for cars. A donkey cart was pulling its way slowly up the mountain road towards Dung Gate. The world looked fresh with dawn, and the silence had a palpable quality, as though nature were listening to see what the new day would bring.

Nick looked out at the wonderful city, as old as time. "Did you know," he whispered, "that *Jerusalem* means *city of peace?* That's a laugh, isn't it?"

As his eyes continued to search the landscape, his mind was racing. There were two things he needed to do before his meeting with Sam tonight. He hadn't planned on arriving in Jerusalem with a young woman in tow, and he knew if they stuck together, their chances of being spotted were significantly greater than if he could move about freely. Still, he could not leave her unless he knew she was absolutely safe.

In the course of his years as an undercover agent, Nick had made many contacts. Like all good agents, he had planned escape routes, safe houses, and caches of clothes and money. However, Leslie was an unforeseen factor. They would have to break cover soon, and the chances of traveling far on the barren hillside without being seen were pretty dim.

The sound of church bells came through the morning air. Nick glanced at his watch and thought, *Six* A.M., *matin bells!*

The church by the Garden of Gethsemane! Quickly, he squatted down beside Leslie.

"We have only a minute. Listen to me. Hezekiah's Tunnel is outside the city walls. That is to our great advantage, because it means we won't need to enter the city until tomorrow. They are bound to be watching and checking every gate."

"Who are *they* ?" Leslie asked.

"Everyone!" Nick exclaimed. "Don't you understand? We are number one on everybody's list. Hal wants me—either to question me or to kill me. The Israelis think I'm part of Hal's organization—all except Levi, and he won't break our cover yet for fear Hal will get wind of it. And Tappin of the CIA is hot on my trail too. The Americans keep tabs on the terrorists, and somehow they have gotten wind of Hamji's group, and they are very nervous about the peace commission. Tappin's been nosing around Sam and me for weeks. He believes we're terrorists, and I suspect he knows more than we think about the ruby and the threat to the city. Only he thinks we're on the wrong side. We're in this alone, kiddo, and if that seems too tough for you to take, I wouldn't blame you if you simply walked out of here and up to that hotel and turned yourself in to the nearest American embassy."

She put her hands on his lips. "Sh-h-h, just go on explaining what we need to do."

"Okay." Nick didn't waste any time on thanks. "You've got to stay put for the day, undercover and safe. I have two things to do."

"What? Can't I help?"

"No. I've got to move fast and do a lot of improvising. But first, we're going to pay a call on an old friend and find out how far friendship can be stretched."

He pulled Leslie up out of the shallow excavation under the scaffolding, and after a quick glance, they hurried across the bulldozed field where the park was under construction and ducked into a centuries-old olive orchard. The trees were gnarled and twisted, with silver-gray bark and slender leaves rustling in the morning breeze. They hurried down the soft path twisting across the face of the mountain, moving downward. Nick kept a sharp eye behind them and to the brow of the hill. Traffic had increased on the road that ran along the summit of the Mount of Olives in front of the hotel, and he could see soldiers patrolling the retaining wall at the side of the road. Once or twice, the sentries paused and seemed to be scanning the slopes of the mountain below them. Nick pulled Leslie down roughly behind a rock, and they remained as still as deer in the forest until the sentries resumed their walk.

At last they came to the foot of the path and entered a magnificent garden. Flower beds, neatly tended, bloomed in profusion, and lush, green tropical trees and bushes swayed in the morning sun. The paths were freshly-rolled gravel, and graceful walls and benches of white granite and marble enclosed the lovely scene.

"This way," Nick whispered, and pulled her through a cloistered door in the wall of the garden. They walked through a small courtyard and twisted through some further walls and passageways until they came to a small antebuilding tucked behind the large elaborate structure of the cathedral, which abutted the gardens.

Nick looked warily to the left and right and then rang a small bell by the side of the door. Leslie heard the faint jangling inside, then there was silence. Far away in the cathedral they could hear the faint sound of men's voices singing a Gregorian chant. It sounded very beautiful in the still courtyard.

Without warning the door was opened a crack, and a voice spoke from the darkness inside.

"Yes, my son, what is it?"

"Father Michael?" Nick asked.

"Yes. What do you wish?" The voice was soft and gentle, but cautious.

"It is I—Nick, the tour guide. You remember, we had a long talk the last time I brought a tour group through. We talked about the peace talks—and you told me of your love for Israel and Old Jerusalem. I have come to you because I really believe you meant what you said. In the name of peace we need help."

"We?" the voice sounded puzzled. "You mean, you and this young woman?"

"No, Father, I mean Israel and Jerusalem. Israel and Jerusalem need your help."

The door closed, and there was a moment of silence. Nick compressed his lips in anger and dismay and turned to walk away. Suddenly the door was opened wide. "Come in, my children. Come in before you are seen."

They hurried through the small door and stood in a darkened room. "Follow me," the priest whispered, and without a sound, Nick and Leslie followed him through a side door, down a narrow corridor, and into a winding stairwell. Bare stone steps led down to a heavy wooden door, which Father Michael opened with a key. Nick and Leslie entered a basement room that was cool and dry, with a spotless stone floor and racks of wine bottles neatly stacked in rows.

"We will be safe here," Father Michael spoke in a normal tone. "No one can hear us, and since I have the only key to the wine cellar, no one will disturb us."

"Won't you be missed at morning services?" Nick asked. "It is important nothing look amiss."

"I had already observed my own morning worship and asked to be excused from formal services today. I had planned to spend the day in seclusion. A day of fasting and prayer for the peace commission, which arrived yesterday in Jerusalem. My every prayer is for peace, not only for my beloved Jerusalem, but for the world as a whole. When you spoke to me at the door in such an unusual way, I thought perhaps God had sent me an opportunity to help bring about the answers to my prayers. He does move in mysterious ways, I know. Speak, and I will listen to what you have to say, with an open heart."

"Thank you, Father. That is all I ask," Nick said solemnly. "I would not have come to you, but you are our only hope. This young woman needs a place to hide today, and I need a change of clothes. We are engaged in a most desperate mission, and I do not exaggerate when I say the fate of Old Jerusalem and perhaps the course of world peace rests on our success."

Father Michael stood quietly in the center of the wine cellar. His neat black cassock hung from his broad, square shoulders in stark contrast to the white walls and floor. He was a man in his early sixties, robust and strong, with a lined, handsome face: honest, intelligent, and unmarked by bitter passions. His eyes were penetrating and wise, with small sunbursts of wrinkles at the corners, which indicated a wry sense of humor and amusement. But at this moment, his eyes were deadly serious as they searched Nick's face.

"That's quite a claim to make, young man," the priest began. "Something in your eyes makes me want to believe you, or at least to believe that *you* believe what you are saying. If it were just myself involved, I would be tempted to help you without question, as you ask. But if I keep the girl here, I involve not only myself but the entire order. How do I know you are anything more than common criminals or smugglers? I cannot misuse the house of God, nor the trust of my fellow priests."

"Even if we were criminals, couldn't we claim sanctuary?" Nick asked desperately. "Sanctuary—just for one day?"

"Ah," Father Michael said. "If it is simple sanctuary you wish, you would have come to the front door. No, I think you want more than to be safe. If anyone were to come asking— and, from what you imply, they may well come—you want me to deny your presence. You want me to conceal you, even from my brothers. And yet, perhaps your being here puts them in grave danger." The priest watched Nick's face carefully as he probed with his questions and deductions.

"Yes, Father," Nick replied steadily. "All you say is true. No one must find us. We have only forty-eight hours, and in that time we must not be intercepted. Will you help us?"

"I will," Father Michael said, "but I beg of you to tell me more."

Nick walked over to the priest and grasped his hand in a firm handclasp. "Since you have trusted us, I will do the same. What I am about to tell you is known to only a handful of violent men and to the secret intelligence services of two nations. Not only the peace commission, but the whole city of Old

Jerusalem is in deadly peril. A powerful traitor is ready to turn our own weapons against us. He is in alliance with the most fanatic terrorist groups. We do not know who he is or how to stop him, but we have the one thing that will make him reveal himself." Nick reached into his pocket and pulled out the ruby. The priest gasped when he saw it. "It is our only hope to save Jerusalem. If I don't succeed, then Hamji and the traitor will."

Father Michael's face went white. "Can this be true? How could this man called "Hamji" wish to destroy a city that is as holy to him as it is to the Jew and the Christian?"

"Because he no longer cares about anything but revenge. If he cannot have Jerusalem, then he would rather see it dead. Its destruction will create international havoc."

"In the tradition of Herod," Father Michael said, his face filled with compassion and sorrow. "Poor blind men who do not know they are children of God. This world is too much with them."

"Herod?" Leslie asked. "What 'tradition' of Herod?"

"When Herod knew he must die, he called the good and noble men from every family in his kingdom to wait at his bedside, and at the exact hour of his death, his soldiers drew their swords and slew the nobles. Herod declared, 'Since the people will not mourn for my death, at least I will ensure mourning in every house in Israel!'"

"Poor Jerusalem," Leslie sighed. "What a blood-drenched history."

Nick turned away and began to pace the floor with anger. "And now this group of fanatic terrorists are saying to the world, 'If you won't mourn our homeless condition, then we will cause all people to mourn by killing this city that is dear to them.' Father, they will do it, too, make no mistake about it."

"How can you prevent it?" Father Michael asked. "It sounds like the authorities are helpless. Either they must accede to the terrorists' demands, or Jerusalem will be blown from the earth—utterly destroyed."

"I can stop them, Father, because I am the final link to the traitor who has access to the weapon. Even if we caught Hal and Ahmud and the others, this traitor is more dangerous than any of them. We do not know who he is, but he is someone in Israel who has power and apparently unlimited access to technological and political secrets. Someone with enough money and clout and knowledge to have built an electronic communicator and installed a computer chip that plots the missile's course, and who has only to put this into action to destroy the city. Until we find out who this man is and stop him, all we will have done, at best, is postpone the inevitable."

"I see," Father Michael paused, "so you are the sacrificial goat. The one chosen to deliver the ruby and discover the man."

"Yes," Nick said quietly. "But things have gone wrong, and I am not trusted anymore, so—"

"So you must operate with stealth and invisibility," offered the priest.

Nick nodded. Father Michael said nothing for a few minutes. His hands were joined, his fingers pointing upward like a tall steeple. He ran his forefingers across his lips as he stood deep in thought. At last he said, "Then, in the name of the Lord, I will trust you. Since you are serving in his behalf for one day, you are entitled to wear his habit. I will return."

Father Michael left the wine cellar, and Nick and Leslie moved closer together. "I am almost persuaded to believe in the miracles of Father Michael's God," Nick said with a half-smile.

"He is your God too, Nick," Leslie answered with a conviction that surprised even herself.

In a few moments, the priest returned. He held two habits in his hands, one for a priest and the other for a nun. He was also carrying towels, washcloths, and a pitcher of hot soapy water.

"You must clean up and change quickly. I will keep Leslie with me in my office for the day. Do you type, Leslie?"

"Yes, a little," she answered.

"Very well then, dress in these clothes, and I will explain to my colleagues that you are a sister, from another order, who has come to help me organize my writings and observations about the peace conference. I have been asked to deliver the benediction at the closing session.

"As for you, Nick. I believe you should put on the priestly clothes, and perhaps you can whiten your hair at the temples with this zinc-oxide ointment. It will age you somewhat, and I have included a pair of wire-rim glasses. It has been my experience that people do not tend to look carefully at the face of people in ecclesiastical clothing. There is a tendency to think we all look alike. Unless, of course, you run into someone who knows you well. I do not imagine there is any disguise that could be effective then."

Nick smiled at the elderly pastor. "If you didn't already have a profession, you would make a terrific intelligence agent."

"In a way, I think that is what I am," Father Michael smiled back. "An agent who has served for many years in a hostile country. My gray hairs tell me that I am soon to be called home. Go do what you must do, my son, and do not worry about me or Leslie. I will guard her with my life." Then, the priest left the room.

"I will step behind the racks," Leslie said. "When you are finished with the water, hand it to me." Leslie slipped behind the first bank of wine racks.

Nick swiftly washed himself. Then he turned to the heap of clothes and quickly changed into the black robe and clerical shirt and collar. There was a small mirror, and with the zinc-oxide ointment, he carefully whitened the temples of his hair, marveling, even as he did it, at the way it aged and softened his appearance. When he put the wire-rim glasses on and looked at his face, clean and shining above the white priestly collar, he smiled. "Even my own mother wouldn't know me," he said to Leslie.

She stepped out from behind the racks, adjusting the cowl of the white habit. She looked up at him, and her face was sweet. "I think my mother would have trouble recognizing me too," she said. "You do know what a difficult and dangerous decision this was for Father Michael, don't you? His heart must be breaking to see these precious clothes worn by impostors."

"He has put all other considerations behind the saving of lives and the preservation of the Holy City," Nick assented. "He is an incredible man. I will go now, but be ready to leave at dusk." Their eyes met for a moment, but they did not touch.

"Are you going to be all right?" Nick asked softly.

"Yes, Nick," she answered. "I am not afraid."

He was gone, and she was alone in the cool cellar. She could hear the echo of her own words. "It's true," she said to herself in wonder. "I'm not afraid. I know I may die in the next few hours, or the world may erupt into war, or Jerusalem and all who are in it may be destroyed. I feel sorrow, but not fear.

"I think I have grown to love Nick," she whispered to herself in astonishment, "and I wasn't afraid to see him go, even though I know we may never see one another again. I only feel joy that I have known him. I've spent my life being afraid, trying to protect myself from being hurt, and suddenly I know there is no protection except the one we build inside ourselves. I will never let the fear of sorrow, fear of being hurt, or fear of commitment rob me of the right to live again, if only to live for a moment. One day of life with faith and courage is better than a whole lifetime of self-protection. How strange. I came to the Holy Land thinking that maybe the dead relics here might give me some kind of belief to build my life upon, and instead I have found the reasons to live in terror, pain, unexpected kindnesses, and the love of a man who is unafraid."

The door opened again, and Father Michael slipped into the room. "Come with me, and we will go to my office now. If we are lucky, we will not pass anyone in the corridors, and I will not have to explain your presence. Since I have asked for a day of seclusion, no one will be surprised if my door is closed."

Silently, they glided through the light stone corridors and came to a small room. When they had entered and closed the door, Leslie was cheered to see that Father Michael's office, though not large, was bright and cheery, with a neat walnut desk and a small typing table. A spray of delicate talisman roses were in a crystal vase on his desk. The walls were bare except for a beautiful olive-wood crucifix, which hung on the wall opposite the window.

"Now, my dear," Father Michael said, "I have here a sheaf of notes that you may work on. It will help you pass the hours more quickly and will relieve me from the responsibility of telling another falsehood. I will simply tell people you are transcribing my journal of thoughts on this subject. I will be in the small chapel next to this room. We will lock the outer door so that anyone entering my office will need to enter through the chapel."

The elderly priest handed her the notes, and she was surprised to see his hand shaking. He had appeared so calm and controlled. She supposed neither she nor Nick had any inkling of the stress and agony they had caused in this good man's orderly life.

She laid her hand gently on top of Father Michael's. "Forgive us, Father," she said. "We had no right to involve you."

He smiled at her. "All mankind is involved, my dear, whether they know it or not. It is my good fortune to be one of the few who has the opportunity to do something about it." He quietly turned to leave her. "Now I will go do what I do best—pray."

Leslie was alone in the sunlit office. With a sigh she picked up the handwritten sheets and began to read a beautiful essay written in archaic scriptural English. It was entitled "Peace on Earth to Men of Goodwill." Soon she was lost in the powerful thoughts of the good priest.

Nick walked up the road toward the tourist hotel at the top of the Mount of Olives. The road was jammed with midmorning traffic. Tour buses had loaded their passengers and were driving slowly down the winding road, as other tour buses arrived and unloaded travelers who were eager to begin their visit to the old city. In front of the hotel were several Arabs dressed in filthy robes, with elaborately bedecked camels, waiting for tourists who wanted to have their pictures taken before leaving the city. Several of the camel owners would have known him as a tour guide, so he avoided walking too close to them.

Security was apparent everywhere. Not only were there young men in uniforms posted along the brow of the hill and along the road leading into the hotel, but Nick observed several plainclothesmen stationed in the milling crowd that entered and left the hotel entrance. Behind one of the pillars on the hotel marquee, he noticed a dark man in tourist garb. The plaid jacket and beige slacks and open golf shirt could not disguise the Arabic appearance of the man's features. The man was watching the hotel entrance with intense eyes, and as he came closer, Nick recognized him as one of the two men who had been with Ahmud in Jericho.

So, Nick thought, *Ahmud is smarter than I thought. He isn't placing all his bets on the gates of Jerusalem. He knows there's a chance I won't enter the city until tomorrow. He knows I bring my tours here to this hotel, so he probably figures I've got contacts here.*

Nick hesitated for a moment, not sure of his disguise. An elderly woman was struggling through the crowd in front of him. She was walking with a cane, and the flow of people hurrying past in both directions was distressing her.

"May I help you up these stairs, my daughter?" he asked.

She looked startled, and then seeing his priestly collar, heaved a sigh of relief. "Oh, yes, Father, thank you very much."

He bowed his head very solicitously and watched her feet at each step. The angle of his concentration hid his face, and the two walked into the hotel. Nick knew the disguised Arab must have observed them, they were moving slower than the rest of the crowd, but he hoped Father Michael was right and his priestly habit would prevent a good look at his face.

"Just a few more steps, my dear, and we will be in the lobby," he murmured to the old woman, more as encouragement to himself than to her. As they entered the door, she reached to take his hand in gratitude, and her cane fell to the ground with a clang. He sprang to pick it up, and as he did so, he glanced through the glass doors. The Arab had not moved from his position and was busily perusing the faces of the incoming tourists.

"So far, so good," Nick whispered in relief.

"What did you say, Father?" asked the white-haired lady, reaching for her cane.

"I said, 'That's very good.' You are all set now. Have a wonderful visit in Jerusalem." He handed her the cane and moved off rapidly through the crowded lobby, keeping his eyes peeled. He spotted several more secret-service agents doing their best to look like tourists or businessmen, but no one showed any interest in him.

In a moment he was walking down the high-ceilinged corridor that led through the commercial wing of the hotel. This wing was a series of lobby shops, which sold everything from souvenirs to fine jewelry.

Nick walked quickly to a small exclusive jewelry shop. The shop's display window glittered with magnificently crafted necklaces, bracelets, and rings. A large amethyst ring set high on a bed of silver twigs frosted with diamonds, an exotic necklace of uncut emeralds spun in gold thread, a bracelet of square-cut sapphires embedded in platinum—everything showed the brilliance of a gifted and untraditional designer. Nick entered the shop. Behind the counter sat a man with a bald head and a waxed mustache that stood out on either side of his nose. His mustache was trembling as he spoke to a customer. The jeweler's voice was agitated and intense.

"Change the curve of this necklace? Are you mad?" accused the jeweler. "It is the curve that gives it style, brilliance, daring! It is the asymmetrical line that declares it a masterpiece. If you wish the ordinary, do not come to me! Go back home to New York, go to your Cartier's or your Harry Winston's—don't speak to me of the ordinary. I break the mold!"

The wealthy American in his Brooks Brothers suit turned away from the jeweler, his face flushed, and walked out of the shop.

"Tourists," the jeweler snorted. "What do they know? I would sell my soul for a customer with taste. Oh—pardon me,

Father. I didn't mean that, of course. Only an expression. What can I do for you?"

Nick was standing with his face turned away from the jeweler and his back to the door of the shop. In a loud voice he said, "I thought perhaps you might have something to show me in a silver crucifix."

"Father, I am sorry. I do not do that kind of work. Only the unusual appeals to me . . . "

Nick turned and looked straight at the jeweler. In an almost soundless voice he said, "Don't look surprised, go on talking about crucifixes and glance out into the corridor to see if anyone is watching us."

The jeweler's eyes widened as he stared into Nick's face, and there was a blossoming of recognition and surprise, but he controlled the reaction and began speaking.

"I have often thought I would like to attempt a crucifix. However, do you think you would be willing to consider something with a truly untraditional design?"

"Good," Nick whispered. "Is anyone out there?"

"No," said the jeweler softly.

Nick breathed a sigh of relief and leaned over the counter. "Have you finished it?" he asked.

"Yes," answered the man, his mustache beginning to quiver with excitement again. "I followed your design specifications to the letter. It is a brilliant job if I do say so myself—although something I would not want people to know I have done. It isn't the type of thing I normally want to do—but this was such an unusual opportunity. You promised I could see the Star. Just to see it—well, as I said before, I would sell my soul."

"What I had in mind for a crucifix was something like this," Nick said out loud, while glancing out into the corridor where people were strolling past. He pulled a handkerchief out of his pocket and unwrapped it carefully, holding it so the jeweler was the only one who could see the contents.

For a few moments the little bald man stood staring at the ruby as though his eyes would memorize it. "Beautiful," he said, the sound of tears in his voice. "Worth a man's soul."

"Nothing is worth a man's soul," Nick replied and folded the handkerchief back into his pocket. "Perhaps you have some samples of your designs that I could take back to my order to show my bishop."

"Yes, yes, of course." The little jeweler was all business because a customer came in. The customer was tall and lean and wearing a pair of nondescript gray slacks and an open-necked, blue-and-white checked shirt. The customer appeared to be engrossed in examining the pieces in the display case. Nick felt nervous and impatient in the small shop. The jeweler rummaged through his safe and returned to Nick with a box.

"You might show your bishop this. It is a crucifix I designed many years ago but have never offered for sale. If he is pleased with the work, please come back, and we shall talk about your needs for your chapel."

"Thank you," Nick said, pocketing the box. "We will be back to you within a day or two. You will find the bishop most generous." He turned and left the shop. The other customer continued to stare at the jewelry case, and Nick watched as the little bald jeweler walked over to ask the man if he could be of service.

Swiftly Nick moved down the corridor. Seeing a public restroom, he ducked into the door and entered one of the booths. He needed a place to be out of sight for a moment, while he planned the next step. The only indication that anything was unusual was the massing of security people. Nick imagined that if security was this tight on the Mount of Olives, Jerusalem must have hundreds of security police, agents, and secret-service men policing the gates and streets.

But what was Levi planning to do about the threat of destruction? Surely he knew it was serious, since he knew about the theft of the computer chip and also of the Star of Chaldea. Were there plans to evacuate the old city? Were they going to give him enough time to find the man who was behind all of this? He had to know what was going on, and he had to have Levi's help. But how? He couldn't talk on one of the public phones—he might be overheard. He wouldn't take a room, because he had no luggage and it would draw attention to him. A room! That was it! He would walk down the hotel corridors, until he found a couple who were leaving their room. He would break into the room and use their telephone. No one would think to trace it until tomorrow when the call would show up on their bill. Even then, the hotel would probably just consider it a mistake. He had to take the chance.

Nick stepped out of the men's room, planning to head for the elevators, and collided with a man hurrying down the corridor.

"Bless you, my son," Nick gasped. The man was the same one who had been looking at the jewelry in the shop when Nick was there. Nick recognized the gray slacks and the checked shirt. Without a word, the man stepped around Nick and hurried on down the hall into a waiting elevator and was gone. Something about the man bothered Nick. He didn't look like a plainclothesman or a security agent in civilian clothes. That was just it. He didn't look like anything. Everything about him—his pants, his shoes, his haircut, his shirt—was totally neutral. It would almost be impossible to say if he were American, Dutch, British, or Israeli. That was the mistake most agents made—especially American agents. They thought if they put on plain slacks and a sports shirt that they could mix with any crowd. What they seldom seemed to realize was that the cut of the slacks, the fabric of the shirt, and especially the quality of their shoes screamed *American* to any observer. Most nationalities could be spotted by a trained man. A slightly different cut, a higher waistline, a fuller pleat, a thinner hem in the sleeves of a shirt—all of these details were distinctive to specific nationalities. But this man in the gray slacks was totally indistinguishable. It set off the alarm bells in Nick's mind. No one could be such a cipher unless he had worked at it, planned it, and understood what clues another agent would be looking for. Nick shook himself. This job was really getting to him. He was beginning to see agents in the air. Why suspect a man simply because there was nothing about him to suspect?

Nick shrugged off the uneasy feeling and walked toward the elevator. Down the hall, he saw a man and woman walking out of a room. They were dressed for a day of sightseeing, and as they passed Nick, he heard the woman say, "James, I want to see everything. I have a wonderful map of the city, and we'll simply walk and walk." James didn't look too thrilled at the prospect.

As soon as the tourists were out of sight, Nick walked to their room. Just as he was fumbling in his pocket for the small rod that he used as a tool to unlock doors, a maid came out of the room across the hall. She was pushing a cart filled with linens and cleaning tools.

She nodded shyly, and he continued to fumble in his pocket, waiting for her to leave, but she stood watching him, still smiling. He withdrew his hand from his pocket and shrugged helplessly.

"I am so absentminded. I left my key at the desk. It looks like I'll have to go back to the lobby." He looked at her helplessly. It was a calculated risk. If she knew the people who occupied the room, she would be alarmed. However, she shook her head at him, still smiling, and held up her ring of keys.

"No, no, Father!" she exclaimed in broken English. "It is my pleasure to help you." She walked over to the door and turned the lock with her master key. "There—I've saved you a walk." She smiled and bobbed him a curtsy.

"Bless you, my child—bless you," Nick said with great feeling and hurriedly let himself into the room. Fortunately, the telephone could be dialed directly. Calls did not go through the hotel switchboard unless they were long distance. Nick dialed the emergency-contact number for Levi.

"Paneastern Travel Agency," a professional voice answered. "May I help you?"

"This is Mr. Levi calling. I am interested in finding out information about tours of Old Jerusalem."

"Yes, Mr. Levi," the clipped voice responded. "I will get someone to give you that information. Will you hold the line for a moment please?"

Seconds later, he heard Levi's voice on the other end. "Yes, sir, I understand you are looking for information about Old Jerusalem. May I ask where you are calling from?"

"It's all right, Levi," Nick said quickly. "I'm at the hotel on the Mount of Olives. I'm in a private room. The phone is clean. Sam will meet me tonight at the Hezekiah Tunnel with the information about the meeting to exchange the Star tomorrow. Leslie is still with me. We'll need a safe house, disguises, and a weapon for tonight and tomorrow. Will you arrange it?"

"Right," Levi answered, "usual drop."

Nick hurried on. "What's happening? What is the peace commission doing? Do they know about the threat?"

"Of course they do," Levi answered. "They know the guidance chip is somewhere in Israel, and they know the Star was stolen and is due to be delivered."

"Have you told them anything about me—or our plans to break the conspiracy?"

"No, Nick. Can't you see? I don't dare say a word—not to anyone. The Israeli traitor could be any one of the men who are in on the decision-making process. If I give you away to the wrong person, you are a dead man—and when you die, our hopes of destroying this threat die too."

"What is their plan?"

"Nothing," Levi replied, his voice as cold as steel. "They are still only acting on speculation, although I think the CIA is close to the truth and may be hot on your trail."

"But . . . " Nick could not believe his ears. "You mean they are still going to do nothing to save lives? What if I fail to stop this man?"

"What can they do?" Levi asked. "The security forces of ten nations are combing the area for any signs of terrorists. All Israeli defense installations within miles of Jerusalem are being searched for the altered communicator, but it all has to be done in secret to prevent panic."

"Why?" Nick asked again. "You mean they will simply let the city and all of its inhabitants be wiped off the face of the earth?"

"This is war, Nick," Levi reminded him. "They can't save Old Jerusalem in any way. There is no existing evacuation plan. There isn't even a way to communicate with the population. Most of them don't own radios or telephones. The inhabitants speak dozens of different languages. The Jewish Quarter won't listen to the Arab Quarter, the Christian Quarter won't associate with the Armenian Quarter—how are you going to organize an evacuation under those circumstances? Where would the people go? All that would result from an evacuation attempt would be wholesale panic, looting, fighting, and death. The international press would tear the world apart, and some people would demand we drop an atomic bomb on every Arab nation in retaliation. The Arab nations will become bitter about false accusations, since they have nothing to do with Hamji and his fanatics, and the Israelis would prepare for full-scale war. No. The peace commission is doing everything they can to avoid public knowledge of the situation as they know it. Friday night, if they have not found the terrorists or the activator, they may plan to evacuate as much of the city as is possible. Whatever happens, it will be disaster."

Nick was silent on the other end of the phone.

"It's up to you, Nick," Levi said. "You have to find the man behind this nightmare—and smash him for good."

"Yeah," Nick muttered.

"Did you visit the jeweler yet? Did he have it finished?"

"Yes, he did. Everything's set. I'd better go now. This place is crawling with special security, and according to you, I'm still viewed as a terrorist—even by the good guys. I'll feel more comfortable once I'm out of sight again." Nick prepared to hang up the phone.

"Wait, Nick!" Levi rapped out. "What are you wearing that has made it possible for you to walk around in the hotel without being recognized?"

"You won't believe it. I'm a priest," Nick told him.

"A priest." Levi gave a short chuckle. "Just to be safe, before you go under cover you'd better go back to our friend in the jewelry store and tell him to lie low for a few days. There's a chance someone on your trail may run across the connection, and I don't think he'd do well under questioning."

"Good idea," Nick said, angry at himself for not thinking of it. "I'll stop by and tell him to go on a week's vacation somewhere far away."

Nick hung up the phone, wiped off his fingerprints, and hurried to the door. He opened it a crack and heard voices coming up the hall. Quickly he stepped back into the room, keeping his ear by the door. The voices stopped, and the key scratched in the lock. Nick jumped into the closet beside the door and squeezed between two garment bags. He heard the door open and a woman's voice, irritated and petulant, complaining, "You know you can't last a day without your antacid pills. Why do you always forget them? Now we've missed the bus over to Jerusalem, and we're going to have to take a taxi. It will cost a fortune."

A man's voice, sounding patient and tired, answered, "Honey, it's all right. You'll be more comfortable in a taxi anyway. Now where did I put those pills?"

There was a sound of rummaging through drawers and footsteps across the floor. He heard a heavy suitcase being dragged across the floor and thumped on the bed. "I could have sworn I had them in the pocket of this bag." The man's voice sounded puzzled.

"James, you are so careless. I declare, it is just like traveling with a little child. Do you think you could have left them in the jacket you were wearing yesterday?" The woman's voice was shrill with impatience.

"No, Vera," the man answered stolidly, "I don't think so."

"Well, I'll just look." Brisk steps moved toward the closet where Nick was hiding. Nick pulled back as far into the corner of the little closet as possible, just as the door opened.

"Vera!" the man's voice exclaimed. "I found them. They were on the dresser beside my shaving cream." The closet door was slammed shut.

"Now can we go?" she asked sarcastically.

"Yes, Vera, I guess so." The sound of defeat was in the man's voice as the couple left the room.

Nick stayed in the closet for a few more minutes. It was stuffy, and he could feel the perspiration under his arms and on the palms of his hands. As soon as he was sure the couple would be out of sight, he let himself out of the closet, left the room, and walked briskly down the hallway. Skirting the edge of the lobby, he retraced his steps to the corridor with the hotel shops in it and stopped once more in front of the jewelry shop. To his astonishment, he saw the shades in the store windows were pulled and a sign written in beautiful calligraphy proclaimed "Closed" in the corner of the door window.

Glancing to the left and right, Nick could see no one watching the shop, so he reached out and tried the door. To his surprise it was unlocked, and he let himself into the dark, windowless interior. The only light in the room came through the drawn shades, which filtered in a little light from the hallway. In the back of the room, by the showcase, he saw a figure bending down. Even in the gloom, he recognized the blue-and-white shirt of the man in the gray slacks. In a single leap, Nick crossed the room and threw his arm around the man's neck in a murderous stranglehold. He grabbed the man's other arm and bent it behind him.

"All right, buddy," Nick said. "Who are you, and what are you doing in here?"

"I'm checking out your dead friend," the man answered, his voice strained from the pressure of Nick's arm on his throat.

Nick glanced onto the floor and saw the slumped figure of the little jeweler, his bald head streaked with blood. "You mean you were killing my friend, don't you?" Nick retorted.

"No," the man in the gray slacks answered. "I would have killed him if I had to, but someone beat me to it. Someone who is now going to be looking for a priest to kill, because your delicate friend has almost certainly told them everything he knows, including the fact that you are dressed as a priest."

"Who are you?" Nick hissed. "And don't give me any more clever answers."

"I'm a man who has been looking for you. I wasn't sure when I saw you in the shop—you were very convincing. I still wasn't sure when I bumped into you in the corridor, but now I know."

"Why are you looking for me?" Nick asked.

"To kill you," the man answered. Suddenly Nick felt a crushing pain in his ribs. The man had worked his arm free and had smashed Nick with his elbow. As Nick reacted to the unexpected blow, the man tore Nick's arm from around his neck and whirled to face him. In the darkness, Nick saw the gleam of a sharp knife blade. The man's arm slashed toward Nick, and Nick felt the blade slice through the front of his coat. With an agility born of necessity, Nick did a handspring over the glass display case and found himself behind the counter. The stranger reached across the width of the countertop, slashing at him again and bringing his hand crashing down onto the plate glass. By some miracle, the glass did not break, but both men knew that the noise of the struggle could not be prolonged before someone in the corridor would come in to investigate. The man in the gray slacks walked around the jewelry case and moved toward Nick, who, keeping his eye on the razor-sharp knife, was backing slowly away.

Too soon, Nick felt the desk and cash register behind him, which sealed off the exit from behind the counter. A grin stretched the mouth of his assailant. He was holding the knife in a bayonet position and was prepared to deal Nick the death stroke. Nick watched the eyes of the assassin, knowing that if his timing was right he had a chance to throw him off balance and slip past him. As Nick crouched in readiness, his hand touched an object in the open display case behind the counter. It was a marble obelisk about a foot high. Nick grasped the marble shaft, and as the knife arched toward him, he swung it at the killer's arm. There was a sharp, cracking sound and a stifled moan, and the knife clattered to the floor. Nick, leaning his full weight against the desk, kicked out with his foot. In the enclosed space he couldn't miss, and the man doubled over. With a quick forward motion, Nick caught his opponent as he fell and landed a powerful right-cross punch on his jaw. Without a sound, the man slumped to the ground.

Swiftly, Nick rummaged in the drawers behind the counter and found nylon tape used to close packages for international mailing. *Perfect*, Nick thought, and taped the man's wrists and ankles generously. Then he propped him in the corner behind the counter, while he searched for something to act as a gag. While he was looking, he heard the man moan. Nick found some handkerchiefs, and he moved over to finish the job. The man was looking at him.

"You're Tappin, CIA, aren't you?" Nick said. "You must be very good at your job if you found out about me."

"I am good," Tappin answered. "I know all about Hal and his bunch of fanatic hoodlums—including you and your brother, Sam. I know what you're up to, I know you have the Star, and I would have killed you. I should have done it the minute you entered the shop."

"Have you told anyone else what you know?" Nick asked. Tappin just looked at him, his eyes unrelenting. "No," Nick answered his own question, "of course you haven't. You were not even sure who I was until I entered the shop a few minutes ago. You don't trust anyone—neither do I. It's a luxury that neither one of us can afford. If it's any comfort to you, Tappin, someday you'll be glad you didn't kill me."

Tappin said nothing. Nick began to prepare a gag to go around Tappin's mouth. "I, for one, shall be forever grateful for the fine American sense of honor, which demands one always give one's opponent a fair fight."

Without expression, Tappin said, "Never again. Our paths will recross, and I promise you I will kill you without a moment's hesitation."

Nick tied the gag around Tappin's mouth and pulled the final knot. "You will only be here for a couple of days. It won't be comfortable, but you'll live. I'm sorry this is the way it's got to be."

Nick stood up and walked to the door. He pulled the blind out so he could peer into the corridor. A family of four was walking down the hall toward the dining room. Nick brushed off his suit and realized the front of his coat was hanging like a flap from the slash of Tappin's knife. He grabbed up a book from the desk and held it against his chest so his arm could pin the slashed fabric against his body. It was the only camouflage he could give to his ruined clothes. When the tourist family was a few feet from the store door, Nick stepped out into the corridor. He had set the door latch from inside and heard it click when he closed the door firmly behind him. The family was now abreast of the jewelry store, which looked neatly closed, with its dark green shades pulled tightly against the windows and the emphatic "Closed" sign still showing.

Nick moved with the family as though he were a part of their little group and walked with them toward the dining room. To his left he spotted a fire door. As they passed it, he nodded to them pleasantly and stepped aside. When they were out of sight, he opened the service door.

Metal fire stairs led through a narrow passageway down to the basement. Nick knew his time was limited. Had someone watched him coming out of the jewelry store? Someone who was looking for a priest? He dashed down the steps two at a time and at the bottom of the stairs found a door with a sign "Employees Only." He opened the door to find himself in a small locker room. On the wall were hooks with janitorial clothes hanging on them and in the corner of the room, he saw buckets, mops, and brooms.

About five minutes later, a janitor—wearing a tan work shirt and pants, a neat visor cap, and carrying a broom—slipped out of the fire door and began sweeping the main corridor of the hotel. He swept past the closed and locked jewelry shop, tipped his hat to the pretty redhead working at the desk in the perfume store, nodded to a group of tourists as they chattered down the hall, saluted the bellhop at the front of the lobby, and proceeded to sweep down the corridor of rooms to the left.

Leslie spent a restful morning and afternoon transcribing the notes of Father Michael's discourse on peace. In the quiet, sunny room she felt a sense of peace herself. For a short while the madness of the world outside and the danger in which Nick was moving seemed unreal and far away.

At midafternoon she heard the faraway jingle of a bell. Father Michael put his head into the office. "That sounds like the garden door," the priest said. "Perhaps it will be Nick. I will go see."

The priest was gone, and Leslie sat in silent anxiety waiting for him to reappear. The door from the chapel opened again, and Father Michael entered the small office, followed by a man in work clothes. When the man lifted his visored cap, she saw it was Nick.

Without thought, she ran into his arms. "Nick! You're safe!" To her own surprise, she found she was crying.

"For the moment," Nick answered. "But we have to get out of here quickly. Ahmud knows I've been dressed as a priest, and he'll almost certainly send his men here to make inquiries. For the sake of Father Michael's safety, we must be gone when they come."

"But where will you go, my children?" Father Michael asked, his kind and wrinkled face creased with concern.

"I have told you too much already. For your own safety, and for ours, it is better if you don't know any more." Nick's eyes were full of gratitude and respect. "You're the finest Christian I have ever known," he said. "I believe you live in the shadow of your Savior."

"Thank you," Father Michael said. "I appreciate praise coming from one of his chosen children."

Nick grinned. "I always used to tell my father I knew we Jews were the chosen people, but I sometimes wondered just what it was we were chosen for."

"Follow me quickly back to the wine cellar," Father Michael said. "I have found some clothing left for the relief of the poor, and I think I can provide you with what you will need."

They dressed in nondescript clothing, with sandals on their bare feet. Leslie wound another cloth around her head to conceal her blonde hair. By now, her face was burnished from the sun, and she used some of Father Michael's shoe blacking on her eyebrows. When she was finished, she looked like any one of hundreds of native Israelis who trudged the streets and sidewalks of the city. "May the Lord bless you and keep you," Father Michael whispered, as he let them out the gate door at the side garden. "May your mission be accomplished."

"Thank you, Father," they replied, and in seconds, they had vanished from sight in the dappled shade of the olive trees.

Less than an hour later, a young novitiate priest came hurrying down the aisle of the small chapel where Father Michael was praying. "Father!" the young man said, obviously agitated, but reluctant to interrupt the older priest's meditations. "There are three men here who say they are from the Israeli secret service and must speak to you at once on a matter of great urgency."

Father Michael rose slowly, with pain in his arthritic knees. "Send them to my office, and I will meet with them there," he said serenely.

The younger priest hurried away and in a few minutes, Father Michael was confronted by three muscular and intense men with eyes like gimlets. The leader of the three flashed a badge and card identifying him as an Israeli counteragent. Father Michael was sure they were impostors.

"Father, we're sorry to disturb you in your house of worship." The man's eyes had no sorrow in them—no emotion of any kind. They were the eyes of a man who was spiritually dead. Father Michael's heart filled with compassion for this child of God who had drifted so far from his own humanity.

His face showing none of his thoughts, Father Michael listened and smiled benevolently at the three men.

"This is a matter of greatest urgency," the leader continued. "I understand you know a tour director named Nick."

"Yes," said Father Michael, "I have spoken to him on occasion when he has brought groups through the church. He seems to be a fine young Arab. Surely you do not hold his race against him. Of course he is Muslim, but nonetheless we share many of the same humanistic values."

The man posing as an Israeli agent cut the priest's answer short with a gesture.

"He is a very evil man, dangerous and an enemy to our country, and it is imperative we find him. We have reason to believe he has been in this area today. Have you seen him?"

"No," answered the elderly priest. "But then, I have not conducted any of the tours today. I had hoped to remain in seclusion, praying for the peace commission's success."

Again the leader made an impatient gesture, as though it were taking all of his control to remain civil. "Not on a tour!" the man exclaimed. "Here—in your chapel—as a fugitive. Have you seen him? I must tell you the entire security of our nation may rest on your answer." There was a cruel intensity in the man's face, and Father Michael felt he could almost smell evil in the room.

"If he had come as a fugitive I would have offered him sanctuary—" the priest began.

"I know! I know!" the angry man burst out. "We don't need a long explanation. Was he here? Tell me the truth, old man. Don't think your gray hair and black robes will save you if you lie to me."

"Why would I lie," Father Michael answered equably. "If we give a man sanctuary, we do not keep it secret."

The three men glared at the priest, their eyes filled with rage and frustration. The leader stepped menacingly closer. In an icy voice, he continued, "We thought perhaps you might know something, because this man, Nick, was seen earlier today in a priest's habit. Would you know anything about this matter whatsoever?"

Father Michael chuckled and gave a relieved sigh. "So that explains it!" he exclaimed. "Early this morning one of our priests woke to find his clothes missing. He had placed his habit outside his cell to be cleaned and brushed. We were afraid perhaps one of the altar boys had stolen it, and we were feeling

very disheartened to think there might be thievery in our clois-
ter. Of course, you are right. This Nick, who has become a
fugitive as you say, must have entered through one of the sanctuary doors and stolen the suit. I am sorry I cannot help you,
my children, and I suppose it is an irony that you, without
meaning to, have helped us. So it is with the work of the Lord.
Manna seems to fall from heaven, and even our humblest
prayers are answered."

The leader of the three men listened to Father Michael as
he rambled on, and his eyes searched the old priest's face like
an X ray looking for one hint, one intimation that Father
Michael was lying.

Apparently satisfied, he turned to his men. "Check the
sanctuary doors and see if you find any sign of them: footsteps,
discarded clothing—anything." He turned back to the priest
who was still sitting at his desk. "Father," the man turned and
tore an olive-wood crucifix from the wall and held it in front of
the old priest. "Father, will you swear to me on this cross that
you have told me the truth?" The interrogator's eyes were like
sabers, and his mouth was pulled back in a vicious snarl. "Swear
to me you have not seen this man, have not helped him, do
not know where he is. Swear it, or I will tear your church apart
stone by stone."

Father Michael rose from his chair to his full height. He
looked down at the vicious man before him and for a moment
the priest's jaw clenched, and his eyes were like blue stone.
With a hand as steady as a rock, he picked up the crucifix and
held it to his breast.

"I swear," he said, looking straight at the terrorist. He
placed the crucifix gently back on his desk. "I did not know,"
Father Michael continued in a calm voice, "the Israeli secret
service was so distrusting, or that it placed so much faith in a
Christian's oath."

With a growl, the man backed up to the office door and
yanked it open behind him, never taking his eyes from the
priest. "My nose tells me something is wrong here," the man
said, "but it may just be the smell of your infidel faith." He

sped out the door and down the corridor. Father Michael could hear the slamming of doors and the heavy shoes of the men, as they searched the anterooms and private gardens. Then there was silence.

Walking slowly, like a very, very old man, Father Michael entered his little prayer chapel. He fell on his knees before the altar with tears streaming from his eyes. Looking to heaven, he clapped his hands and whispered, "Father, forgive me, for I have sinned. I have deceived my brother priests, I have given your holy habit to be worn by the unordained, I have put my desires for worldly service above my vows to spiritual law, and worst of all, I have sworn upon thy holy cross that I had told the truth, when in truth, I had lied, and so I have dishonored thy Son as well as myself. But I beg forgiveness for even thou hast at times shown it is right to deceive evil men in order to protect the righteous. I bid thee, Lord, remember Sarai and Abram and how thou commandest them to say Sarai was Abram's sister in order that they might live and raise unto thee a mighty nation. It is to protect that nation that I have done what I have done. Oh Lord, have mercy upon me."

Father Michael bowed his head upon his clasped hands and continued to pray. As the sun began to sink behind the summit of the Mount of Olives, the stained glass windows of the little prayer chapel glowed richly in the fading light of the evening.

Chapter Nine

By any definition, King Hezekiah was a hard-luck king. He inherited a throne that was a vassal throne to the Assyrian Empire, he inherited a kingdom that was little more than a battleground for the warring nations of the known world—especially Egypt, Babylon, and Assyria. He was a man of faith and goodness in a nation that had forgotten both. Nonetheless, Hezekiah reigned with courage, hope, and a determination to be free. Unfortunately, his desire for freedom led him into disastrous alliances, which eventually brought the wrath of nations and of God upon his head.

Even the things he did that were fortunate turned against him. He was miraculously cured of the bubonic plague and then, in rejoicing at his recovery, foolishly displayed the treasure rooms of Israel that had been hidden. He angered God and Assyria and finally had to strip the treasure rooms, the temple, and even the golden doors of the city to buy back their favor. Poor Hezekiah, a good man in evil times. But one thing that he accomplished outlasted his reign, the Babylonian captivity, and even the temple of Solomon.

In order to secure the city of Jerusalem against siege, Hezekiah ordered an aqueduct tunnel to be carved through the stone of the mountain on which Jerusalem rested. The tunnel curved under the walls of Jerusalem and down to the spring of Gihon, a source of clear water flowing above the Valley of Kidron. The underground aqueduct led the water up into the city where it fed the pool of Shiloah, which was joined to a second reservoir called the Lower or Old Pool. This system of fresh water supply was the only way in which the walled city, which had no source of water within its walls, could withstand the threat of siege. Through the centuries the tunnel that Hezekiah built remained as it had been in the days of the king's reign.

It had become a splendid tourist attraction. On a hot, arid day, it was a joy for tourists to walk down the cool steps into the deep stone tunnel with its smooth walls and the sound of fresh flowing water echoing through the hollow rock arch.

Intrepid tourists could walk the distance of the tunnel on the narrow stone pathway by the side of the pool. Sometimes the water was high, however, and the stones became slippery. At such time, the tunnel was hazardous and closed to tourist traffic. It had been an unusually wet spring season, and as Leslie and Nick hurried toward the tunnel entrance in the dark, they saw a sign written in six languages that declared the tunnel closed.

Nick took Leslie's hand and helped her over the barriers at the entrance. Swiftly, they made their way down the smooth stone steps into the dark interior. They could hear the sound of flowing water and the dripping of interior springs. A shaft of evening light gleamed through the entrance down the center of the stairs, and in its glow they could see the path beside the spring, wet and close to the deep water. It looked dangerous and narrow. Further down the path, they saw a dark obstruction where the path widened a little.

"Looks like a rock slide," Nick said. It was cold in the tunnel and Leslie shivered, not only from the cool air but from the unearthly feeling of the aqueduct.

"This place gives me the creeps," she whispered. "It's as though there is nothing living here, a place of death."

"Not true," Nick replied, pulling her against him and chafing her arms to warm her. He pointed to the water. "That is life. Without it, everything above us would have blown away like the sands of the desert."

"M-m-m," she said, holding her body close to him and feeling the warmth of his nearness wash over her. "How long will we need to wait?"

"If I'm right, and this is where Sam meant for us to meet, it shouldn't be too long. Maybe an hour or so. In the meantime, we had better see to making ourselves comfortable." He had grabbed a sweater out of the clothes that Father Michael had given them. "Put this on," he told Leslie. She did as she was told, and they sat down next to the stairs. Nick put his arms around her, and they sat very close.

"I believe this is called huddling," Leslie laughed self-consciously.

Nick was silent, and she could tell he was preoccupied.

"Do you have the Star with you?" she asked. He shook his head.

"No. I don't carry it. Too risky," he answered.

"Where is it?" she wanted to know.

"Safe," he answered, his mind on other things.

"Don't you think you should tell me where it is, so if anything happens, I will be able to get to it?"

"No," Nick replied, his voice weary. "If I die, it is better if the Star dies with me. It will never be found. At least that may avert this destruction, even though it won't have any effect on future attempts."

Now Leslie was silent. "You're worrying about Sam, aren't you?" she whispered after a while.

Nick stirred irritably. "I don't want to talk about it," he said. "Please, Leslie, let's sit and wait."

The minutes passed as slowly as the dripping waters. In the cold, damp gloom, Leslie felt the chill of despondency settle in her heart, as the chill of the stones crept into her bones. It all seemed hopeless to her. Even if Sam delivered the message, as soon as they left the tunnel they would likely be discovered, and if Ahmud had his way, they would be killed. She didn't even want to think about the Israelis and CIA, who also thought they were the enemy. Would Sam come? Would he be able to help them? She didn't know, and the long minutes held no answers.

Suddenly she felt Nick grow taut. His head snapped up, and he seemed to be listening. "Sh-h-h," he whispered. "Someone is coming." They pulled back into the shadows in a deep corner behind the stone stairs and watched as a pair of legs descended.

"Sam?" Nick whispered. The person walking down the stairs turned in the direction of Nick's voice and shone a dim flashlight into the corner, illuminating Leslie and Nick's faces. The flashlight turned off, and the man came toward them.

"Nick," the voice was resonant with feeling. It was Sam. The two men embraced in the darkness. "You figured out my message on the plate!" Sam exclaimed. "I knew you would. I knew you'd come."

"Are you alone?" Nick asked.

"Of course," Sam answered loudly. "You don't think I'd lead somebody to you?" While he was speaking, Sam gave a quick affirmative nod and a look of understanding passed between the brothers.

"No," Nick almost shouted, "but you might have been followed. Give me your flashlight." Nick ran up the stairs, turned off the flashlight, and looked around the sloping hillside. Nothing was visible. Nothing moved in the pale evening light. Satisfied, Nick bounded down the steps.

"I can't see them," he whispered. "Maybe you lost them. Quick, Sam. Tell me what I'm supposed to do with the Star, and then let's get out of here."

"They let me go this morning without making me tell them the message I got for you. I knew they let me go just to follow me to you. Hal came to Hebron himself, and he told Ahmud to stop hunting for you. He had full confidence you would finish your mission if Ahmud would leave you alone. Hal still believes in you. He told me he understood you had to protect Leslie from Ahmud. 'Nick's smart,' is what Hal said. 'He knows we can't afford to have that girl turn up dead yet, not like this hothead Ahmud.'"

"Good," Nick continued to whisper. "They let you go. But Ahmud's followed you for sure. How did you get to Jerusalem?"

"On Ahmud's motorbike. It was picked up down by Potter's Field, and I rode into town this afternoon. I've been lying low ever since, waiting to come here to meet you. I tried to lose

them. I used every trick I know." Sam's eyes looked as old as
time. "But I think I've led them here. I feel it in my bones."

"What's the message?" Nick asked urgently. "Where and
when do I deliver the Star?"

"Three o'clock tomorrow afternoon in the street of the gold
merchants in the market of the old city. You remember, it's a
dead-end street. You go into the last shop on the right-hand
side. El Sharif is the name of the shop. You are to ask for a
golden Star of David, and the shop owner will tell you he has
some fine specimens in his back showroom. Then you are to
say, 'I have also heard you have some fine replicas of the Star
of Chaldea.' That's the password."

"Not very imaginative," Nick muttered, "but appropriate."
Sam nodded.

"We'll part company now, Sam," Nick said, "until this terrible time is over, and then, dear brother, we shall take a long,
long vacation together. On a night like this, I can fairly see the
Alps and the long slopes of snow with the two of us skiing
straight down, powder flying beside us." Nick chuckled. "Why
did we ever leave all that to become involved in this?"

Sam started to say something, but he paused and cleared
his throat. "I'm staying, Nick. Whatever happens now is my
fault. If I've led them to you . . . we'll face it together."

Nick was silent for a moment, then he laughed. "What are
you talking about, Sam? You know an agent running alone is
the safest and surest bet. I'm sending Leslie with you. Take her
to the American Embassy in Jerusalem and tell them it is imperative to keep her under wraps for a few days. Get out while
you can. It's not your fault. You did everything right, Sam. If
Hal is convinced I'm loyal, then Ahmud is my only concern,
and I can handle him."

There was an awkward silence. "Nick," Sam said very mis-
erably. "They only let me go to lead them to you. I was so sure
I could shake them . . . "

"You did everything right, Sam." Nick's voice was calm.
"You know how these things work. Nothing matters right now

but my making the rendezvous with the Star. You've made that possible. Now take Leslie and go."

"What about me?" Leslie asked hotly. "I want to stay with you. I've been a help so far, haven't I? Please, Nick, you can't do it alone."

"That's the only way it can be done, Leslie," Nick said firmly, his voice ringing in the dark tunnel. "Get going."

Sam spoke, but his voice was faint and vague. "Is everything set then? Do you have the Star with you?"

There was a long moment of silence, and then the sound of a footstep came out of the darkness. Leslie heard Nick's voice answer Sam, "Yes, of course."

Leslie was so astonished she could hardly believe her ears. "Nick," she gasped, "you told me—"

"Be quiet," Nick hissed. "There is too much talk and not enough doing around here. Every minute we're in this tunnel increases our chance of being caught. We have a lot of empty hillside to cover tonight before any of us make it to Jerusalem."

"Why don't we go through the tunnel together and separate once we're in the city?" Sam suggested. He was panting slightly, and his voice was almost inaudible.

Nick paused for a moment. "All right," he said carefully, "if that's the way you want to do it, Sam. Give me the flashlight."

The three of them began to work their way along the slippery rock path beside the swift, deep water. There were places where the water lapped up onto their shoes, and they had to grasp projecting rocks to maintain their balance. Several yards into the tunnel, Nick shone the flashlight on a pile of rocks that had collapsed over the pathway. The path was wider at that spot but was heaped with boulders and stones.

"Looks like we'll have to climb over," Nick said, moving forward.

Just then, a blinding light hit Nick, and he threw his hand up to shield his eyes. From behind the powerful beam, a voice spoke. It was Ahmud.

"You've led us in a merry chase today, Nick. Sam was easier to follow. Just give me the Star, and we'll let you go. You know the Israeli secret service as well as the CIA are probably combing this hillside for you right now. It would seem you are caught between the devil and the devil. Get Sam to tell me the rendezvous place and time. No amount of torture could get it out of him. Of course if we'd had more time . . . but at least he led us to you. He was not as quick as usual. Couldn't give us the slip. Once I have the Star in my hand, you can head back to Jordan a free man."

Nick stood absolutely still, his hands dangling at his sides. "I think, Ahmud, I would rather take my chances with the Israelis. Just how much do you imagine a promise from you is worth?"

Ahmud's voice was a barely controlled scream. "The ruby, Nick. Now!"

Nick reached into his pocket and pulled out a box. "Catch!" he shouted and threw it hard at Ahmud. The powerful flashlight curved in an arc and fell into the water as Ahmud frantically lurched to grasp the box with both hands. Somehow Ahmud managed to snag the box just as his flashlight sank into the stream, plunging everything into darkness.

"Duck," Nick whispered. Leslie and Sam flattened themselves on the path. A shot rang over their heads. Then, a flashlight behind Ahmud lit the cavern with grotesque shadows, and Nick saw Ahmud raise a pistol and aim it straight at his head. If Nick had been alone, he would have dived into the water, but he knew the swirling current would carry him away from Leslie and Sam, and they would be killed. Sam had never learned to swim. It was the one athletic thing he had never mastered, and Nick did not know if Leslie could swim or not. In that awful moment of indecision, the thought flashed through Nick's mind that he was going to die here in this cold, underground cave. Leslie had been right. This was a place of death. He heard a shot ring out, but he felt nothing, only the echo of the detonation as it rang down the stone walls.

Looking up, he saw Ahmud standing near the top of the rock barrier with a surprised expression on his face. Slowly, he watched Ahmud tip forward, as though he were bowing farewell. Then Ahmud fell down the heap of rocks and splashed into the icy stream, where his body was whirled into darkness.

As Ahmud fell forward, his gun clattered onto the rocks. Nick sprang forward to retrieve it, and as he did, he saw the thug who had accompanied Ahmud taking aim with his gun. Nick dived to the base of the rock and grabbed Ahmud's pistol. Before he could fire, another shot rang out in the echo chamber of the tunnel. Nick squeezed the trigger, and the thug dropped his flashlight and fell into the water with an awful scream.

The tunnel was pitch black again, and Nick felt his way back along the passage, feeling for Sam's flashlight. He found it and turned on the weak beam. Clinging to a rock, Leslie faced him, her eyes wide with horror. Behind her, on the stone path, Sam was clutching his stomach in silent agony. Blood was oozing out between his hands, and his face wore the expression of a schoolboy who has been punished for something he didn't do.

"Sam!" Nick screamed as he ran over to his fallen brother. "Sam—it was your shot that hit Ahmud. You saved my life. It's going to be all right now." Nick knelt beside Sam and held his head and shoulders in his arms. "I'll take care of you. Haven't I always taken care of you? And you . . . you've always taken care of me. We're strong, Sam. We'll make it together."

Sam shook his head, but there was a smile on his face now. "I did all right, didn't I, Nick? I was afraid I'd led you into a trap, but it was the only way to get the message to you. The mission . . . we have to succeed, have to find the madman. Traitors. I've had my fill of it all. It's got to get better sometime, doesn't it, Nick? People have to start caring about each other. Not killing. Always killing."

"Yeah, Sam. You did the right thing."

Sam continued to smile. "No," he said, and coughed up some blood. "I thought I heard something in the tunnel. Figured they'd followed me. Tried to warn you . . . asked about the Star . . . code word . . ."

"I know, Sam," Nick said. "You pulled it off. We're safe now. Tomorrow, everything will be all right because of you."

Sam slumped in Nick's arms. "Tomorrow . . . " he whispered in a broken voice.

Nick felt for a pulse in Sam's throat. "Gone," he said, his voice ragged with grief.

For an ageless time, Nick sat on the cold wet stone, holding his brother in his arms. Finally, Leslie touched him. "Nick, if there are Israeli agents on the hillside, they might have heard the shots. Someone could be on the way to investigate. Shouldn't we go?"

Nick seemed to shake himself. "We can't let them find Sam," he said grimly. "It will give them too much to go on." Gently he lifted his brother and slipped him into the cold, clear spring. "He is like this water," Nick said. "He has given life."

Picking up the flashlight, Nick hurried along the tunnel, lifting Leslie over the boulders and onto the narrow path. They toiled on in the uncertain beam of Sam's flashlight, pausing now and then to listen for signs of pursuit. Finally, they broke through the barricades at the Jerusalem end of the tunnel, skirted the pool of Shiloah, and hurried out into the sleeping streets of Old Jerusalem. Through the narrow, endless alleys and twisting, erratic streets they raced, pausing frequently in dark doorways. Finally, in the early hours of morning, they wound their way through the Arab Quarter and crossed behind the Dome of the Rock. There a neglected park ran alongside an old stone wall. To their right loomed the vast, heavy bulk of the buttresses of the unused East Gate. Broken and neglected steps led from the park to the back walls of the temple site to which there was no access from this area. Nick pulled Leslie toward a splintered door beneath the steps. It was a decrepit garden closet, with hoes, rakes, and the musty smell of decay. Using the flashlight, Nick found a musty burlap sack, which he shook out and placed on the ground. The two exhausted warriors sat down together and were asleep almost instantly. Each dreamed his own dread thoughts.

Nick woke to Leslie's shaking. "Nick!" she said frantically. "The Star! The Star! You don't have it. Ahmud took it with him when he fell. What are we going to do?"

"It's all right, Leslie. I didn't have the Star. That was an empty box. I left the Star with Father Michael, and he transferred it to Levi. It will be with our things at the safe house."

"And where is the safe house?" Leslie asked.

"That's what we're going to find out," Nick said. "Come on, let's go."

They went out into the faint light of dawn, and Nick led her down a steep path next to the ancient walls of the city. They skirted along the walls, until they came to the East Gate. The gate was set like a tall square tunnel in the wall. It jutted out on either side of the city wall like a long narrow building. The gate was enormous, tall, and massive, impressive in every proportion. As they rounded the wall of the gate and looked through the passageway, Leslie gasped with amazement. The opening of the gate was filled with enormous boulders. The length, breadth, and height of the gate was piled with massive rocks that blocked every crevasse of the passage.

"The Turks," Nick said in explanation. "Centuries ago. The gate has not been used since for obvious reasons." Leslie stared in awe at the tons of stone blocking the noble entrance.

"It's not supposed to be used again until the Millennium," she whispered.

"Well," Nick said ruefully, "I imagine that's one prophecy that has a good chance."

Nick continued walking past the ruined opening of the gate and on to the far side. Between the gate and the wall was an indentation. Nick pulled Leslie into the shadows and counted six stones from the ground up. He glanced over his shoulder at the empty park, and then pulled against the stone in the wall. To Leslie's amazement, she saw the weathered, moss-veined block moved. It was a panel, with a facing of stone. Inside was a bundle of old clothes. Hurriedly Nick pulled them out, closed the panel, and stepped back into the cover of the walls. The clothes were Arabic: a long dark robe and veil for Leslie, a soiled caftan and headdress for Nick. In the veil was a bottle of black hair dye. "For you," Nick said. "That blonde hair is like a beacon."

They dressed quickly. Nick took a rag from his shirttail and used it to dab the black dye on Leslie's hair. Soon there was no trace of her golden shade. She pulled back the wet black locks and made a tight knot at the back of her neck. Nick looked at her critically.

"Uncanny," he said, "what a difference color makes."

When they were finished, Nick took the flowing Arab head-dress and prepared to place it on his head. He looked carefully at the heavy cord that secured it. With strong hands, he pried the cord apart and took a piece of paper from inside the strands. "Here it is," he said. "The place to wait until rendezvous time."

The address on the paper was located on a side street close to the Via Dolorosa, between the Muslim and Christian sections of the city. From that location, it would be a short walk through the market district to the street of the gold merchants.

Wearing the Arab robes, Nick and Leslie hurried through the early morning streets. A few donkeys with baskets heavy with produce were wending their way toward the market. Inside the stone houses crowded along the winding cobbled streets, and reaching three and four stories above the narrow thoroughfares, they could hear the early morning sounds of waking families: babies crying, a woman's voice scolding, a young child singing. A few stray dogs and cats were slinking along the buildings, and Nick and Leslie caught whiffs of the smells of oil heating and rice frying. Leslie was so hungry, the scent of food almost made her ill.

They hurried up the streets, keeping their heads down. Nick continued to glance sideways and front and back, but he knew such surveillance was hopeless. If a professional were following them, they would not see or hear a thing until it was too late.

Finally they located the doorway to which they had been given directions. "Keep walking past it," Nick whispered. "Don't

even look up." They walked to the end of the narrow street
and turned the corner, then Nick drew her to a stop.

"We will wait here five minutes," he whispered. They stood
silently against the wall of an old stone house on a nameless,
winding street. Every house looked like all the others, and
Leslie thought that if she lost Nick, she would never find her
way out of the warren of stone paths and the canyons of stone
buildings. Suddenly she was reminded of Petra, the stone city.
Old Jerusalem was a stone city, too, only man had built these
stones, not nature.

"Now," Nick said, and they swiftly backtracked and turned
the corner onto the street where the safe house stood. No one
was in sight. "It looks like we've made it." Nick heaved a sigh
of relief, and the two of them hurried to the green wooden
door and pushed it open.

As soon as they were inside, Nick pushed a heavy iron bolt
shut, and they dashed up the stairs leading from the tiny ves-
tibule into the room above.

Leslie gasped. It was a beautiful room. The floors were covered with priceless Oriental rugs; the walls were hung with silks
of every hue. There were soft deep cushions on the floor, and
a low table was set with a beautiful enameled decanter and
cups. Glowing fruits were heaped on a brass tray, and fresh
bread and cheese were laid beside them. Behind a screen, they
discovered an old-fashioned tub, and beside it hot water was
boiling on a brazier.

Nick reached down to the table and picked up a piece of
paper. "This home belongs to an Arab who is my dearest friend.
He has the desire for peace and brotherhood as strongly as I.
We work together for that dream. Our hopes are fastened on
you today, Nick. Rest and prepare for the final thrust. Levi."

Nick handed the note to Leslie, and she read it with tears
in her eyes. With a weary hand, Nick reached out to the bowl
of fruit. On the top of the arrangement, a perfect orange glowed.
Nick picked it up and pulled back the turgid skin. Leslie watched
with fascination as he peeled away the sections, revealing the
brilliant ruby glowing in the heart of the fruit.

He took the ruby out and wiped it carefully and deliberately on a napkin. Then he held the magnificent gem on the flat of his palm and stared at it. "The last step of a long journey," he said with a sigh. "I hate this stone. It is too expensive."

Leslie left him and went behind the screen. Wearily, she pulled off the filthy clothes and lowered herself into the tub. The water was cool, but she reached over and took the heated basin and poured the boiling water into the tub. The steam rose to ease her aching muscles. The hair dye was permanent, so she soaked her hair and washed it. Finally, she pulled herself reluctantly from the water, knowing if she stayed longer she would fall asleep, and she needed to eat first in order to conserve her strength.

The filthy clothes by the side of the tub repulsed her, so she grasped one of the lengths of silk hanging from the wall and wrapped herself in it. She took one of the thick turkish towels, and rubbing her long blackened hair, she moved back into the main room.

Nick had put the ruby away and was lying among the pillows staring at the ceiling. When she entered the room, he raised himself on one elbow and looked at her.

"You are beautiful, you know," he said, his voice flat and emotionless. "You are beautiful, and I thought I might be falling in love with you, but now, since Sam, I think I will never feel an emotion again—not hate, not love, not warmth, not passion. I'm as hollow as that orange peel." He pointed to the ruined peeling on the table.

"Oh, Nick," Leslie cried. She ran to him and threw her arms around his shoulders. "You've got to let yourself cry for him—you've got to. You can't go on holding it in any longer."

"I can't cry for him, not for him and not for the people of the city. And not for this whole crazy human race, which is so bent on destroying itself. If you start to cry, there is no place to stop."

"Nick," she whispered, holding him tightly against her as though he were her child. She rocked him gently, stroking his hair. "Sam wasn't the whole world. He was your own dear brother. You loved him and took care of him all of your life. He loved you too. Everything between you was fine and precious. You can't let the ending blot all of those years away. Remember him as he was. Remember how he always laughed at danger. Remember how he looked when you first saw him, starving and brave in that awful camp and how you knew, the minute you saw him, that he was your brother."

"You wouldn't have believed him in that camp," Nick whispered, bowing his head on his hands. "He was ready to take on the world, and when my father held out his arms to him, he sort of lighted up. It was like he knew us right away, and it was joy, you know, pure joy. That's what he carried around in his eyes. He'd seen the worst, so he treasured the good—and fought the rest." Nick sat up straight.

"He was a scrapper too. Father didn't like that because he knew it meant Sam still remembered everything: the injustice, the suffering, the prejudice. Father hated those things, and he wanted Sam to forget them. But he didn't understand Sam. Sam wasn't fighting because he wanted revenge. He was fighting because he wanted to change things. He didn't hate this country. He loved it."

"And your father? What did he feel?" Leslie asked, hoping she could keep Nick talking.

Nick took a deep breath and stood up. "Father had no interest in politics. He hated the prejudice against the Arabs and the fighting between our countries, but he was a pragmatist and he didn't think anything could be done about it. His philosophy was 'Avoid it. Ignore it.' He couldn't leave Israel because of his business interests, but he told Sam and me from the time we were young that he didn't ever want us to live here. He tried to convince me by telling me privately that Sam could never live a happy life in Israel because of the restrictions on Arabs. He worked on Sam by telling him that I was too hot-blooded and was bound to get myself killed if we remained in such a volatile country. To insure we didn't stay, he sent us to prep school in Switzerland and then to university in England."

"How on earth did he allow you to come back and work at something as menial as guiding tours?" Leslie asked.

"He doesn't know we're here, doesn't know what we're doing," Nick answered shortly. "A few years ago, after a particularly nasty flare-up with the Arabs, Father wrote and begged us not to come back to Israel except for an occasional vacation. He told us he would arrange to meet us once or twice a year in America or Europe, and he wanted us to spend a while enjoying the world. It was his guilt about Sam, you know. He felt it was his fault Sam had such a terrible childhood, and he wanted to make it up to him with a lifetime of fun and games. He sent us an allowance every month—a very generous allowance—and we wrote to each other through a box number in Switzerland.

"It was easy for Sam and me to return to Israel in secret. We made contact with the Israeli secret service, met Levi, and received our first assignment to get ourselves recruited into Hal's terrorist group. The Israelis had tried to penetrate Hamji's group for years. They suspected they were planning something big, but didn't know what or when. I have posed as an Arab for nearly five years now." Nick sat down again and pressed his face into his arms. "I don't even know who I am anymore. What is an Arab? Or a Jew? Sam and . . . we . . . had postcards written and mailed to Father from all over the world, and once or twice a year we would manage to meet him at some resort and play together for a week. It made Father very happy to think his sons were far away from the untidy world of Israel."

"Your father must be quite a businessman," Leslie commented, "to support you in such style."

"He is," Nick said, "but then he works hard at it. He only has two interests in his life: making money, and his sons . . . " There was a long pause, and then Nick added in a muffled voice, "His son."

"Are you like him?" Leslie asked, searching desperately for a way to prolong the conversation.

"I don't know," Nick said restlessly. "How does anyone know what he is like? Sure, I guess I'm like him—strong-willed, stubborn, with a chronic case of tunnel-vision. Sure, I'm like him in those ways. But Sam—Sam was like him in all the fine ways. Sam was loving and loyal, tender and selfless. He was the best, and they killed him because he had a tender, vulnerable heart, caring more about me than he did for himself."

"But the good times, Nick. Those won't die. He lived with hope; he died with hope. Remember the good times, Nick, and make Sam's hope come true."

Nick's shoulders were shaking with grief and anger. He pounded a pillow with a muscled fist. "That poor, wonderful, scrawny little kid. Fate just couldn't leave him alone. The world wouldn't let him live, it kept after him and after him until it finally got him. Everything we could do, me with my strength and Father with his money, just wasn't enough. They got him, don't you see? They got him. All the meanness and hate—it got him. Hate has to destroy. It has to destroy everything that knows how to love."

Leslie sat silently beside Nick. She did not touch him or move, and gradually the muscles in his back relaxed. His weariness overtook him, and he slept.

"But love can win . . . " Leslie murmured, and moved to a pile of rugs, where she fell asleep as the city came alive in the morning sunshine outside the window.

Leslie woke around noon. The room was shadowed and cool, but outside in the narrow street, the sun beat down upon the cobblestones. The citizens of Jerusalem were scampering indoors for their noon meal and rest until the sun moved further across the heavens, leaving the streets in shade once more.

Nick was up, standing against the wall, flat by the side of the window. He was peering down at the street below without being visible himself.

"Can you see anything?" Leslie asked, all of her senses instantly alert.

"No," he said, turning to her with a reassuring smile. "Caution is a good habit for a man in my profession."

He had bathed and shaved and was wearing a clean loose caftan, which he must have found in the room somewhere. His strong brown feet were bare, and he looked rested and assured again.

"Welcome back," she said, smiling up at him.

He strode across the room and sat down on the floor beside her. "Maybe not back yet, but on the way. Thanks." They looked at one another for a moment and the air was heavy with unspoken emotion. Leslie was the first to look away.

"I keep forgetting to eat because I'm so sleepy," she said. "I think we should have something to eat to keep up our strength."

She went toward the table, but Nick put his hand around her wrist and stopped her. "I'll fix it," he said.

He moved over by the table, and taking a small brass plate, he began to select the best fruit. He took seedless grapes, a ripe rosy peach, which he peeled and sliced, and a melon, which he also prepared with his strong, careful fingers. Next he peeled an orange and arranged the sections in a circle. From the cheese tray he cut small cubes of creamy cheese and placed them on thin slices of unleavened bread. He poured a glass of amber liquid from the decanter and brought the plate to her. She took a section of the orange and put it to her dry mouth. The juice flowed sweet and cool onto her tongue. She sucked the fruit until it was juiceless, and then reached greedily for another. Once started, her appetite rampaged, and she took each perfect section and each piece of fruit and filled her mouth with its sweetness.

She felt the juice from the peach running down her chin, and she could not stop to wipe it off. She must have another piece and another. All the while Nick watched her eating with a delighted smile, as though he were watching a child perform. Finally she took a long drink of the amber fluid. It tasted of honey and lemons, and at last she felt the frenzy of her hunger abate. With a sigh of pure contentment, she leaned back and took a last piece of bread and cheese and began daintily picking at it, putting tiny pieces into her mouth with leisurely pleasure.

"Well," Nick said, "I'm glad to know there was a bottom."

"I know," she assented, her mouth filled with bread and cheese. "It must have been an awful sight. Ravenous woman attacks plate."

Nick looked at her with a smile of gentle irony, and Leslie took a deep breath and put down the food. She wiped her hands on a damask napkin and then looked up at him steadily.

"Nick," she said, "I think we need to talk. Now isn't the right time or place, but there may never be another. Nick, I think I love you. No matter what comes after all this, if we never see each other again, I love you."

Nick bent toward her and gathered her into his arms in a tender embrace. "Oh, Leslie," he whispered. "Here and now, in the most crucial moment of my life, when I have to be free to act and do whatever needs to be done—what a time to hear you say it. But I wanted to hear you say it, Leslie. I wanted it more than you can ever imagine."

Nick gently took her face between his hands and bent and kissed her until she felt herself falling through the sky into some vast, glorious sunlit land.

"It's time," he said, breaking the spell. "I'm going now. You wait here, and if I'm not back by four o'clock, call Levi at this number." He thrust a penciled note into her hand. "Memorize it, and destroy the paper."

She was befuddled with emotion. "But I'm going with you. You can't leave me here."

She struggled to her feet. Nick went behind the screen, and she heard the rustle of clothing. He moved from behind the screen and swiftly walked toward the stairs. "Remember," he said, "four o'clock."

He was wearing a nondescript cotton shirt and slacks that would blend into any street scene—tourist, Israeli, or Arab. Over the shirt, he shrugged a wrinkled cotton jacket.

"Where is the Star?" she whispered anxiously.

"Taped to my body," Nick answered. "They won't get it unless they get me—and they won't get me," he added with a grin and showed her a slender, deadly automatic pistol in the inside pocket of the jacket. "Wish me luck." He reached for her with one arm and kissed her again.

"Luck," she whispered, "and all the blessings of Father Michael's God and mine."

He looked at his watch. "I think I will wait a few more minutes," he said. "The less time on the street the better."

"I had better get dressed too," she said. "What should I wear in case I have to go out?"

"Wear the skirt and sandals," Nick said. "The Arab robes are too restricting in case you need to move quickly. No one will recognize you with that black hair."

She changed rapidly behind the screen, brushing out the shining black-dyed hair and leaving it straight down her back so that it became her most striking feature.

When she returned, Nick had taken up his post beside the window and was peering down the street, which was rapidly filling with people now that the sun was beginning to lower: merchants, peddlers, women going to market, clusters of tourists, as well as young men in khaki uniforms carrying rifles, and sober-looking men in neat suits.

Nick took a deep breath. "The troops are out," he said. Leslie was standing on the opposite side of the window, looking at the other end of the street. There were several sidewalk merchants sitting by their wares. The one nearest their house was wearing a hooded, striped caftan, and he was slumped beside large, open gunnysacks of pistachio nuts and almonds. The other produce sellers were noisily importuning everyone who passed to buy their wares, but the nut merchant seemed indifferent to potential customers. *Sleeping on the job*, Leslie thought, and turned away, but out of the corner of her eye she saw the Arab shift position, and quickly, almost imperceptibly, he raised his head and for a fraction of an instant stared at the window. The look was so penetrating that Leslie almost felt he must have seen her, even though she was well to the side of the window and flattened against the wall.

"Nick," she groaned. "It's Hal Johnson—Hamji! He is sitting on the sidewalk across from our door. He's waiting for us to come out."

Nick frowned. "Are you sure?"

"Positive. His head is covered, but I caught a good look at his face. It was Hal all right."

"He can't be sure we're in here, or he would have broken in. He's going to wait another few minutes, and if we don't appear, he'll head for the street of gold merchants and stop us there."

"You said *us*," Leslie whispered.

"I can't leave you here," Nick answered. "It isn't safe anymore. If he's waiting by the front door, that must mean there is no other way out of this building, but Levi would never choose a place with only one exit." Nick began to walk quickly along the back wall of the room, knocking the wall gently. Behind the screen, he rapped an area that sounded hollow. He tore the silk hangings from the wall, and they could see a disguised door, flush with the wall. Nick pounded his fist softly down the line marking the door. At the third position, the door sprang open.

They walked rapidly into a dank-smelling passageway, so narrow one person could barely fit. They hurried along as the passage dipped lower. The tunnel became darker. Whatever source had lighted it was lost, but they could feel their way easily along the wall, and the footing beneath them was like soft sand. Above them they heard clattering and an occasional muffled shout.

"I think we are tunneling under the street," Nick whispered. Soon the passageway moved upward again, and a dim light was visible ahead. They came to a closed door at the end of the passageway.

"Will it open?" Leslie asked, her voice quivering with apprehension.

Nick leaned against the door, and it swung silently out into a small, bare room with a glassless window. The room had no other exit.

Nick hurried to the window and looked down. They were one story above a narrow pathway. The alley fronted the wall of Jerusalem, which ran, in this section of the city, alongside a jumble of flat-roofed houses. The top of the city wall was about a story above them. The old wall was several feet wide and, in centuries past, had served as a pathway for sentries and soldiers. Daring tourists would occasionally find one of the many sets of stairs that led to the top of the wall, and they would walk around the city. It was a time-consuming undertaking and, in one or two places, quite hazardous—but it could be done.

Nick looked down the fifteen feet to the cobblestones below. The winding alley was deserted. "We'll need to drop," he said. "Do you think you're up to it?"

"If you go first," Leslie answered. Just then they heard a sound. It was soft and muffled, but was unmistakably the thud of running feet coming through the passageway.

"Jump!" Nick commanded, and Leslie, without hesitation, climbed out the open window, clung to the window ledge, and dropped. Pain jarred every joint in her body when she hit the stones, and her ankles groaned with the strain, but she kept her balance and staggered a few steps. Nothing was broken. In an instant, Nick followed her, and she heard a soft grunt as he landed. He grabbed her arm, and they began zigzagging along the alley. As they turned a corner, they heard the smack of shoes on the cobblestones behind them and knew their pursuer had also hit the pavement.

They turned another corner, and Nick moaned. The backs of the tenement houses abutted the old stones of the city wall. There was no exit from the narrow cul-de-sac. Stairs were carved into the stones of the city wall beside them.

"Up!" Nick yelled, and they scrambled up the uneven, mossy stairs.

They dashed along the narrow pathway at the top of the wall of Jerusalem. On one side of them were the narrow cobblestone streets and tangled roofs of the city, and on the other side was a sheer drop down the wall to the sharp, stony hillside. It was a dizzying route, one demanding caution, and yet they ran along the uneven stones, heedless of the danger of falling, conscious only of the need to evade their pursuer. Occasionally, through an open window, they would see an astonished face staring at them as they ran headlong along the wall.

Leslie could not bear the tension of not knowing, and she turned her head to look behind her, expecting to see Hal in his flowing, striped robes running behind them. Instead she saw a man, tall and thin, wearing wrinkled gray slacks and holding a revolver in his hand.

Scattered pedestrians on the street had observed the chase, and several were stopped, watching with intense interest.

"It isn't Hal!" Leslie gasped to Nick. "It's someone else."

"I know," Nick's voice was hardly winded, but it shook with the force of his uneven running. "It's Tappin. He'll shoot as soon as he's within range. He doesn't care who sees him. All he wants is to stop us. He thinks we're the enemy. We've got to get off this wall. We're too visible."

There were no steps in sight, but a few yards ahead of them, the houses veered more closely to the wall, and a line of flat roofs ran parallel to the city wall.

"Do you think you can jump the gap?" Nick asked, pointing ahead to where a span of several feet separated the wall and an adjacent roof.

"I'll try," Leslie responded.

They arrived at the area, and Nick leaped off the wall and spun across the space with the unforgiving cobblestones far below. He landed on the roof and rolled to his feet. "Jump!" he shouted to Leslie. She had turned, but as she prepared to leap, she looked down and saw the steep drop to the murderous stone.

"I can't," she gasped. Tappin had dropped to his knees, and Nick could see him sighting his revolver carefully. Nick threw himself flat on the roof as the bullet sang just inches above his head. Tappin did not move. He brought his two arms straight in front of him as though he were at target practice.

The shot had galvanized Leslie, and as she saw Nick fall to the ground, she sprang from the wall, her powerful legs giving impetus to her leap. She landed barely a foot from the edge of the building, but the force of her jump threw her forward, and she skidded across the roof, her knees and elbows scraping against the tile. Nick grabbed her hand. Crouched and running, they moved over the flat rooftop. The buildings were joined to one another, and the roofs were crowded with clotheslines, fenced-in play areas, cooking pots, and an occasional small hut built on the top of the roof like a tenement penthouse. Nick and Leslie wove among the paraphernalia, grasping at whatever cover they could find. Finally they could hear no sound of pursuit, and they dodged into a small building on the rooftop. It was a square stone hut with an open door and windows and a sandy floor. They moved into the blessed shadow of the hut and stood exhausted in the corner, breathing heavily.

The next rooftop was tile and had a sharply slanted roof. "We have to get down from here," Nick whispered. "It's only a matter of time until someone reports this disturbance to the soldiers—and we'll be stopped. Stay here, I'll go out and look around."

Nick eased himself out of the small hut, and then sprang back. "It's Tappin. He's here, right on this roof. I don't want to shoot unless I have to. There are soldiers in the street."

"I know you're in there, Nick," Tappin's voice said. It was coming from just outside the hut, near the front door. "You're not coming out alive."

Leslie and Nick remained in the dark corner. Outside the door, they could see bright sunshine and hear the hum of insects. Everything was silent, except for the filtered sounds coming up from the street.

"Stay here," Nick's mouth was against Leslie's ear. He grabbed up a handful of sand, and moving like lightning, he sped across the hut and leaped out into the sunlight. Leslie saw him throw the sand and heard a muted gasp of pain. She heard the sound of Nick's feet dashing across the roof and then the thud of a tile hitting the ground far below. Seconds later, she heard a second pair of feet running.

She could not stand being in the dark secrecy of the hut, and she ran out the door. Nick had left the flat roof and was carefully picking his way across the slanted tile roof. Behind him, Tappin was also moving slowly across the slanted tiles. Nick was nearing the next roof, a flat expanse with several places for dodging and concealment. Tappin, realizing Nick would soon be away from him, stopped progressing across the tiles and raised up on his knees. With a deliberate motion, he raised his gun, and Nick, slow and awkward on the slates, became a perfect target.

"Nick!" Leslie screamed. The sound of her voice startled Tappin, and his foot slipped. It seemed to Leslie that everything that happened next was in slow motion. Nick reached the flat roof and turned to watch as Tappin slid, calmly and with a strange dignity, down the steep roof. The man seemed to float in the air. He hit the awning of a fruit stall three stories below, which shattered beneath him as did the tables of fresh fruit, and then he rolled out into the center of the street and lay absolutely still.

Leslie hurried across the roof and found the exit stairs. With shaking feet, she dashed down the four flights of stairs and stepped into the street. The superstitious residents had run into their houses, so she found the street deserted. Far down the street, she saw a man in native dress gesturing wildly to two soldiers, pointing down the street where the fallen man lay. Leslie did not know if she should run back into the house or down the street to where Nick was, or if she should go check on the man who was lying apparently dead on the cobblestones.

As she stood in indecision, she felt a hard object shoved into her back. Hal's deep voice spoke to her, "Don't make a sound, Mrs. Brinton. I think your long journey is almost finished. Walk slowly over to the dead man, and when the soldiers arrive, tell them he is your husband and his murderer has just run into the building over there, across the road." Hal pointed at a building directly across the street from the building where Nick had last been seen.

"All right," Leslie answered. "I'll do as you say."

"As soon as the soldiers are out of the way, you and I shall go into the building where Nick is hiding. I think when he sees I have you, he may choose to show himself. He only has ten minutes until three o'clock anyway. I think he will have given up making the rendezvous by then. I will deliver the Star myself."

Leslie went over and stood looking down at the body of Tappin, lying amid the ruins of the fruit stand.

Hal jammed the gun into her back with great ferocity. "Cry," he whispered fiercely. Tears sprang to her eyes as she looked down on the man who had slipped from the roof, and it seemed to her the whole world had somehow slipped awry. Where was Nick? What would happen if Hal killed him? Would Hal deliver the Star? And would this whole ghastly venture end in a giant cloud of destruction as the ancient ruby signaled the warhead to come home, home to Old Jerusalem, bringing its deadly gift with it?

It all seemed so useless and suddenly Leslie knelt beside the man she had never known. A man who had tried to kill her. And she wept in earnest.

The soldiers came panting up beside her, and she raised her tear-streaked face. "His killer ran into that doorway! You must catch him! Hurry! Hurry!"

The two soldiers turned and sprang through the open doorway of a tall tenement building on the opposite side of the street, and she could hear their boots pounding through the hallways, the butts of their rifles banging against the doors.

"Very good," Hal growled. "Now stand up, and we shall go hunting for Nick."

She stood, but she refused to move. "You may shoot me here, Hal. I will do nothing to compromise Nick's position."

"That won't be necessary, Leslie," Nick said, as he stepped out of the darkened doorway behind the fruit stand. He had his shiny automatic in his hand. "Let her go, Hamji."

"Don't be stupid, Nick," Hal replied. "I have this gun pointed in her back—straight at her heart. If you do not drop that weapon instantly, I will blow a hole through her that will let you see the daylight."

Nick stared at Hal and dropped his gun. "All right, Hamji," he said, "you've done it. First Sam and now me. We're two of a kind. You can come get the ruby, but let Leslie go first."

Hal chuckled. "It isn't going to be that easy, Nick. I'm hanging on to her until the Chaldean Star is in my hand. Then I'll let her go."

Hal shoved the gun in Leslie's back and prodded her toward Nick. "No, Nick!" she cried. "Don't give him the ruby. Run for it! It's the only way to save the city." But Nick stood his ground. In desperation Leslie turned around and swung at Hal's arm, but he was too fast for her, and with a powerful fist he struck the side of her head and knocked her to the ground. She lay on the cobblestones, dazed and weak, and Hal knelt beside her and aimed the gun at her temple.

"Nick!" Hal ordered. "Walk over to me slowly and hand me the Star, or she gets it right now. I finally figured out you're an agent for the other side. What a fool you made of me, but I shall have the last laugh."

Nick reached inside his shirt, and there was a sound of tearing. He pulled out a ragged strip of tape wrapped around a solid object. Slowly he walked toward Hal, who was holding his hand out, and laid the Star in Hal's outstretched hand.

"Now," Nick said, his voice trembling with menace, "let her go."

"Right you are, Nick," Hal said, whirling onto his feet facing Nick. He pointed the gun at Nick. "Good-bye, lover boy."

A sudden explosion rang up the narrow street, and Hal fell to the ground, his caftan billowing around him. Leslie looked around in amazement. In the midst of the fruit a blood-stained man was propped on one elbow, a smoking revolver was in his hand. Nick ran over to him.

"Tappin!" he exclaimed. "You're alive! But why did you shoot him and not me?"

Tappin managed a crooked smile. "It took me a minute to decide which one I ought to shoot. But I figured if Hal wanted to shoot you, you had to be worth saving. Besides I, like Hal, was beginning to suspect you were something other than you seemed."

"When I visit you in the hospital, I'll explain all about it," Nick said, smiling.

"You won't need to," Tappin replied, gritting his teeth against the pain. "I think I've pretty much figured it out. Don't you have something to do?"

"Yes, I do," Nick said. "I've got to get out of here. It seems like I'm always leaving you in tough conditions—but you'll make it, I know you will."

Nick ran over to Leslie, who was crouched on the ground beside Hal. Nick grabbed her hand, and they started running down the street. They ducked through an alley and along a winding street and then burst out into the main market thoroughfare.

"Five minutes to three," Nick panted as they squeezed their way through the crush of people walking along the two crowded lines of stalls. Vendors and hawkers impeded their way, and knots of sightseers blocked the street. Nick walked in front breaking the way. Leslie walked as close to him as possible.

"Nick," she whispered, "there's something you should know. Hamji wasn't dead when he fell. He spoke to me before he died."

"What did he say?" Nick asked.

"He laughed and said, 'It doesn't matter if I die or not. Nick won't succeed.' Then he whispered something. He was gloating. 'I know about the street of gold.' That's what he said. Oh, Nick! I'm frightened. He must have men posted there waiting for you."

As they continued to walk, Nick thought furiously. They were passing a small bazaar that sold children's clothing. Nick stopped suddenly and reached into his pocket. He pulled out a bill and thrust it at the woman. "Those red shorts and white T-shirt," he said, pointing to a pair of shorts for an older child and a plain white shirt. The woman handed him the clothes and began rummaging for change in her money box, but Nick and Leslie were already hurrying up the street. Nick pushed Leslie into a crevasse between two buildings and handed the clothes to her.

"Here," he said, "put these on. I'll guard the way so no one will see you."

He heard the sound of rapid dressing, and in a few moments, she stepped out of the opening in the skin-tight T-shirt and shorts. "Nick," she exclaimed, "this is indecent!"

"That is exactly what I'm counting on. I'm sure Hamji must have men waiting for me. To Arabs, immodesty in women's dress is infuriating. They will automatically turn away from the sight of you. Do you have enough courage to walk up the street of the gold merchants, by yourself, looking like this? If you can distract those watching for me, for even a minute, I may have a chance."

Nick stopped by a vendor and haggled to buy his clothes. In another few minutes, Nick was swathed from head to foot in an Arabic burnoose. In these strange clothes, they reached the entrance to the street of the gold merchants.

The main market street of Old Jerusalem was crowded, noisy, and shadowed. The buildings on either side were so close together that they blocked out most of the sun. Each tiny shop displayed its wares in open profusion—no sacks, market bags, boxes, or display cases. Fruits were laid on tables or heaped in baskets. Rugs and fleece were piled; caftans, shirts, embroidered blouses, and shawls were hung to blow in the wind like colorful flags. The street was teeming with color and life and avarice: rich scent of spices, curry, ginger, and almonds; buckets of flowers; tables of leather; shelves of olive-wood carvings; sharp-eyed shopkeepers haggling for money; and wary buyers haggling for bargains.

The street of the gold merchants turned off at a right angle from the market street, and it was a different world. The street was one block long. A dead-end street, wider and cleaner than the market street, with lower buildings and tidy shops with heavy doors and lettered signs. Some of the shops even had display windows barred from within, but open enough so that one could see the gleam of gold on tantalizing display. The men who ran these shops were sleek and handsome, with trim beards and western suits or sparkling white robes.

Tourists wandered into the street of gold a little awed by the shine of wealth on display in the narrow shops. This was no place for the bargain hunter or for tourists who wanted cheap souvenirs. The fare offered on this street was precious and priceless, and only money spoke the language of these merchants.

Even this street was fairly crowded. Many tourists were wandering in and out of the shops, and Arabs, a few Hasidic Jews, and several businessmen in three-piece suits were slowly strolling along the smooth stones. Leslie saw the storefront that Sam had described to them—El Sharif. It was at the far end of the street.

"It's one minute past three," Nick whispered, and with a rush of courage, Leslie stepped into the sunlight, which flooded the sidewalk. Instantly, she caught the eye of a young, handsome Arab who was standing in front of one of the shops bargaining with the owner over a gold bracelet. She saw outrage and fury in the man's eyes and realized what Nick had meant. Her clothing was an affront to the Muslim. Perhaps this diversion would work after all. She put her hand on her hip, and although everything in her cringed, she began walking slowly up the center of the road. She kept an indifferent look on her face, looking from shop window to shop window as though she were a bored tourist taking in the expected attractions. She had no way of knowing which of the men on the street were part of Hal's terrorist group, and so she could only hope she was being seen by the right ones. Even the American tourists were outraged by her poor taste, and she saw them whispering to one another as she walked on. At one point she noticed two young Arabs expostulating together, staring at her and pointing. For a moment, she almost panicked and began to run. She was sure they had recognized her, but she pulled herself together.

They are expecting someone with blonde hair, remember? she told herself. *It's just my costume. They could kill me for that. I'm a public disgrace—but not a threat. At least they aren't even looking at my face.*

Had Nick made it to the shop? She had no way of knowing. Perhaps she should try to prolong the distraction another minute. Ahead of her, she saw a solid American couple. The man looked tired and bored, and the woman was talking exuberantly. "Did you see that gold chain? Have you ever seen anything so beautiful? Imagine, ten thousand dollars just for something to wear. Have you ever?"

"Mrs. Warren!" Leslie called. "Mrs. Warren!" She ran up and hugged the woman, who stepped back in astonishment. "Oh!" Leslie said, laughing with embarrassment. "Would you believe it, I thought you were Mrs. Warren from my tour group. I seem to have gotten myself lost, and I've been wandering around this market for hours trying to find someone I knew. I surely thought you were Mrs. Warren—you look just like her. I do declare!"

"Young lady!" the affronted woman exclaimed. "You should be ashamed of yourself." The woman's voice was shrill with insult. "You certainly have no right to speak to a stranger like that, and what do you think you are doing in those kinds of clothes. Why . . . why . . . you are a disgrace to your country, that's what!"

A small crowd had gathered around to listen to the interchange, and she saw smiles of satisfaction on several faces as the woman gave her a thorough scolding.

Leslie began to back away, her face flaming with embarrassment, which was not an act. "I'm sorry," she said. "I really did think you were Mrs. Warren—I'm sorry."

Leslie moved away from the center of the street and escaped through the door of the last shop. She let herself in quickly and closed the door behind her. The room was gloomy, and there was no one in the store but a man behind the counter and a robed Arab. Leslie recognized the robe. It was Nick.

She heard him ask about the Star of David, and then she heard him give the password. "The Star of Chaldea." The shopkeeper proceeded to take Nick into the back room, and a moment later the keeper reentered the shop alone and came toward Leslie. "I am sorry," he said, "you must leave the shop. I am closing."

Leslie was standing near the door, and as the shopkeeper came to her he saw that she was crying. "Please," she whispered. "Can't I stay here for a minute or two until those people leave? I'm not dressed appropriately, and I know that I've lost my tour group. I just can't bear to go back out onto the street until that woman leaves. Please? It will only be a moment."

The shopkeeper looked at her for a moment, and his eyes softened. "Perhaps I can make it possible for you to leave without further comment," he said. "Wait a moment."

He was a man with a white beard and a worldly face. Leslie had the feeling he knew a great deal about women. In a moment the man returned from behind the counter holding a simple white caftan. "This is sometimes worn by my assistant, when she is working after the shop has closed. It is what you Americans would call her housedress. I do not think she would mind if you bought it from me."

Leslie smiled. The man was generous, but he was still a businessman. "I have . . . I have lost my purse," Leslie whispered. "I think I left it on the bus. Do you think she would take my watch? It is quite a good one."

She held out her hand, and the gold dealer looked at the watch with a practiced eye. "That is worth much more than a simple cotton robe," he said. "Are you sure you feel it is a good trade?"

"Well," Leslie said slowly, "perhaps you might add a small piece of jewelry as well. Then the trade would be more even." She smiled at him with a touch of mischief, and he laughed. She could tell he loved to bargain. His eyes sparkled.

"Already you are learning," he said. "If it were another day I would say 'Let us see,' but I am afraid that today there is no time. You will have to leave the shop either with or without the robe—it is your decision—but you must leave. I am closing right now."

Leslie's mind searched frantically for a way to buy time, but she knew it had run out. Slowly she pulled the watch off her wrist. "I think the robe is worth it," she said ruefully and began pulling the white garment over her head. While her head was still inside the slender robe, and she was struggling to pull it down over her shoulders, she heard the shop door opening. The keeper walked over to the door. She still could not see, but the dress was sliding down. It was terrible to be tangled in its folds as the unknown person stepped onto the threshold.

"I am sorry," the shopkeeper said, "we are closing."

"Where is the man who came in here?" a harsh voice asked. Leslie pulled the caftan into place and stared at the insistent man, who was standing next to the doorway and the shopkeeper.

"What man?" the shopkeeper asked. "If a man came in here, I have not seen him. As you can see, only this young lady and myself are here, and she is leaving."

"If you don't mind, I think we'll take a look in the back." The man grabbed the shopkeeper by the arm and pushed him toward the door at the back of the shop.

Leslie followed the two men. "What are you doing?" she yelled at the dark man. "You can't push a person around like that. This shop belongs to this man!"

The intruder gave her a murderous look. "Get out of here," he growled.

The shopkeeper turned and hit the terrorist with his open hand, but before he could strike again, the man pulled out a snub-nosed handgun and shot him. The shopkeeper spun across the room and slumped onto the counter, knocking the golden bracelets and necklaces onto the floor.

At the sound of the shot, the rear door flew open, and Nick leaped into the room and shot the assailant before the man had time to turn. Leslie had followed the man toward the back of the shop, but Nick motioned to her desperately. "The metal grill, Leslie!" he shouted. "Drop the metal grill in front of the shop!"

Leslie ran to the front of the store. Out on the street, she could hear people screaming and shouting in reaction to the sound of the shots. Feet were running in panic, and people were stampeding to get out of the street. She could also see several men trying to push against the tide of people flowing away from the area, and she knew it would be only seconds before they reached the storefront and burst in upon them.

The heavy metal grill was folded up in front of the store like a movie screen. "Where is the button to lower it?" Leslie whispered. She searched the front of the store, looking for a telltale switch. There it was, at the side of the door. Quickly, she reached out and flipped it, and the hum of a small motor began.

Very slowly, she saw the iron screen begin to descend. Two men had broken through the fleeing crowd and were sprinting toward the store where the two men lay dead. Nick had reached down and taken the dead man's pistol from him, and now he was running toward Leslie.

"Get down!" he shouted. "Duck behind the counter. Hurry, Leslie—there's no time to waste!"

But Leslie could not move. She felt she was watching the end of the world. The metal grill continued to descend with slow deliberation, and the men were running closer and closer. It was as though she were condemned to watch the bars descend, as though she knew if she stopped watching, the screen would stop moving, and the men would pound into the shop with their automatic machine guns and destroy them all.

Nick grabbed her by the hand and pulled her to the floor just as the heavy protection grill clanged against the sidewalk, and the running men, unable to stop their furious impetus, crashed into the solid interlocking bars.

"Stay down!" Nick shouted. "We're not safe yet." The two men outside stood back from the iron grill and pulled the auto-

matic rifles, which were slung across their shoulders, into firing position. They began to rake the store with a rain of bullets. Glass, wood, and noise filled the little room. After a minute
or two of solid firing, they ran up and smashed their bodies
against the grill time after time, but the heavy grill held. The
men ran across the street calling instructions to two other men
who were running toward them. The storefront was completely
destroyed. The glass windows and the door were shattered by
the heavy bullets. Leslie lay in a daze on the floor behind the
heavy wooden counter. Both she and Nick were covered with
broken glass and shards of wood. They carefully picked themselves up, trying to avoid the shattered glass around them. As
Leslie lifted her head, she saw, deep in the shadows of the rear
room, the figure of a tall man wearing a dark suit and a white
shirt. She could not see his face—only the gleam of his eyes as
he watched them.

Chapter Ten

When Nick saw Leslie step into the street of the gold merchants, his heart twisted. He thought in his whole life he would never see a sight so brave as Leslie's head held high while she was wearing those red shorts, as though she were above the rules of society and the regard of her fellow beings. He knew what it had cost her tender, dignified spirit to walk into that street and be the object of stares, distaste, and ridicule.

"Someday I'll make it up to her, I swear," Nick whispered to himself. It was working. He saw, even more clearly than Leslie did, the shock her appearance caused and the anger on the faces of the Muslims, to whom modesty in women is a sacred commandment.

In Leslie's wake, he slipped along the sidewalk in his generous robes, pausing to look in shop windows and check the faces and attitudes of the crowd around him. No one seemed to notice his progress, and when Leslie caused the scene in the center of the street with the woman tourist, he gratefully slipped into the shop just minutes after the appointed time.

Everything had gone smoothly. The shopkeeper had recognized the password and had taken him into the back room and left him alone. The room had no windows and was lit by a single shaded lamp on the desk.

The chair to the desk had a high back, which was turned away from the door. Nick sat down facing the desk and waited. The chair swiveled slowly toward him, and Nick, wordlessly, watched as the lamp lit a dark suit and a spotless white shirt with a gleaming silk tie. Gold cuff links and fine, long-fingered hands showed as the man behind the desk placed them palm-down on the blotter. It was the hands that told Nick. He did not even need to hear the voice or see the face.

There was a moment of incredulous silence in the room, and then the man spoke. "You—" his voice was harsh with horrified anguish. "How can it be? Why?"

Nick's eyes had become accustomed to the gloom, and through the shadows above the lamp, his father's face came into dim focus. The two men stared at one another across the desk.

Nick could not think. His mind refused to understand, refused to accept what was happening. In that empty moment before the shock could buffet him, he said the only thing that was in his mind.

"Sam is dead. You've killed him."

He saw his father's shoulders slump. "But you were in Switzerland for the spring skiing." His voice was still disbelieving. "What are you doing back in this forsaken land?"

"We have been working the past five years for the Israeli secret service. This is the land that bred us, Sam and me. It is our country, our bone and sinew—our blood. Until this land is healed, we could not rest. You should have known that. We learned it from you. Never abandon a thing you love. Isn't that what you taught us?"

His father bent his head forward and leaned it on the desk so Nick could not see his face.

"You have the Star?" Nick's father asked in a muffled voice. "You are the messenger from Hamji?"

"From Hamji, yes, but working to destroy him—and you. I was to deliver a bullet with the ruby. Why, Father?" Nick's voice was a wail of anguish. "You hated politics. You avoided contention, you sneered at diplomacy, you ignored power— what are you doing here? Surely not for money. You wouldn't do this for money."

"No, my son, not for money. I did it for bitterness, revenge, and for hate. How can nations deserve to live when all they have to give is hatred? Such ones do not have the right to go year after year, decade after decade, century after century, fanning the flames of centuries-old enmities, murdering innocent women and children, scarring the land of Abraham, their father. We need to be punished, all of us. We need to fight until we either rip ourselves off the face of the earth or cleanse ourselves of this evilness and exhaust the bitterness that lies between us. If only ten people of each nation survived, perhaps they could find the thing that you and Sam found—that brotherhood and love can span the differences of centuries. I've thought about it ever since I found my son starving in the camp like a stray dog, his mother killed slowly by privation. I could not forgive myself for having failed them. I could not forgive the nations that had caused this thing." The voice was flat and dull, like the voice of an automaton, and Nick realized that his father was mad. Somewhere along the way, somewhere in the years of self-incrimination, the years of sorrow and strain, his father had lost sight of reality.

"You were trained as an engineer, weren't you, Father?" Nick whispered. "That's what you studied while you were in London, wasn't it?"

His father nodded. "I have run the experimental division of Israeli defense for twenty years. My import business was a front so I could be free to travel and consult anywhere in the world. My identity and true occupation were kept secret for security reasons."

"You built the atomic system, and you had the computer chip installed," Nick stated.

"Yes," his father nodded. "All is ready. Now, you must give the Star to me. They have killed Sam, and they must pay for it."

"No, Father," Nick whispered. "That isn't the answer. Somewhere inside of you, you know it isn't the answer. You don't answer hatred with hatred. You don't save innocent lives by taking innocent lives. Please, Father, give yourself up."

"Give me the Star, Nick, and leave. This has nothing to do with you. Get out of Israel now—tonight. Go where you can be free of this awful heritage. Leave this cursed land, Nick. Give me the Star and leave, so that I may do what I must."

Nick shook his head.

"You see," his father began, speaking softly, more to himself than to Nick, "the ruby belonged to Father Abraham. It was the symbol of the triumph of good over evil. He brought it with him when he escaped from the blind and wicked superstition of a corrupt civilization. I will take it, and when I have destroyed the corruption that chokes this civilization, when I have brought them to their knees—Arab and Jew alike, the children of Father Abraham, brothers still—then . . . then the Star will once again shine as a symbol."

His father's face was wet with perspiration, and his fine hands were trembling with fanatic fervor.

"No, Father." Nick's voice was soft, but firm. "You are not Abraham. You cannot heal wounds by pain. You cannot build with destruction. You can't bring peace with death. I will not give you the Star, Father."

His father said in a voice that came like a dream, or a nightmare, "Then I must kill you too, Nephti." He had not called Nick by his childhood name for many years, and Nick's heart moved with sorrow.

"Fathers do not kill their sons," Nick whispered.

"Abraham was told to," his father answered, so softly that Nick could hardly hear.

Just then, there was the sound of a shot in the outer room. Nick sprang from his chair and threw open the door in time to see the shopkeeper collapsing on the gold counter and an armed man wheeling to shoot again.

Chapter Eleven

Leslie stared at the tall man standing in the back room. "Nick," she whispered. "Who is he?"

Nick was sitting back in the corner under the front display case, loading his revolver. "It's only a matter of time before they break in," he whispered urgently. "You must get to the phone and call Levi. Have you memorized the number?"

"I'm on my way!"

The street outside was deserted, and the four men with automatic rifles were conferring. Nick knew it would only be a matter of minutes before they broke through the grillwork. He watched as Leslie moved to the back counter. An old telephone hung on the far wall. She began to dial the number, and Nick saw his father come to life. He began to move out of the back room.

"Stay away from her!" he called to his father. His father walked like a man in a trance. He walked straight down the center of the store, his dignified body so dear and familiar to Nick that he thought he would cry. He looked at his father's face and was astonished to see tears streaming down the tanned cheeks. The jaw was clenched, but the eyes were as vacant as agate crystals.

"Give me the Star, Nick. Don't be difficult. You always were stubborn—just like your mother. Not like Sam. Sam would have given his soul for someone he loved. Give me the Star, Nick. Now. I will not ask again."

Nick stared at the ravaged man, who had nurtured him and had been father and mother to him for most of his life. Something in his heart lurched, and almost like he was hypnotized, he reached into his pocket and pulled out the crystal. He raised himself to a kneeling position, and as his father came and stood in front of him, he raised the gem toward his father like an offering.

His father's strong, gentle hand reached out and closed over the ruby, and his right hand rested for a moment on Nick's head. "My beloved son," Nick's father whispered. The hand remained for the briefest of seconds, but Nick felt a glorious warmth run through his body, as though his father's hand were imbued with some rare power.

The spit of an automatic rifle shattered the silence, and Nick's father clutched the ruby to his heart and fell forward onto the floor, which was littered with broken glass. Nick raised a gun and fired through the shattered window and heard the cry of a man being hit.

Leslie came running back. "I got through. He said help would be coming in three minutes. Can we hold out that long?"

"As far as I can determine, there are only three of them," Nick said, "but I only have eight rounds of ammunition, and those men are carrying automatics. The odds don't look very good. They're going to do everything they can to assault that grill. What we have got to do is find a way to slow them down."

"There's nothing to stop them," Leslie moaned. "The street is as empty as the sky."

"No one's going to come out either. They're all in their rooms behind those doors and windows, and they won't come to help us. People value their lives more than anything," Nick said bitterly.

He looked at his father, lying on the floor with the ruby clutched in his dead hand. "No," he whispered to himself, "that's not true, there are other things men value, both good and bad, sometimes more than their lives."

"Of course, Nick!" Leslie exclaimed. "Can you cover me?"

"What?" Nick asked.

"You know, like in the movies. Shoot out the window so the men won't come close for a minute."

"All right," Nick said, "but remember I only have eight rounds." Leslie crept across the shop under the cover of the display cases. A round of automatic fire stopped her, but Nick answered the fire, and the man drew back into the street. Nick fired again, and Leslie grabbed a basket and started filling it with gold. She grabbed coins and bracelets, charms and amulets, and threw herself on the floor under the shattered window. As Nick fired again, Leslie took two handfuls of gold coins and threw them out onto the cobbled street. In the momentary silence the coins clinked like bells, and the gold glittered in the afternoon sun. A burst of rifle fire followed the shower of gold, but Nick answered the fire with another shot, and the gunman withdrew again. Leslie threw out another rain of gold that sparkled and glittered as it fell. Suddenly some children darted into the street and began picking up coins, their mothers following. Leslie grabbed another handful of gold charms and threw them with great force. A shout went up from the far end of the street, where people had been crowded at the entrance of the gold merchants' cul-de-sac. A surge of tourists and street hawkers flooded forward.

The men with the automatic rifles stood before the crowd, holding their rifles in menacing positions, but the crowd, impelled by the force from behind, fled past them, knocking them aside. For a precious minute, the men stood undecided. Should they shoot into the crowd? Would the crowd disperse, or were they so gold hungry they would simply attack?

The scene was madness. Men, women, and children fought over the coins and necklaces. Leslie continued to throw gold from the window, and the crowd went into a frenzy, thronging against the grillwork and reaching greedy hands through the openings.

"Nick!" she cried. "The gold is all gone. The basket is empty. What do we do now?"

At that moment, the Arab terrorists made their decision. They began to fire sharp bursts above the heads of the crowd, and again, panic and fear seized the street. Leslie and Nick watched as the crowd surged away once more, and as the street began to clear, the armed men gathered together, although they still remained on the far side of the street. A new man had joined them.

"Why aren't they coming?" Leslie whispered to Nick. The terrible, ominous quality of the waiting frightened her. Nick raised his head and looked at the terrorists. The new man was drawing his arm behind him, preparing to throw something.

"It's a grenade!" Nick yelled. "Get back!" He grabbed her arm and dragged her to her feet, and they lunged into the back room. They dived over the desk, and as they hit the floor behind the heavy mahogany barricade, there was an immense explosion. The whole world seemed to vanish in a black, roaring voice. The shop lifted from the ground and blew apart like a shattered toy. Plaster, glass, wood, and a concussion of air slammed through the wall of the small office, and the desk, like a malevolent beast, hurled them against the wall.

It was a few minutes before Leslie's head cleared. The ringing in her ears would not stop, and she could not see through the choking dust that filled the room. "Nick!" she screamed. "Are you all right?" She tried to move, but her legs were pinned by the desk. "Nick?" she repeated, her voice rising in alarm. "Where are you?"

From beside her there was a movement, and the heap of plaster dust and chips moved. She brushed away the debris, cutting her hand on a sliver of glass. "Nick, are you hurt?" He raised his head, his hair white with dust, and shook himself slowly.

"No," he said, "I don't think so . . . are you all right?"

"My legs are pinned under the desk . . . please help me."

He sat up slowly, pushing against the desk. Leslie moaned. "I'll have to work myself out from behind the desk and lift it," Nick said. "Can you hold on that long?"

"Yes," she said, "but hurry!"

Nick began to move gingerly. He was pressed between the wall and the desk, but was trying hard not to shift the position of the desk resting on Leslie's legs. "Just one more second, and I'll be out," he encouraged her. "Hold on."

He inched a little further and jostled the desk. Leslie gasped with pain. "Do you think they're broken?" he asked.

"No," Leslie answered, "I don't think so. Just pinned."

From the outer room, they heard a sound that made their hearts stop beating. The shop was still filled with swirling dust and visibility was poor, but across the littered, ruined floor, they heard the crunch of cautious footsteps. Helpless behind the desk, they stared through the swirling haze, watching the torn doorway, expecting at any moment to see the barrel of an automatic penetrate the gloom and strafe the tiny room where they were imprisoned. Nick reached for Leslie's hand and gripped it to give her courage. He could feel the blood from her cuts seeping through his fingers. In one day, he would have lost everyone and everything he loved, but he had saved the city— not a bad way to die.

A man's form stepped into the room. A rifle was held in firing position. Through the shadowed, dust-filled room, it was impossible to see. Only the figure of a man, no face, no identity, just a man who was commissioned to destroy the enemy. Nick steeled himself.

"Is anybody there?" a voice called, and another figure stepped through the dusty doorway.

"Levi?" Nick shouted in a hoarse voice. "We're here, behind the desk. Leslie's legs are caught. Help us!"

"Quickly, men!" Levi shouted, and two other men sprang through the door. The four of them grasped the capsized desk and carefully lifted it from Leslie's legs. She drew a deep, shuddering breath.

Levi knelt beside her and gently touched her legs, feeling carefully for broken bones. "Do you think you can stand up?" he asked solicitously.

Nick put his arm around her waist, and Levi steadied her on the other side. They lifted her up and placed her lightly on her feet. "Can you support your own weight?" Nick asked, gradually releasing his hold, so she could test her strength by degrees.

"Yes," she said tentatively, and then she felt her legs supporting her, so she repeated the word. "Yes. I'm fine. A little sore, but no damage done." She was laughing with relief and joy. "We made it, Nick. We're going to be all right. It's all over. We made it!" She turned to him and tears were streaming down her dust-streaked face. "I can't help it. I'm so happy to be alive. I'm so happy you're alive." She turned to Levi and threw her arms around him. "I'm so happy to see you, Levi! I've never been happier to see anyone in my whole life."

Levi flushed with embarrassment and pleasure, and his men looked away with amused smiles at his discomfort.

"Got here in time to catch those terrorists clumped together like a bunch of daisies. They were just preparing for their final assault on the shop—waiting for the smoke to clear, I guess." Levi mumbled to cover his awkwardness.

Leslie turned back to Nick. "It's all over, Nick. I can hardly believe it. The nightmare . . . it's all over . . . "

There was a moment of silence, and then Nick looked at Levi and said, "Not quite. Levi, come with me."

Levi and Nick walked to the front of the store, or what was left of the store. Nick's father's body had been thrown against the side wall by the explosion. He was lying under the empty shelves, one arm covering his face, his hand still clutching the magnificent ruby.

Without a word, Levi walked over and moved the arm. Nick saw him start with shock as he saw the face. "Nick," Levi said with horror. "I had no idea. Who would have guessed? One of our greatest patriots."

"You knew?" Nick asked in anger. "You knew my father's real position, knew who he was, and you never told me, never let on. You just let me go on thinking that he was an apolitical businessman. I'm glad I don't have your job, Levi." Nick's voice was bitter. "It takes a lot of guts to play God with other people's secrets."

"I wasn't playing God," Levi answered compassionately. "I knew of your father's secret-weapon work. He was one of our greatest national resources. It was not my secret to share, not even with you. But how? Why? I don't understand this. He couldn't have been corrupted—not by money." Levi's face reflected honest anguish and sorrow.

"I don't expect you to understand, Levi. I'm not sure I understand myself. Maybe the strain of his double life just got to him, but somehow he began to see things through a distorted image. In the strange realities he created for himself, he thought he was doing the right thing—the noble thing. I think perhaps he was playing God. He felt that God had failed, and that maybe he could put it right." Nick's face was a mask of agony.

"We've got to clean up here and fast," Levi said sadly. "It's only a matter of minutes before the army or the police swarm. There can't be any trace of what has happened. The peace commission is appreciative that the threat has been eliminated, but they are adamant that no word of what has happened shall ever go beyond locked doors."

"And my father?" Nick asked. "And Sam?"

"Officially, there can be no record of how they died. Of course, their deaths will need to be announced, but they will be attributed to a car accident. The country will mourn suitably for the wealthy importer, Joseph Samuelson, and his youngest son. They will be buried at private family services." Levi was thinking out loud.

"Have you found Sam's body?" Nick asked.

"Yes, the bodies were retrieved from Hezekiah's Tunnel this morning."

"And Tappin?"

"He's going to live. Hal is dead, but Tappin will recover from his injuries. His people flew him out by helicopter. By now, he is probably on a hospital ship in the Seventh Fleet. Officially, he was never in Israel."

"He's a good man," Nick said, "a real professional."

"That's funny," Levi grinned. "He said the same thing about you."

"What about Leslie and me?" Nick asked. "How do you clean us up?"

"I think perhaps we should get you back to Switzerland. That's where your father said you were. You will receive notice of his death there. As for Mrs. Brinton, we will arrange passage back to California—"

"No," Nick interrupted, "I think she will send a wire to her friends saying that she will be spending a few weeks in Switzerland for her health."

"We'll see," Levi considered. "I think, Nick, it will be best if you don't come back to Israel for a time. Your cover has been effectively blown, and even if we have brought our boot down on a nest of vipers, who knows whether or not some of the small ones have escaped and are still looking for you. They can be very venomous."

"That's all right, Levi," Nick answered softly. "I think I have lost my taste for the work, at least for a while."

Levi reached over and clasped Nick's hand in his own and shook it with emotion. "Thank you, Nick. You have performed a great service for your country and your fellowman. It is no less great because you and I will be the only ones who will ever know."

Levi drew himself up and became all business. "Now, tell me how you want to make the arrangements to leave."

Nick answered in equally businesslike tones. "I have three requests, Levi. First, I will bury my own dead. At the end of Sabbath, after sundown, I want a truck loaded with two coffins carrying my father and my brother. I also want tools for burial—shovels and picks—and I want papers for free passage. No one is to follow me. I will bury them in secret, and you may release whatever story you want to the press.

"Second, I want you to drive Leslie and me to my father's apartment and leave us there. We will pick up the truck on the road leaving through the Valley of Kidron at ten o'clock tonight.

"Last, I want a private plane with clearance, fuel, and a pilot waiting on the old landing strip outside of Meggado at dawn tomorrow. In the plane, I want papers and luggage for Leslie and me to enter Switzerland as tourists, and also, while you're at it, have your wonderful counterfeiters make us two false sets of papers with alternative identities in case those vipers you mentioned should ever track us down."

"Done," Levi said. He reached down and took the ruby out of the dead man's hand, prying open the fingers. "I'll take charge of this," he said, looking at the brilliant stone with weary eyes. "What a lot of grief this thing has caused."

"It wasn't the Star that caused the grief," Nick answered. "It was men. The Star is an inanimate object. It is harmless. We can only be hurt by one another."

The two friends stood for a moment looking at the glorious stone. Even in the dim and dusty room, it seemed to glow with a private light.

Levi turned to go and said, "I will give the order." He nodded to the plainclothesman standing on the street in front of the bombed-out shop. "The lieutenant will escort you to your father's apartment as you requested."

Nick came out of his father's shower room into the spartan bedroom. Although his father loved fine things, in this, his most personal room, everything was austere. It showed another side of the man. The large platform bed was covered with a dark brown down comforter and two plain pillows with clean white pillowcases. The closet was a monument of order. Nick had taken out a pair of British tailored slacks and soft, glove-leather moccasins and an oxford sports shirt. He and his father wore the same size, and it gave him an odd sense of comfort to wear his father's clothes.

After the shower, he stood for a few moments examining himself in the bathroom mirror. He was covered with a network of bruises and cuts. In the past few days, he had lost weight and his muscles stood out like knotted cords, but the biggest change was in his face. There was nothing of the cocksure tourist guide; nothing of the vapid playboy; nothing of the spoiled, rich, Oxford-educated Israeli left. He could never play those parts again. His face was harder, tougher, older, but nonetheless there was something else he could never erase—a harsh wisdom and, strangely enough, a look of tenderness and compassion. He thought he looked like a man who had seen the worst life had to offer and yet could understand; and if not understand, then still care.

He walked into the sumptuous living room of his father's apartment. "This," he said to Leslie, who was curled on the couch, "is the New Jerusalem." The room was exquisite, with a thick white rug and modern, overstuffed couches. The accent colors were deep blue and rust, and everywhere in the room were lovely works of art, china, enamel, brass, and ivory from around the world. A bouquet of fresh Iceland poppies stood in a crystal vase on the glass coffee table, and a shot of pain ran through Nick as he thought that just hours ago, his father had placed them there. They were still fresh as dew, untouched by the horrors of that day.

Leslie saw the shadow of pain cross Nick's face, and she wanted to go to him, but she felt she had to wait until she had sorted out her own feelings.

Leslie was sitting, bathed and fresh, wrapped in a huge Turkish robe that had also belonged to Nick's father. Her hair, black and shining, bloomed around her face. Nick stared at her for a moment without really seeing her, and then he seemed to collect himself.

"When we get to Switzerland, you are going to have to see if there is any way to remove that dye," he remarked.

"I have a more immediate problem than that," Leslie said. "What am I going to wear to get to Switzerland? I can't go out on the streets in this robe."

Nick smiled and came over to sit beside her. "That's right, you can't. It looks like we're stuck here." He bent over and kissed her, and she returned his kiss shyly.

"Well," Nick said, "I guess I'll go see if I can rustle up something for us to eat."

Leslie jumped to her feet. "Let me fix supper for us. You go out and see if you can buy a dress and some shoes for me."

As she stood up, he looked at her bare legs and feet under the robe. The legs were bruised and the shins were raw. Her feet were torn. Slowly he perused her. Her hands were scratched and Band-Aids covered the glass cuts. Her face, one side red and bruised, reminded him of the blow from Hal. She, too, had changed forever. He looked into her eyes. Although they had been cold and dead when he had first seen her boarding the tour bus, they were now the eyes of a woman who had become open, vulnerable, and courageous. She looked at him squarely, and he thought, *I would trust my life to her.* Then he smiled at the thought and added to himself, *I already have.*

"Very well," Nick said out loud. "I will go out and find something for you to wear, while you cook like any good barefooted woman should do. And when I test your cooking, if it's good enough, I may even decide to marry you."

She burst into startled laughter. "If you married me for my cooking, you'd get a bad bargain." But her face was grave.

Leslie walked into the kitchen, and Nick went into his father's room and took some money out of the top dresser drawer. How strange to think it was his money. If it hadn't been for Leslie's needs, he wouldn't have touched it.

An hour later, Nick came back from shopping, his arms full of packages. The sound of happy humming and the smell of steaks frying came from the kitchen.

"Is that you, Nick?" Leslie called out, her voice trembling. She peered apprehensively out of the kitchen door. He dropped the packages and, with one swift move, crossed the room to embrace her.

"You don't need to be afraid anymore, Leslie," Nick whispered. "You're safe now."

She sighed, and he could feel her body trembling. In that minute, he knew it would take many years to wipe away the events of the past days from her tender mind.

"It's all right," he said, patting her gently on the shoulder until the trembling subsided.

"You startled me, that's all," she murmured. She smiled at him and said, "What did you get me?" He pointed to the packages on the couch, and she lighted up with anticipation. "It looks like a birthday!" she cried, and started to move toward the parcels.

"Hold it," Nick said, laying a restraining hand on her arm, "not so fast. I told you I was going to get you something to wear, and I have. Here!" He took a small box from his jacket pocket.

"Open it," he said, "and see if it fits."

With shaking fingers, she opened the box. Inside, on a small velvet cushion, was a solitaire diamond that was cut like a teardrop. "Do you like it?" Nick asked.

"Oh, Nick . . . of course I love it. But I can't . . . I mean . . . what is this all about?"

"It was my mother's," Nick said softly. "My father had kept it for me to give to my wife when I married. I found it in his cash drawer, and I know this is what both he and my mother would have wanted." Nick took the ring and gently put it on Leslie's bruised finger.

"Leslie," he said, "will you help me to build something of value and worth out of all this unhappiness? Will you help me to build a family—one that Sam would be proud of?"

Tears stood in Leslie's eyes like diamonds. Nick reached out and pulled her to him in a bittersweet embrace. He kissed her with such strength that she could scarcely breathe, and their hearts, pressed together, beat as one living thing.

She moved away from him, and he smiled at her. "You notice, I asked you to marry me, even before I tasted your cooking."

She did not raise her eyes to meet his, and her face remained pensive and troubled. "I don't know what to say, Nick. Please, can we eat and talk later?"

He was puzzled, but knowing all she had endured in the past few days, he was reluctant to press her. "Okay," he said. "First things first."

After they had eaten, they sat on the couch and watched night descending on the modern sparkling city before them. "New Jerusalem!" Leslie exclaimed. "It is like a different world. How can two such diverse cities exist side by side? It's as though the ancient world and the modern world were colliding here."

Nick did not answer. He was sitting deep in thought, and she knew he was mourning the past. Finally he stood up and walked to the window in silent meditation. She remained sitting on the couch where he had left her, understanding his need for solitude. He turned to her as the night sky deepened.

"It is time for us to be going," he said. "We will drive Father's car to the Valley of Kidron, and then Levi will dispose of it. I am almost finished with what I need to do here."

She looked at him, puzzled. "Wait here, for a moment," he said.

Nick had bought her a silk blouse and a linen skirt with a matching jacket in a pale ivory shade. He had also bought her slender ivory-colored sandals, and she sat alone on the couch smoothing the lovely fabrics with her hand, luxuriating in the wonderful sensations of cleanliness and comfort.

Nick walked into his father's study. She heard the frantic sounds of drawers being opened and furniture being dragged and shuffled. "What are you doing, Nick?" she called, alarmed at the sounds of such strenuous activity.

"Start the fire in the fireplace," Nick called. She looked over at the spotless modern fireplace.

"How?" she asked.

"Gas jet, by the side of the hearth," Nick called back. She found the jet and some long-handled matches, and she started the fire. It glowed cheerfully around the ceramic log.

In a moment Nick hurried into the room. His arms were full of papers. "Start burning them," he ordered. "I don't want one piece of paper left that could implicate my father in any way. I want him to be remembered as the man he was—not as the man he became."

Together they combed the apartment and burned every scrap of personal paper that existed. Files, drawers, desks, closets, they cleaned out everything, and the hungry fireplace turned the pile to ashes. When they were finished, Nick sat staring into the flames. He took the last item. It was a picture of his father with his two sons, Nick and Sam, when they were still in high school. The three of them were looking directly into the camera. Nick's father's arms were resting on each of his sons' shoulders as they stood beside him, and anyone looking at Sam and Nick's handsome, resolute, happy faces would have known they were sons of the father. Nick stared at the photograph for a long minute and then placed it gently on the flames. He watched as the flames ate into the paper, and the picture curled and burst into fire.

"No identification can be left, either," he whispered.

They stood up stiffly and walked toward the door. As they stepped out of it, Leslie gave one last look at the beautiful rooms. "Are you sure there's nothing you want to take with you, Nick?" she asked "A keepsake?"

Nick looked around one more time and shook his head slowly. "Nothing. All the things I want to keep I already have."

They sped through the night down the road that led around Mount Moriah past the sleeping city of Old Jerusalem. Levi had said the bombing of the gold merchant's shop was going to be reported as a terrorist demonstration against the peace commission, which was quickly brought under order. It would become just one other incident in a lifetime of incidents for the residents of Old Jerusalem.

As they drove down the valley road between Mount Moriah and the Mount of Olives, Nick stopped the car. They were near the Garden of Gethsemane, with Father Michael's church looming in the dark beside them and the silent olive orchards behind. "I want to run in here for a minute," Nick said. "I want to speak to Father Michael and give him something."

He reached in the back of the car and pulled out a large, heavy book bound in tooled leather. It was an ancient book, but beautifully preserved and magnificent.

"It's an illuminated Bible. My father bought it years ago from a rare-books dealer in Rome. I think Father Michael will like it."

"*Like* it?" Leslie said, examining the precious volume in the dashboard lights. "He will *love* it. What a wonderful way to say thank you."

Nick dashed into the dark night. Leslie shivered with apprehension as she waited for him, but he was back very soon. "Let's get on our way," he said, slightly out of breath from running, and the powerful car roared down the road. A mile further on, they came across the truck waiting on the side of the road. A young soldier was standing guard. He did not speak to Leslie or Nick. They climbed into the cab, leaving the other car pulled off the road behind the truck. The keys were in the ignition and transport papers were in a neat envelope on the seat.

Within seconds, the truck was speeding down the Valley of Kidron. The young soldier climbed into Nick's car and drove it away, back towards Jerusalem.

In the garden chapel, Father Michael wandered down the corridor from his monastic chamber to the little entrance door in the back garden. He had been awakened by the pealing of the garden bell.

Who on earth would be ringing at this time of night? he wondered. *Only someone with an urgent need would come out in the darkness.* He had thrown a dark robe over his nightshirt and had thrust his bare feet into his sandals.

When he opened the door of the antechamber, he was surprised to see the small courtyard empty. The moon shone down on the white stones and the empty benches, and the smell of mimosa and sweet ginger hung in the air.

What a prank, he thought in exasperation, but as he turned to close the door, his eye fell upon a dark object at his feet. He bent to pick it up and saw that it was a very old and beautifully illuminated Bible.

He was astonished and puzzled. In the book was a scrap of paper, sticking out like a bookmark. He pulled out the paper and examined it in the small nightlight above the door. There was no name and no message—only a Biblical reference printed in a careful hand—"Matthew 25:34-40."

Father Michael closed the heavy Bible and held it cherishingly in his hands as he looked out into the velvet night, where the olive trees rustled.

"Thank you, Nick, my poor, valiant son," he whispered to the empty courtyard. As he turned and made his way back down the cool corridor to his bed, the words of the quote from

Matthew came sweetly to mind . . . "I was a stranger and ye took me in . . . inasmuch as ye have done it unto the least of these . . . "

Chapter Twelve

They drove for nearly an hour in the cool, dark night. Nick wanted to be alone with his thoughts, so Leslie did not speak or interrupt the laden silence.

"We're going to Hebron," Nick said, breaking the quietness with a voice that sounded resolute and calm.

"Why?" Leslie asked.

"Ephron's Field," Nick answered. "That's where Abraham is buried, Ephron's Field, the cave of Macpelah, in Hebron. I am taking them back to him."

Leslie did not understand what Nick was saying, but she did not want to probe any further than he was willing to go by himself. She was silent again for a few moments, and then she spoke. "You loved your father very much, didn't you, Nick?"

He looked at her, but did not speak. "But still," she went on, "there is one thing I don't understand. As much as you loved your father—you wouldn't have put your love for him above the lives of the whole city of Jerusalem. Why, Nick, why did you give him the Star? Was it because you thought that none of us would leave the shop alive? Did you think he wouldn't use it? It just didn't make sense. Why did you give it to him?"

"Because," Nick said, "there was no point in defying him, no point at all. You see, I didn't have the Star."

"What!" Leslie gasped. "But I saw it. I saw you hand it to him; I saw Levi pry it from his hand."

"No, Leslie, you saw something that looked like the Star— but it wasn't. It was a duplicate—paste—that's all it was."

Leslie sat, trying to take it all in. "You mean, we struggled, fought, contrived, deceived, for a worthless piece of paste glass!" she exclaimed.

"No, Leslie. At first it was the real ruby. I switched to the fake one at the hotel in Jerusalem. Hal must have killed the jeweler before he could tell him about his masterpiece—the fake Chaldean Star."

Leslie stared out the window at the side of the road, the stone fences on the floor of the valley slid past like crooked shadows in the night.

"You see, Leslie, it didn't matter if I gave him the Star or not. As a matter of fact, at that moment, I felt that nothing mattered at all."

"But things do matter, Nick," Leslie whispered, still staring out the window. "That's what you have taught me. People matter, and causes matter, and even learning to love ourselves—that matters. If people like us quit, then the others have won. I know that now."

The road began to look familiar, and Leslie stared at the mountain with Hebron at its summit, rising in the distance. They turned a corner, and she realized they were driving beside Potter's Field. In the distance she could see the black, burned-out ruin of the old shed. In the moonlight the humps of the sleeping sheep moved restlessly. They looked like little clouds in the dark night of the field.

Nick drove through an opening in the stone fencing, and they bounced across the rough field toward the ruined hut.

Nick got out of the truck and came to the door on Leslie's side.

"I want you to stay in the truck," he said. "I do not want you to get out or watch me. Sleep. I will call you when I am ready." His voice was determined, and she knew she should not argue. With a tired yawn, she lay down across the seat in the cab of the truck. At first she listened carefully to the sounds of the pick crashing into the earth, the scraping of the shovel, and the thud of earth. After a while, though, her weariness got the better of her, and she slept.

She didn't know how much later it was when she awakened to the sound of heavy scraping in the rear of the truck. Looking out, she saw Nick pulling a long, heavy plain box toward the ruins. She had promised not to look, so she put her head back down. She heard the second coffin being dragged from the truck, and then the rhythmic thud of the shovel once more. She dozed again.

When Nick awakened her it was the dead of night. The moon had set, and the stars were so brilliant they almost hurt her eyes. She stumbled sleepily out of the truck.

Nick held her arm, and they walked over to the ashes and charred foundation of the shed. There was not a sign that anyone had been there. Nick had rearranged the burned timbers and blackened soil so there was no trace of the two graves.

"I do not know if this is Ephron's Field," Nick said, "but somewhere near here Abraham is buried, and I have brought two of his children home."

Leslie remembered back to her thought as they had traveled in Jordan. Was it only a week ago? *They are all his children,* she had thought.

"Abraham had two sons, you know," Nick went on, almost to himself. "Two sons. They fought as sons will, they debated the birthright, and they went their separate ways, but Abraham knew."

"What?" Leslie asked.

"Abraham knew the answer to their quarrels. He knew. Somehow he reached out to them and touched them. He helped them remember that they were brothers first and always. It was his love that did it. It healed the rift."

"How do you know?" Leslie asked.

"Because," Nick answered, "Ishmael and Isaac came together to bury their father. They put aside all the anger, the humiliations, the bitterness, for love of him. But their children forgot and continued to fight." Nick heaved a sigh. "Perhaps the answer lies buried forever in the grave of Abraham. Perhaps he is the only one who can remind his children who they are."

Nick turned away from the ruined site. "It's time to be going," he said.

They tramped across the field, and Leslie felt a sense of ineffable sorrow for the verdant land underfoot. The sheep bleated restlessly, and the citadel city of Abraham raised its silent walls to the ancient skies. She glanced up at the stars and thought of the invisible satellites winding endless, unknown routes around the planet with the power to bind or to destroy.

"Nick!" she exclaimed. "The Chaldean Star! You never told me what you plan to do with the real one. Will it be returned? Will Israel keep it? You must consider carefully what you will do with it."

Nick laughed a mirthless chuckle. "I have considered it carefully."

"Where did you hide the Star, Nick, after you got the duplicate?" she asked.

"In the olive orchard behind Father Michael's chapel. I buried it under one of the trees. When I took him the Bible, I also retrieved the Star."

"Then you have it with you? Oh, Nick. I don't want it. Get rid of it. It has brought nothing but misery—and it promises more." Leslie's face was harsh with anxiety. "Please, Nick."

"It's all right," Nick said. "The Star is at rest."

"What do you mean?" Leslie asked. "I'm tired of puzzles and innuendos. Where is the Star?"

"I have returned it to Abraham too," Nick answered.

The full implication of his words sank in. Leslie knew that somewhere in the vast bosom of the field, the Chaldean Star had been returned to the earth that had spawned it. She nodded her head and thought of the jewel returned to the place it belonged. It seemed right, somehow. All things felt solace in returning to their place of belonging.

She was silent and thoughtful as they turned to drive northward through the night. As dawn pinked the eastern sky with the glorious color of a clear summer morning, they drove on to the open plains below the excavations of the city of Meggado. Winding through the pleasant green fields and rolling hills, they turned and bounced across an open plain, which stretched before them.

"Only a few more miles to the landing field," Nick said. The land was verdant, but there were few signs of habitation, and no traffic had passed them for over an hour.

Nick pointed to the plain. "The plains of Armageddon," he said. "The first battle of recorded history was fought on those plains, and it is prophesied that the last one will be fought there as well—the battle that will signify the end of the world."

Leslie looked away from the plain and shuddered. "This spot," Nick continued, "is the crossroad of the world. The ancient meets the new, the East meets the West, Christian meets Muslim, dark meets light, continent meets continent."

Leslie looked at him with inquiring eyes.

"I am giving my last tour," Nick said, attempting a smile.

"No, you're not," Leslie answered. "You are saying farewell to a land you love. You love it so much, I do not think you will be able to say good-bye to it, not for long."

In the long, smooth valley nestled between the low hills, they saw a rough and unused runway. At the end of the runway was a small, beautiful jet perched like a white gull.

"Levi is as good as his word," Nick smiled.

They left the truck and ran across the cracked asphalt and climbed aboard.

A jaunty, young pilot with white teeth flashed a salute at Nick and a dazzling smile at Leslie. "Welcome aboard," he said.

"Contact Levi has asked you to communicate with him before we depart. I believe everything is in order, so if you wish to use my radio—I have it on scrambler. We can leave whenever you say."

Nick ducked into the cockpit and put on the headphones. "Contact Levi," he said. There was a crackling sound and then Levi's voice unscrambled. "Password!"

"Star."

Levi's voice came again. "Dreadful word, but that's why I'm calling you. It was the imitation Star you gave your father of course. Where is the real one? I have people clamoring to know."

Nick pressed the talk button. "Lost," he said.

The radio crackled explosively, "Lost!" Levi's voice was like a rifle shot. "How could you lose a thing like that?"

"In the line of duty," Nick answered. "Isn't that how you account for all major losses of material—when a car gets wrecked, or a plane gets dunked, or you need to make a major payoff? Doesn't accounting just throw it into the slush pile . . . lost in the line of duty?"

There was a moment of silence. Nick waited. He wondered if Levi would order him back to Jerusalem. If there would be a board of inquiry. Things could get very nasty, but it would all have to be hush-hush. The peace commission couldn't afford to have anyone know that a weapon had been designed to strike and destroy Jerusalem. Israel could not afford to let it be known that the top man in their defense organization had played a major role in stealing the weapon and turning it on his own country. They also couldn't afford to let the public realize that they had known of a devastating threat to the lives of tens of thousands of people and had kept the threat a secret, risking all of those lives. Nick could almost hear Levi weighing all the facts in his mind.

The radio crackled. "Very well, Nick. I understand. Whatever you've done, I trust it was right. Very busy days you've had—lots of physical abuse, changes of clothes and location, and all that. Difficult thing to hold onto something as small as the Star. You hung on to the imitation one, at any rate, and that was the one that brought the whole thing through. Kept your eye on the important things, didn't you."

Nick pressed the radio transmitter. "I knew you'd understand if you thought about it for a few minutes, Levi. I promise you, I don't have it. I promise you, it is truly lost. I'm sorry. Give my regrets to Tappin. Tell him it was a pity I lost his ruby. I think he'll understand too."

Another crackle and then Levi's voice came one last time. It sounded a little petulant and harassed. "Devil of a mess you've left me to clean up here!" he said. "Your father's place as empty as a drum, all the cover-up stories, and now a dozen sticky explanations about how my first-rate agent somehow managed to lose one of the most valuable gems in the world."

"It was never ours anyway, Levi. We hadn't earned it," Nick said. Nick smiled to himself and took off the headphones, the radio still crackling. He went back into the small passenger section.

"I think it's time we left," he said to the pilot, who was carrying on an animated conversation with Leslie. "You can change the frequency on the radio now. All we're receiving is interference."

The pilot saluted and entered the cockpit. In a moment, the engines were roaring, and the lovely plane darted across the empty field and leaped into the glory of the morning sky.

It was a smooth and beautiful takeoff, and Leslie sat by the small window and watched as the green fields beneath her widened. Soon she could see the horizon of the world curving to the East, with the shimmer of the golden desert sands brushing the rim like gold dust.

Nick took off his seatbelt and crossed the narrow aisle to kneel beside her.

"Below us," he whispered, putting his hands over hers and lifting his head toward her, "are the excavations of the stables of Solomon's chariots. He was a great warrior, a horseman, and a magnificent poet."

Leslie stared into Nick's dear face, and she smiled, but there was sadness in her eyes.

Nick frowned with concern as he looked into her eyes. "What's the matter?" he asked softly. "Something is troubling you. What is it?"

Leslie turned her head from his gaze for a moment as though struggling to organize her feelings. She took a slow, deep breath, and then turned back to face him once more.

Slowly she twisted the ring he had placed on her finger and drew it off and handed it to him.

"Nick, I can't marry you. I can't stay in Switzerland and pretend I'm someone I'm not—anymore than you can."

With an abrupt and angry gesture, Nick clenched the ring in his hand. "What do you mean?" he growled. "I thought you loved me. I didn't realize you were pretending."

"No," Leslie protested. "I wasn't pretending to love you. I did—I do love you. But what I was pretending was that we were different people than we are. I was pretending to think love between us would be possible."

Nick turned away from her. "Leslie, I'm too tired to play games. I love you, and I want to marry you. I never thought I'd feel that way about anyone."

"But don't you see, Nick? You don't feel that way about me, about the real me. You feel that way about a fellow warrior, a companion who joined you in the thick of battle—who fought by your side—who believed in you and stuck by you. That's the woman you love. I was that woman for five days of my life.

"You don't even know the woman who is a quiet biology professor, an American, a widow . . . a . . . oh, all the other pieces of my life. I don't think you would love that woman—she's too placid, too serious, too traditional."

"This is nonsense," Nick interrupted. "I would love everything about you." He paused and smiled. "And what I didn't love, I could change."

She didn't smile in return. "No, Nick." She shook her head gently. "Change isn't that easy. I know."

"I love you, Leslie," Nick said quietly. "I love you, and I want you—it's as simple as that."

Leslie shook her head. "For now. And maybe tomorrow. But then, one morning, you will wake up and remember Sam, or see a headline, and you'll think of Levi and your father and the land that you love more than anything else in the world. You can't change either, Nick. You will find a way to go back to Israel. You will find a way to continue your fight for peace."

Nick began to protest, but she laid her finger gently on his lips. "No, Nick. You won't change. You must not try to change. That fight—those loyalties—are the finest part of you. They are your life. If I forced you to turn from them, you would grow to hate me, and even worse, you'd grow to hate yourself."

Nick was silent for a moment, then he nodded.

"But you could join me, Leslie," he murmured. "It could be our fight."

Quietly, Leslie shook her head. "I believe in your cause, Nick, but I am not a warrior. I am fighting my own battle. Long ago, I lost something more precious to me than the Star. I lost my faith, and with it, I lost my purpose in living and even my desire for life.

"You and Sam gave me back something more precious than you can ever know. Because of you, I began to see beyond sorrow, struggle, and ugliness to the beauty of the human heart. I saw how tenderness, loyalty, and love can survive evil and tragedy. I began to see beyond the seeming meaninglessness of life to something that can transcend the horrors and pettiness.

"I'm not ready yet, Nick, to be whole for anyone, but I have at least, through all the pain and triumph of being with you and Sam, found my way back to a place where I can begin again.

"Can't you see, Nick? I have come too far from the things I once knew to be true. I have a long journey ahead of me, which I must travel alone, to discover who I am. I'm confused, and I must return, like the Star, to where I belong."

"And what is it you expect to find at the end of this journey of yours, Leslie?" Nick asked softly.

"The things you have taught me," Leslie murmured. "Hope, faith, loyalty, and . . . love."

Nick's jaw clenched tightly, and he looked away from her for a few moments. In the deep silence Leslie could sense his thoughts and emotions. He was turning her words over in his mind, testing them, searching for the truth for both of them.

When he turned back to her, his eyes were calm but filled with power and resolution. He smiled at her, and she saw certainty in his smile.

"And when you find those things, they will bring you back to me," he said. His voice was quiet and sure. "Perhaps you are right, we each have unfinished tasks that we must accomplish alone now, but somewhere there is a destiny that brought us together, and that same destiny will return us to one another.

"A love such as ours, forged in grief and joy and sealed with tears, cannot be denied and will not be dimmed by time or distance. I do not know how or when, but I do tell you, Leslie, no matter what you say, as surely as the stars shine eternally over Ephron's Field, we shall be together again."

Her small, cut and bruised hand was closed into a fist on the armrest between them, and Nick reached over and enclosed her hand in his own large, muscular grasp.

In his firm and gentle grip, her closed hand fit comfortably and completely as though in its own perfect glove. Almost unbidden, Leslie felt her hand opening as naturally as a flower, and in the tender warmth of Nick's touch, she thought she felt the wounds and bruises beginning to heal.